One Small SPARK

GENNY CARRICK

Cover design and illustration by Melody Jeffries

Edited by Cindy Ray Hale

ISBN (ebook): 978-1-957745-20-6

ISBN (paperback): 978-1-957745-22-0

 Created with Vellum

WHAT TO EXPECT

This book includes one-sided enemies to lovers, loads of banter, discussion of parental abandonment, a main character with anxiety, and a fade to black.

*For the loud girls, the unfiltered girls, the ones who aren't afraid
to take up space.
Never stop being you.*

And for my dad. I love you big.

ONE
WREN

IS this what it's like to claim an Oscar onstage? It's got to be a close second.

I walk up the pine tree-lined residential street carrying two boxed pies, my body fizzing with triumph. After months of gentle prodding and a tiny bit of bribery—the pies, obviously—I finally snagged an invite to one of the most mysterious clubs in Sunshine, Oregon. Today is the day. At long last, I get to sit in on Ada and Isabel's smutty book club.

To be clear, I adored their romance pick for the month—a Highlander hero, this one wheedling his way into marriage via blackmailing his intended with her embarrassing letters to an imaginary beau. It automatically went on my favorites list. But I've pictured Ada and Isabel's secret meetings as something subversive for too long for me to just stop referring to them as risqué.

Even if I'm now included in the get-togethers.

I've got a dopey smile on my face when I ring the bell of the classic single-level ranch house. I fully expect every woman in this club to be at least twice my age, but I haven't been this excited to be part of a group since middle school. Maybe it's silly, but it's *mine*. And I need something that's all mine right about now.

Ada swings the entry door open wide. Her chic gray bob accentuates her sharp eyes and bright smile. "Well, if it isn't the newest member of our little enclave. Welcome in, Wren."

She waves me inside, and I step over the threshold into the cozy home.

Enclave. I like that. I'm one of the lucky few included in their super-secret, ultra-exclusive—

"*Callahan?*"

Several older women mingling throughout the open-concept living room and kitchen turn at my outburst. But standing in the middle of them wearing a blue flannel shirt layered over a black tee like a grunge rocker among cardigan-clad grandmas is Shepherd Callahan.

How is this my life?

For a second, he's frozen mid-conversation, a polite smile stuck on his face. But his smile morphs into a smirk I know all too well.

That smirk sets my teeth on edge and makes my heart rate kick up as I wait for his next move. He's way too amused, like he knows something I don't. I *hate* him knowing things I don't. And right now, I'm so far out of the loop, I'm not entirely sure what the loop *is*.

Ada leads me to the kitchen table and I set down the pies, but I don't take my gaze off Callahan. What the heck is he even doing here? I doubt any of these ladies had a bicycle break down on their way to book club and had to call an emergency mechanic. So? What gives?

Ada introduces me to the other women. I nod along but can't pretend I'm memorizing anybody's names. Safe to say I'm too distracted by the Callahan of it all.

He has no right to be here. This was supposed to be a gray-haired lady zone, with a *No Loitering* sign for lanky men with scruffy hair and short, dark beards. Don't even get me started on his stupid brown eyes.

Finally, she gestures between the two of us with one pale finger. "I'm guessing introductions aren't necessary here."

He shoves his hand out to me, ready to be properly introduced. I roll my eyes and lightly smack it away, but touching him is always a mistake. A zing of awareness lights up a panel somewhere in my nervous system labeled *Inconvenient Attraction*. It's like my body never got the memo that the man's a life-ruiner, and instead gets fixated on useless things like *warm, strong hands*.

He makes a rumbly sound in the back of his throat, as amused with me as ever.

"Fill your plates," Isabel instructs. "We're pretending it's still summer and having our discussion on the back deck."

"The patio warmers are already toasty for us," Ada adds. "And we've got a big stack of blankets if you need an extra layer."

It's only early October, but I still expect some kind of complaint from the group. Nobody seems fazed by the revelation, though. I would have worn more than the light hoodie I've got on if I'd known we'd be hanging around outside for book club.

Right now, the chill in the air isn't my most pressing concern.

Callahan shifts to the back of the crowd around the table, letting everyone else go first as if he's some kind of gentleman. I'm waiting for him to realize he wandered into the wrong house by mistake and sneak out, but my dreams remain dashed.

Rosetta, Sunshine's library director, turns from the food to face me. Her beautiful brown complexion is complemented by her silver-streaked hair, twisted into a braided bun atop her head like an ornate crown. "We're happy to have you with us today, Wren. It'll be good to hear another young person's opinions on our book."

"Who is the other young person in the group?" I ask. Because the obvious answer makes no sense.

"Does that mean you think I'm not in the group or not a young person?" Callahan's low voice is like a shiver up my spine, equal parts pleasant and unsettling.

"Only one of us is under thirty." I've still got a year to go. Not even he can take that away from me.

Rosetta chuckles. "We have a more generous definition than that."

"Krause can be a stickler with details," Callahan says, eyes on me.

"That's a relief," the woman next to Rosetta pipes up. Nora, I think. "Most of us forget the finer details of the books before we ever get together to discuss the...ahem...broader aspects."

They'll be sincerely disappointed in me, then, since I was expecting to discuss the *broader aspects*, too. By which I assume we mean the kilt-wearing hero.

But I should probably come up with something a little more specific to say about the actual romance. "Well...I think the hero believing that love is a lie is relatable when you consider—"

Rosetta raises a hand to stop me. "Oh, no, no, no. No literary discussion just yet. Not until we've got our food and are settled in."

"There's a structure to it," Isabel says.

"Oh. Right." I look past them to the table where the other women are piling their plates. Along with the pies I brought sit a couple of vegetable dishes, a fruit salad, some kind of spicy chicken, and a hearty loaf of bread.

"Krause is eager to discuss her skepticism about love." Callahan's gaze stays stuck on me as the women titter over their plates.

"Yup. That's me." I grab his hand. *Mistake.* Too late to do anything about it now. "You don't mind if I steal Callahan for a minute, do you?"

Pretty sure fresh laughter rolls around the group as I drag him to the relative privacy of Ada's hallway. It's lined with framed photographs of what I assume is her family and an old-fashioned travel poster of Mount Bachelor. It's also only about twenty feet from the crowded table, but shutting ourselves up in a bedroom would be wrong on so many levels.

"How are you here?" I hiss at him.

He smirks down at me. Just a twitch of his lips beneath his short beard, but it's enough. He dips his head, sending locks of his mouth-length dark hair over his forehead.

Mouth-length? No. That's not a thing. Ear-length. Somewhere in the vicinity of his cheekbones. Nowhere near his mouth, which I'm definitely not looking at. Whatever the length, his hair is perpetually windswept and messy, like he just hopped off a motorcycle.

Which isn't really the point right now.

"Rosetta invited me," he says.

"When?"

"A few months ago."

A few months? I've been finagling my way in for at least that long.

"Why?"

He lifts a shoulder. "I enjoy reading. And we were in the library. Just in case 'Where?' was going to be your next question."

"You don't even read romances." I have no basis for this assertion, but the other option is too absurd to comprehend.

Shepherd Callahan, sitting around reading about love and romance and relationships? Never.

"You make a lot of assumptions about me."

He squeezes my hand, and I'm horrified to realize I didn't let go of him when I dragged him back here. I make up for it now and drop his hand like it's on fire.

"They don't let anybody into their group," I hiss again. My gaze darts past him, but nobody's followed us into the hall. "They keep it a big secret. It took me forever to get them to invite me."

Isabel tried to pretend ignorance even though she's come into Blackbird's to buy desserts for the book club several times.

His smirk widens. "We're a very exclusive group."

"Ugh." My hard-won invitation doesn't seem so special now. Not if they hand them out to just anybody.

"What? Am I not allowed to read books and discuss them with some of Sunshine's most interesting minds?"

No. Not really. He can join some other book club. Not the one I've been so desperate to get into. I can't believe he's been privy to the inner workings of Ada and Isabel's romance club for actual months.

"But it's *romance.*"

That word seems wrong spoken out loud to him. I don't like having it in the air between us. It's a giant, invisible mosquito I want to swat away.

He purses his lips. "Krause." He drags the word out slowly, teasing me with my own name. "Judging me for reading romance? That's not very enlightened of you."

I take a step closer to him. My traitor gaze skims up his open flannel shirt and the tight, black T-shirt underneath. Unhelpful. As is the flush of warmth creeping up my neck. But stepping out of his space would count as a win for him. Better to stand my ground.

"Just tell me what you're doing here," I seethe.

He inhales so slowly, I almost think he's breathing in my orange and lavender perfume. Which would be crazy. Obviously. This is Callahan. He's probably trying to suck all the air out of the room before I have a chance to breathe it.

Then, I have an out-of-body experience. His gaze dips from my eyes to my mouth. He tilts his head a fraction of an inch closer. The heat on my neck becomes an inferno. Is he—? He wouldn't. I suck in a breath, frozen in place.

He snaps his gaze back up to mine.

"Maybe I need more romance in my life."

I snort. Mostly at myself. One tiny movement, and I'm dreaming up forbidden kiss scenarios? I blame the Highlander romance novel I binge-read over the last two days.

Along with the dozen other romances I read this month. I really need to switch to thrillers.

"That wouldn't be hard to achieve," I finally say.

He quirks his eyebrows at me. "Flattery will get you everywhere."

I make a sound of disgust. Naturally, he would take what I say the opposite of how I mean it.

"Are you two ready?" Ada calls from the kitchen. "Better get your food before there's nothing left to eat."

"That won't happen." He whispers as if we're sharing secrets back here. Which I suppose we are. "They always send me home with leftovers."

"Is that why you come here? For the free food?"

His lips purse beneath his trim, dark beard. "You've figured out my scam, Krause. Brilliant sleuthing. Are we done in the hallway or did you want to hold my hand some more?"

My mouth falls open, but I'm pretty sure anything I want to say would get me kicked out of Ada's house. I storm past him, ignoring the hand he's holding out to me and knocking my shoulder against his in the process. The move always looks so perfectly dismissive in the movies, but in real life, it's more like an unintended full-body caress.

Sick burn, Wren.

We're the last to fill our plates. I keep my focus trained on the food, willing my brain to erase the last five minutes of sensory input. I can still salvage this, Callahan notwithstanding. Just because he somehow managed to score an invite to their book club first doesn't mean I can't prove myself to be a valuable part of the group. What would he even have to say about romance books?

I kind of hate how much I want to know.

Outside, I'm in for another unpleasant surprise—the ladies have taken up all available seating except for a snug-looking wicker loveseat. They've thoughtfully draped a blanket over one cushion, as if inviting Callahan and me to share it.

Ha. Never going to happen.

He sits, and I can't help but notice his jeans-clad thigh doesn't quite stay on his half of the loveseat. I hover behind him, staring at the sliver of leg that's clearly crossed a boundary.

"Come sit down, Wren," Isabel says amid the low chatter. "Shepherd won't bite."

He looks up at me. Something in his brown eyes promises that yes, he absolutely will bite if given the opportunity.

But there's nothing I hate more than backing down from one of his challenges, spoken or not. I round the loveseat and sit next to him. I lift my eyebrows at him, lobbing back his little dare. I will sit here and eat this delicious food and talk about a Highlander jaded to love, all with our thighs and arms pressed together on this too-small loveseat, possibly while sharing a blanket.

It doesn't bother me at all.

TWO
WREN

ACTUALLY, it bothers me a lot. I can't think straight. It's not like he's full-on manspreading, but his leg is encroaching on my cushion. I press my thigh against his, thinking he'll get the message and, I don't know, cross his legs to the other side. But he doesn't move at all, and our legs stay plastered together from hip to knee.

Plus, I'm sweating. It's these dang patio warmers Ada's got out here. I thought it'd be chilly, but between the heat pouring off the metal poles and the close quarters on the love seat, it's sweltering.

Also—this seems key—nobody's talking about the romance book we were supposed to read. The ladies are eating and chatting about gardening tips and how Fran got the green beans so tender and whether we'll have early snow this year. It's not the deep-dive into smut I've been looking forward to. Maybe that'll start up after we finish eating?

"When are we going to get to the romance part of romance book club?" I ask low so the others can't hear.

"We have social time first," Callahan says. "Everyone catches up while we eat."

"Are we supposed to *talk*?"

He chuffs a laugh. "You're so horrified."

"Look who they stuck me with."

Which I don't actually do. The man takes up my entire peripheral vision as it is. If I skate my eyes to the side, I'll be confronted with his flannel-covered goodness. Badness. Him.

It's bad enough I can smell him. I would love to say he smells like roadkill in the sun, but the light woodsy scent I'm catching isn't terrible. It's giving "I live in a forest where woodland creatures visit me daily to watch me chop wood." The least he could do is bathe himself in sinus-clearing body spray like a normal guy.

I focus on devouring my plate of food.

"You could pretend you like me," he offers, as if that's a practical solution.

"Sounds like a nightmare."

Callahan doesn't flinch. Not sure what I thought he'd do. Burst into tears and beg my forgiveness? He probably doesn't even remember saying that about me. Honestly, he might have said worse since then. It's been two years, after all. Who knows what else he's told people behind my back.

"How is the hunt for your own personal Greek god? Any luck yet?"

I finally swivel my head to face my nemesis. Of all the stupid things for him to overhear me say. Fresh off of an evening listening to my best friends gush about how grotesquely happy they are with their impressive boyfriends, Callahan caught me at a weak moment. I might have mentioned something about wanting someone of my own, never guessing he was lurking in the shadows.

Incidentally, that was months ago. So. He can remember *some* things.

"It's going great. I've got several potential Greek gods on the line as we speak."

Lies, of course. My dating life is deader than the souls in the Underworld, but I'm not going to admit that to Callahan. Not after he suggested I go for Hephaestus. The monstrously ugly one.

According to some websites I looked up, also the least adulterous one, but still.

He leans a touch closer as if he's buying my garbage. "What's your criteria to decide who wins your heart?"

As if he cares.

"He needs to be a reader, obviously." Except, no. That's unhelpful when Callahan's here with me at a book club. I don't want him to get ideas. "Not outdoorsy."

He ticks an eyebrow. I don't care that every woman in my life is currently loved-up by some strapping mountain man. That's not the road for me.

"Indoor cats only," he confirms. "What else?"

He's shifted even closer, taking up way too much space on my half of the loveseat. Heat courses up my spine straight to my scalp. I almost tug at the neck of my hoodie that has *First of all, I'm a delight* printed on it above a raccoon's face. Stupid patio warmers.

I nudge his shoulder with mine, but he's immovable. "Can you not loom so hard?"

"Sorry." He shifts back to his side of the small couch. At least, his upper body does. His leg remains firmly pressed against mine, but I refuse to give up my space. "Continue with your list of requirements in a boyfriend."

"Taking notes, are you?"

"Extensive ones."

I'm not a fan of this conversation. Not just because I've got his undivided attention. Callahan's focus on me always leaves me a bit unmoored. If he's looking for faults, I've got plenty to find. As he apparently knows all too well.

But it's been so long since I really dated, I feel like a fraud to even talk about it. What do I want, assuming all I had to do was ask? Finding someone steady and loyal but up for anything would be the dream. Someone to talk and laugh with and—ugh—cuddle with would be even better. But that's too ooey-gooey to say out loud.

Instead, I describe the polar opposite of the man who owns the bike rental and repair shop right next to our family's bakery. "I want someone outgoing and popular. The life of the party. Cerebral. Skilled in the kitchen."

I just know he lives off ramen and cold cereal.

"Is that the only room he should be skilled in?"

I shrug. "I don't want to make you self-conscious about your shortcomings."

"You're so thoughtful."

I take a bite of the bread I slathered with butter and moan. His eyes narrow, and his jaw ticks beneath his beard. I don't care if my response is over the top, this bread is heaven. "This is what I'm talking about."

"It's that good?"

"It's a perfect boule. Chewy crumb that's light and airy with the right amount of flavor and a crisp crust begging to be an entire meal." My focus in culinary school was pastries, so I know bread. I'll need to ask around to find out where this one came from. "I would marry a man who can make bread this good."

Callahan's slow smile sets something off in my stomach. Indigestion, probably.

"Thank you." His gaze is back on my mouth. "I'll keep that in mind."

I stare, my lips parting. "You couldn't," I breathe out. "I can't even make bread this good."

Not consistently, anyway.

His smile widens until it's comically large. "I don't want to make you self-conscious about your shortcomings."

"Where did you—"

"Is everyone ready to discuss?"

Ada's loud question startles me out of my confusion. Well, mostly. *He* made the bread that has me drooling for more? Impossible.

The theme of the day.

"Callahan said he made the bread we're eating." My interjection makes me sound like a ten-year-old tattler. I don't care. No way will these ladies let it go if he's taking credit for something somebody bought.

To my dismay, a chorus of compliments about his bread follows. Apparently, he brings it every month, at their request. The bicycle mechanic moonlights as a bread wizard.

Distressing.

"I've married men for less," Fran says, aiming a slow wink his direction.

He twists so he can whisper in my ear. "Two proposals in one day. How will I choose?"

I elbow him back to his side. "Nobody wants to marry you."

His dark brown eyes sparkle at me. "Not even with the promise of endless bread?"

I mean...the bread is good. But, no. It's not so good I'd sell my soul for it. Or marry a guy who can't stand me, which is basically the same thing. I set my empty plate aside and cross my arms, bumping him needlessly in the process.

"For our newcomer," Ada says, waving over at me, "our book discussions are casual, as you can see. Everyone can jump in whenever they like, but we ask that nobody hogs the conversation entirely."

She shoots a pointed look at the woman to her left.

The woman I'm pretty sure is named Barb seems unfazed by the call-out. "It's fair to discuss the rules of the ton when we're reading historical romances."

"We never got a chance to talk about the book," Nora points out.

"But now we'll know when we spot historical inaccuracies."

A few of the women groan over that.

"Who would like to open discussion of this week's book?" Ada asks.

She's watching me, but I don't want to go first. I *will* talk about this romance book, but I'm still cramming the fact that Callahan made that bread into my brain. I can't also discuss why the Scottish hero with the unscalable emotional walls was so swoony when he finally dropped them.

"I thought it was heartbreaking," Nora says. "The hero had been abandoned and never loved properly, and the heroine had lost everyone she ever loved. But then, it was infuriating, too, when the hero wouldn't just admit how he felt about her."

"Isn't that always the way?" Barb asks.

"Do men ever just admit how they feel?" Ada's eyes dart to Callahan, but she's not questioning him.

I wish she was. I'd like an answer. *Do* men admit how they feel? They must, right? All the women I care about now have men in their lives who must have verbalized a sensitive notion or two at some point. I've sure never experienced that, but I don't hate the idea of it.

"Isn't that why we read romance novels?" I put in. "So we can pretend men have a normal range of human emotions?"

"The heroine wasn't forthcoming with her feelings for him, either," Callahan says. "Most romance novels would end pretty quickly if the main characters said everything they were feeling the moment they felt it."

"Read a lot of romances, have you?" I mutter.

He dips his head closer. "I'll show you mine if you show me yours."

Ugh. This man.

"That's why we love them," Rosetta says. "The delicious tension of the push-pull where as the reader you know the characters are falling in love, but their histories make it impossible for them to admit it to each other."

"There's nothing like a good enemies to lovers," Isabel adds. "They hate each other, but really, they don't."

"If they don't hate each other, then it's not enemies to lovers," Barb says.

I want to add my two cents that love interests don't need to have knives at each others' throats to count as enemies, but Callahan splays one hand on his thigh, and I lose the conversation. The tip of his pinky finger rests against my leg. It's some kind of power move. It has to be. One more nudge over the line that's supposed to exist between us.

I can't stop staring at that tiny point of contact. Crazy how much heat transfers from his pinky fingertip, through my leggings, to my skin. I should brush his hand away. Make it clear he can't manspread *and* handspread.

His hand is kind of nice, though. If you're into that sort of thing. Long fingers and a generous palm. Bigger than my hand, but not so enormous mine would look like a miniature in comparison. A myriad of shimmery scars dance over his skin. Probably from when he gets all up in some bike gear shaft or whatever he does in his shop.

Higher, a dark line at his wrist marks the beginning of his tattoo sleeve. It's a stark transition from lightly tanned skin to dark gray ink. Both his arms are covered in mysterious black-

and-gray tattoos with little pops of color I've never looked at too closely. They're currently covered by his blue flannel shirt, but that visible sliver at his wrist before it disappears beneath the cuff bugs me.

The fact that I want to know what his tattoos are bugs me the most.

His fingers extend and flex once, brushing that pinky fingertip a few centimeters across my leg. I shiver against my will.

He grabs the blanket he'd moved out of the way when I sat down and offers it to me. "Cold?"

"Yes." I gladly take the excuse and the blanket and spread it over my legs.

"Wren, you had something to say about the hero earlier, didn't you?" Rosetta asks.

I stare at her, needing a minute to figure out what I'd planned to say. I took a lot of notes while I read, all of which have slipped my mind. "Uh..."

"Something about love being a lie," Mr. Helpful offers.

"Right! Yes!" I'm a little too triumphant, but the clarity of thought is welcome after my brain fizzled out over his freaking hand. "The hero doesn't think love is real because he's never experienced it before. Both his parents abandoned him, and he never had anyone in his corner. But the heroine's mad he's not more romantic. If you don't have any context for love, how can you be expected to search for it the way the heroine was?"

"The heroine didn't have a lot of context for love either," he argues. "But she still wanted it."

"Because she's the heroine. In a lot of romance novels, the heroine is desperate for love and affection no matter what she's been through."

"That's a good point," Rosetta says. "There's an expectation that women are always looking for love."

"Exactly. The hero gets to be all stoic and detached from his feelings and only stumbles into love after it's already fallen in his lap. The heroes are more relatable because they *don't* think love is for them."

Silence takes over the patio. Great. My first foray into a romance book club and I've all but admitted I don't actually believe in it. Even Callahan's watching me closely—big surprise, the creeper.

My smile is mostly cringe as I try to recover. "But, hey, those shirtless scenes were fire, am I right?"

THREE
SHEPHERD

THIS AFTERNOON HAS BEEN full of revelations. When Wren walked into Ada's house, I froze, sure *I* would be the one revealing more than I intended. But here she is, unveiling tiny, glimmering pieces of herself without meaning to.

I scoop up all the shiny pieces and tuck them away in my hoard. I collect little glimpses of the woman beneath the snark to treasure like a covetous dragon over his gold.

"Ooh, those shirtless scenes." Nora fans herself. "Sorry, Shepherd, but you know how we feel about them."

I laugh at her faux apology. "I'm not offended, Mrs. Gonzales."

"Nora, please. How many times do I have to remind you?"

I nod, but it's a tough habit to break. "Nora."

"You don't call me by *my* first name," Wren grumps next to me. "You could mix it up, you know."

An interesting request, since she's the one who started the last name business. But I don't trust myself to try. Our game has gone on so long now, saying her first name out loud would probably fall under the "revealing too much" category.

"Whatever you want, kitten," I return.

She glares, sending a rush of heat through me. I'm a simple man. An idiot, but a simple one. I'll take any reaction from her I can get.

"It's when the hero rolled up his shirtsleeves that did it for me," Isabel says. "A small gesture, but a mighty one."

"Hmm..." Ada pats a finger against her chin. "My Harry never does that. I can't quite imagine it."

"How can someone never roll up their sleeves?" Fran asks.

Ada sniffs. "He has skinny elbows. They don't stay up."

Fran's gaze lights on me with naked enthusiasm. "Maybe Shepherd would demonstrate for us."

The ladies seem to like this idea—all but one. My seatmate rolls her eyes.

"How am I supposed to do it?" I'm game, I just don't know what they want. I've read the sorts of passages they mean, and was frankly surprised to learn it's a recurring piece of imagery. I assume it's something to do with a buttoned-up man letting loose a little. Doesn't really apply in this situation, since I'm nothing close to stuffy.

"Just roll up your sleeves so we can see your forearms," Ada directs.

"Slowly!" Fran adds.

I shake out my arms as if I need to gear myself up for it, and a couple of the women laugh.

Wren huffs at my side. "They're objectifying you," she mutters. "Like you're their *boy toy* or something."

I lean in so I can whisper in her ear. She freezes, her big blue eyes wide as she watches me draw closer. "It's all good. Everyone here has my consent to objectify me."

"Gross."

It's really not. Sure, it can be eye-opening to sit in on conversations where women twice my age admire fictional men, and discussion of sex scenes has been illuminating to say the least, but I'm not uncomfortable. These women look at me more as a surrogate son or nephew rather than some potential conquest.

But if boy toy is where Wren's mind goes, I won't object.

I unbutton the cuff on each sleeve of my flannel shirt and roll twice before pushing them a couple of inches higher. Nothing, right? It's a move I've done a hundred times, but here, it earns a round of applause. I don't understand the appeal, but I'll take it.

Then again, I have no room to criticize. Wren could expose anything right now, and I would lose the ability to speak in coherent sentences.

The ladies discuss the wonders of forearms for another few minutes. Wren doesn't add to the chatter. She's quiet, her gaze stuck on my arms. Most likely, on my tattoos. I doubt she realizes how often she stares at them. I haven't figured out if she likes them or can't stand them. It'd be a shame if she hated them, since I have no plans to get all this work lasered off.

Her gaze shifts to meet mine, and she narrows her eyes, silently daring me to say something for catching her. Of course, I can't resist.

"Are good forearms on your list of Greek god requirements, too?"

"*No.*"

Her heated response isn't selling the denial.

"What do you like?"

Her gaze skims down over my chest, all the way to my knees before it pops back up to my eyes. Pink blooms across her cheeks, making my own blood heat.

"Brains." She flashes a patronizing smile, her doubts about mine obvious.

I can't help my smirk. It's second nature around her and never fails to fire her up. "Same here."

I could list more qualities I want in a partner. Motivation. Loyalty. An excellent sense of humor. Fire. But she doesn't ask.

Conversation moves to the heroine's emotional journey, but soon the ladies get distracted again.

"You know what I've never seen?" Fran pipes up. "A doorway lean."

A couple of them nod agreement, but Nora asks, "What's that?"

"When the guy puts his hands on a doorframe and leans in," Rosetta explains.

Barb frowns at her. "That's appealing?"

"Oh, yeah. It's so sexy and confident, and just—" Wren snaps her mouth shut.

More shiny bits for my treasure hoard.

"I need to see that one," Isabel says. "Shepherd?"

"There's no doorway out here for me to lean against."

Fran points over my shoulder. "Use the French doors that lead into the kitchen."

"This is ridiculous," Wren mutters.

It really is. This is my fourth month in the book club, and they've never asked me to do anything like this before. It's usually typical book club fare—we chat, we talk about the characters, I learn more about romance tropes and clichés with each visit.

Today, they need visual demonstrations?

But it doesn't bother me and seems to make Wren squirm. Whatever it takes.

Before I can get up, she pops out of her seat. "I'll show you."

I twist to watch her stalk across the patio, open one of the doors, and step inside. When she turns around, the spark of defiance in her eyes could burn down this entire neighborhood. I'm already on fire, smoldering in silence.

She rests one shoulder against the door frame, arms crossed. "Look at me all casual and manly. I'm leaning."

She goes on glaring at me as though she thinks she's showing me up. She's so cute.

"Or they do a one-hand version." She shifts and places a hand on the door frame at about eye level. "All I have to offer you are these two hands and the kilt on my back."

She's deepened her voice and narrowed her eyes, doing her best Blue Steel. Behind me, the ladies chuckle at her impersonation of a generic romance book hero.

Wren slides her hand higher in the doorway and turns toward the frame, raising her other hand as though caressing an invisible face. "I'm not like other guys. I'm...built different."

Her saucy wink at her audience tears a laugh from me.

"What about the one where their hands are on the top of the doorframe?" Fran asks.

Wren lifts her arms, but her fingertips only graze the wood.

Rosetta *tsks*. "I guess we need Shepherd, after all."

I get up before I think to do it. I don't love this much attention on me. I don't like performing and I'm terrible under pressure. A shiver of anxiety washes through my stomach, but I can't pass up this opportunity. I'm at the doorway in a few steps, staring down at Wren. I lift my hands, easily resting them on the frame above us.

Her blond hair is wild today, loose and free, unlike the slick ponytails she prefers when she's working in the bakery. I catalogue her sassy hoodie, the latest in a seemingly endless collection of shirts printed with sarcastic sayings. Even though it's torture, I breathe her in. She rotates her perfumes, so I never know what I'm going to get. Today, I fill my lungs with a fresh, citrusy scent.

I lean down a touch, tilting my head closer to hers. She glares up at me, her chest rising and falling with quick breaths.

My nearness affects her, but I'm not naive enough to trust that she'll magically drop her walls. She'd rather fight with me than fall into my arms.

I don't pick up on subtle flirting cues and am far from smooth, myself. If I thought she legitimately hated me, I would keep my distance. But this...it's not hate. I don't know what this dance we're doing is, but I can't make myself give it up.

Wren licks her lips, staring at me as if waiting to see what I'll do next. Like with most of our dance, I let her take the lead.

Doesn't mean I can't push her a little.

"Okay there, kitten?" I ask low.

She huffs out a breath, placing both hands on my chest to move me out of her way. I step aside, but her touch lingers as she brushes past, leaving my skin heated and my fool heart wishing for more.

After closing the door, I follow her to our loveseat, where we're flooded with appreciation from the rest of the book group.

"Thanks for indulging us, you two." Ada beams as though we acted out the entire book. "That was very helpful."

"Yes. Very illuminating." Rosetta sounds a little too pleased for my taste.

"Maybe we should do some more," Fran says.

"Hmm." Wren seems to think about it. "The heroine in our book kneed the hero in the face. We could demonstrate that."

"They were in a compromising position when that happened," I point out. "How book-accurate do you want to be for our demo?"

She purses her pink lips. "I don't see you wearing a kilt."

"Ask nicely and you might."

Her lips part as if to fire off something else.

"Maybe we should get back on topic," Nora says. "Like the heroine's predicament of needing to marry to keep her estate."

They discuss inheritance laws and societal norms of the

time. Barb is almost feral to share all the facts she's researched. Talk gradually moves from Regency England to the patriarchy and back to kilts for some reason. Finally, before wrapping up for the day, we vote on next month's reading options. In a close vote, a contemporary wins out.

"Phew," Wren says. "I'll be glad to get back into the modern world. It was a little annoying to read about a character five years younger than me, lamenting how she's never going to find a man. Have some dignity, girl."

"The heroine in this one should be more relatable." Ada's eyes twinkle in the afternoon light. "She's convinced she hates the broody cowboy hero, but I have a feeling he's going to change her mind."

Wren's excitement fades, leaving a hollow smile. "Yay."

Inside, we pack up the leftovers, and women slowly start heading out. Ada grabs her phone off the kitchen table. "Give me your number, Wren, and I'll add you to our group chat."

"Do you discuss books as you read?"

"We try to keep spoilers out of the chat," Rosetta tells her. "But we like being in touch."

"Maybe Shepherd will give you his bread recipe," Barb suggests.

"If you ask nicely," Nora croons.

"Maybe he'll even give you a one-on-one lesson." Fran's gleeful smile completely misses Wren's growing grimace.

"Maybe we can knead the dough together, *Ghost*-style." Wren's lack of enthusiasm almost makes me laugh.

So does the lack of subtlety in this group.

"Take these with you." Ada foists so many containers of leftovers into her hands they almost topple.

Wren glances at me as she juggles the food, and I can't hold back my "I told you so" smirk. Her frown deepens, but she switches to a smile for Ada.

"Thanks so much for inviting me."

"We're glad to have you join us. You're the perfect match for..." Ada takes a deep breath, drawing out the pregnant pause. "Our little group."

"I'm always looking for my next book boyfriend."

"What about a real one?" Fran asks.

"Find me a guy with a kilt and a castle, and we'll talk." She backs toward the door, avoiding eye contact with me. "I like my men like I like my coffee: tall, dark, and fictional."

A couple of the women shake their heads at her silly expression.

"Is that from one of your shirts?" I ask.

Her gaze hits mine like a thunderbolt. She's almost smiling. "Trademark Wren Krause. Don't steal my idea."

With that warning, she slips out the door. I watch her out the front window until she disappears from view.

Rosetta sidles up next to me. "That's a wildfire just waiting for a spark."

I chuckle at her perfect assessment. I've been looking for a match for years.

FOUR
WREN

IF I WERE A SWEETER, kinder, more demure woman, I would have already forgiven Callahan for horning his way into the romance book club *I've* been trying to horn into. I would say, "It is what it is," smile, and move on.

But I am a wretched woman full of snark and Dr. Pepper, so I barge into my house dreaming up ways to exact my revenge. Subscribe to junk mail in his name. Put up fliers around town that say "Get in Gear sucks." Sneak into his house and burn all of his stupid flannel shirts.

Wait. Nope. Bad idea. That would leave him wandering around shirtless, and nobody wants to see *that*.

Nobody.

Even if I am kind of curious. Do the tattoos just stop at his shoulders or what?

Inside, a little voice shrieks, "Wren!" and all my frustrations melt away.

"August!"

My nephew hops off the kitchen chair where he was coloring and flies into my arms. I lift him up, and he squeezes me tight, his head on my shoulder, his little heart beating out his love. This is the good stuff. Better than cream cheese brownies, a deep tissue massage, and *The Princess Bride* combined.

With one arm around my neck, he uses his other hand to brush his pale blond hair away from his forehead. He's overdue for a trim. "Are you going to watch the movie with us?"

"I don't know," I tease. "Depends on which movie."

"Robin Hood and Little John."

I die every time he mispronounces "l" sounds. His speech impediment makes it *Yittle John.*

Never get old and jaded, my sweet boy.

I squeeze him around the middle until he giggles like I found all his tickle spots. "One of my favorites! But I always want to hang out with you."

I've seen this little munchkin practically every day of his life, and I always want more. He and my sister Tess lived right here with me and Mom up until a few months ago. I practically pushed Tess to get her own place and now only have myself to blame for how my sad little heart aches whenever I walk by their empty rooms.

Forget sleep, exercise, and staying hydrated. My mental wellbeing rests entirely on nephew snuggles.

I set him back on his feet. "What did you do today?"

"I rode my bike and played with Dutch and built Legos and ate ice cream!" Words tumble out of his mouth faster than I can keep up, but I think I get the basics. It's a good day.

"Ice cream for dinner? I didn't know Nana was that much of a pushover." Actually, I did know. Everyone melts for August.

"He didn't have ice cream with us." Mom walks into the dining room from the kitchen, smoothing her hands over her disheveled hair. "He had a boys' afternoon with Ian."

Speaking of melting for my nephew, Tess's new boyfriend has become the mushiest. He started out as a Viking-styled hermit and now acts like the sun rises and sets over Tess and

August. I'm here for it. They deserve to be cherished by someone who realizes their worth.

He's also part of the reason August spends at least one night a week with us at the house. It gives Tess and Ian some alone time and affords endless cuddles for Mom and me.

"Ice cream was a treat, silly." August grins, showing off a new gap in his smile. At six years old, this kid is losing teeth at an alarming rate. "Daniel made sausage and potatoes for dinner."

As if answering a summons, Mom's silver fox beau emerges from the kitchen. Sheriff Daniel O'Grady. He looks kind of rumpled, too, his short hair askew in the front and his T-shirt wrinkly.

Oh. Oh, no. They were making out in the kitchen again. For shame. You'd think a bakery owner would be more hygienic than that.

That's another big change around here. Not only did Tess finally move out and meet a fantastic man, but Mom's dating again. It took her twenty years after Dad left, so it's a big deal. I'm glad she's happy. But when I asked her if we were getting a stepdad, I meant it as a joke, not a wish. Daniel isn't here twenty-four-seven, but it's only a matter of time.

It's a fresh reminder I need to get a place of my own. I paused my apartment search after meeting one mild-to-moderately creepy landlord too many. Now, I'm waiting for my best friend, Hope, to move in with her fiancé so I can swoop in and take over her apartment. It's a genius plan.

"There's leftovers if you want some," Daniel offers. "Mo wasn't sure if you'd be hungry after your book group."

Mo. He's given Mom a nickname that never fails to make her blush. I didn't even know the woman was physically capable of blushing up until the summer. Suddenly, she's fooling around at every opportunity and blushing up a storm.

Gross.

"They fed us, but I'm always in the mood for a tasty potato." I head for the kitchen, but Daniel cuts me off.

"I'll get a plate for you. You relax with your mom and August."

"Uh, okay. Thanks. That's...nice."

I sit next to August, who has returned to his Avengers-themed coloring book. I make a mental note to find a pin-up of Thor in there and hide it somewhere for Tess to find. She might have her own real-life Thor now, but that doesn't mean I'm going to forget about her old crush on the hunky superhero.

Mom sits across from us. "Daniel just wants to be helpful," she whispers.

"I know," I whisper back, even though I have my doubts about our privacy. Aren't law enforcement officers required to have supersonic hearing or something?

She lifts an eyebrow, telegraphing, "Then act like it."

I'm trying, but it's a lot to get used to. It's been the three of us for so long—and then August made four—it's hard to adjust to the new dynamic. Plus, it's awfully soon to cozy up to my mom's new man, right? They've only been dating a little while.

I'll just ignore the fact they've basically been in love and yearning for each other for years.

Daniel returns a minute later with a plateful of roasted red potatoes topped with a few seared sausage chunks. He sets it in front of me along with a fork and takes a seat next to Mom. His arm automatically goes around the back of her chair, and she leans into him, placing a hand on his leg.

I avert my eyes like I'm avoiding Medusa's stare. It's my signature move lately. Every important woman in my life has paired off and become *mushy*. And then there's me. Tough, gristly Wren.

"How was the romance book club?" Mom asks.

I take a bite of potato and automatically wish I had a slice of Callahan's bread to go with it. My tastebuds are traitors, but they know good food.

"It was neither as exclusive nor as scandalous as I was led to believe." I wonder if I can get them to spice things up with a little paranormal action one day. A vampire could be good. Maybe a werewolf. I bet Fran would be into that.

"I think you led yourself to those conclusions, honey."

"They were fishy and weird whenever it came up. Obviously, I'm going to assume something racy." Aside from their questionable Callahan-ogling, it was literally just talking about romance books.

"Are you going to stop going now that your curiosity's been satisfied?"

"Oh, no. They're stuck with me." Now that I know Callahan's involved, I'll never drop out. Not unless he does first. I'm locked in.

"What's next?" Mom asks. "Another historical?"

"Contemporary cowboy." I wrinkle my nose. I'm not bothered by the cowboy. It's the hints about how the main female character falls for the guy she doesn't like that make me doubt the book choice. I can only suspend so much disbelief.

"We're going to try that new ramen restaurant in town this week," Daniel says casually. "Want to join us?"

"I like ramen!" August pipes up.

Daniel's smile warms. "You're welcome to come, too, pal."

August lights up at that. Daniel's focus swivels to me, that same kind, fatherly expression on his face.

I genuinely don't know how I'm supposed to respond to it. My dad left when I was eight, and after a few half-hearted visits, dropped out of our lives. It's easy for August to soak up attention from Ian and Daniel because he's never had a man in his life. I have, and I know how it crushes your soul when that man decides he doesn't love you enough to bother anymore.

Stalling, I chew another bite of surprisingly delicious potato. What is it with men and their excellent kitchen skills today?

Unfortunately, that makes me think of when Callahan mentioned skills in *other* rooms, and I almost choke on my food.

"I don't know if I can." I've been meaning to try the restaurant, but I'm a third wheel often enough as it is. We're together practically all the time at home. I don't need to join them on their nights out, too. "I might need to read up for the next book club."

"That's a month away, isn't it?" Mom says.

Busted.

"It's not just that. I've also got..." I scramble for something, anything else going on in my life. I'm not involved in any other clubs or groups. I don't have a side hustle. I don't have a boyfriend, and all my closest friends are occupied with theirs. It's just me and my newfound crochet addiction against the world. "Things to do."

An exquisite excuse.

"That's okay." Daniel's unfazed by my rejection. He probably has a lot of experience from trying to make perps confess their crimes. Or whatever he does. "You can join us another time."

I make a finger gun at him but immediately ball my hand into a fist. That's probably offensive and could possibly be seen as a threat. Arresting me might put a damper on his relationship with Mom. "Another time. I'm going to change, and then I'll be down for movies."

I mostly say this to August, who cheers as I leave the table to tuck my empty plate into the dishwasher and run upstairs.

Shutting myself into my bedroom, I breathe easier. I change into soft flannel pajama pants, take off my bra with a deep sigh, and put on a T-shirt that says *In your dreams*. Then, I flop onto my bed and check my phone.

> Hope: How did book club go?
>
> Hope: I need to know
>
> Hope: I keep imagining those sweet, elderly women saying the most unhinged things
>
> Hope: Please help a girl out

I put her out of her misery and press *Call*. She picks up right away.

"Are we disappointed or relieved book club didn't go into overtime?" she asks.

"A bit of both." I wouldn't have minded talking about the book longer, but my seatmate left a lot to be desired.

"So? Was it everything you hoped?"

"It was...illuminating." To quote Rosetta. "Considering it took them forever to admit they were reading romance novels, they sure have no shame discussing shirtless men."

"It's their happy place," Hope says with a laugh. "And now it can be yours, too. You can discuss imaginary men to your heart's content."

Just one flaw in her plan. "It would be my happy place except Callahan was there."

Just saying it out loud makes my stomach flip. I am never going to get over this.

"Shepherd was visiting or something?" It's gratifying that even Hope finds his presence absurd.

"Nope. He's part of the group. And has been for longer than I've been buttering up Ada and Isabel." It's rude, honestly. I don't know how he did it, but I just *know* he did it on purpose to get at me.

"So you guys talked about romance? Together?"

"Not only that. The ladies asked us to—" I clamp my mouth shut. Maybe I don't want to share about Callahan's manliness demonstrations. Hope has specific delusions about the two of us that I don't need to encourage.

"They asked you to what? Act out the scenes?" She laughs. *Laughs.*

Because what could be more hilarious than Callahan and me pretending to be romantic?

After a few seconds of silence on my end, her laughter dies out. "Wait. You really did?"

I sigh all the air out of my lungs before launching into a recap of my afternoon. Forearms, doorway leans, and all. Books played a very small part.

"You have to admit, it's really sweet they invited him," she says when I finish. "They must like him a lot."

"I don't have to admit anything. You know how I feel about him."

"Right." She drags out the word as if she hasn't listened to at least one rant a week about him for endless months. "But it's been a long time since all that stuff between you went down. Maybe things have changed."

I sit up and punch my pillow into a better shape. Then punch it a few more times. "Not for me."

"Hear me out. I didn't think I liked Griffin—"

In the background, her fiancé shouts. "I'm standing right here!"

She laughs again. "But when we reconnected, we both realized we had each other all wrong."

"And you realized you were madly in love with me." His voice sounds closer than before.

"That, too."

The line goes suspiciously quiet for a minute.

"And I realized I'm hopeless without you, sweetheart," he says.

Ugh, these two. Adorable, yet disgusting. Like baby pandas before their fur comes in.

"All I'm saying is," she finally continues, "just because Shepherd said some things about you in the past, it doesn't mean he feels the same way now."

Hope is way more forgiving than I am.

"I think you misheard him," her fiancé says.

And Griffin is an idiot.

"I straight up heard him tell his coworker how awful I am. I didn't *mishear* anything."

People have said worse about me, but not the guy I'd been bantering with ever since he opened his bike shop. Not the guy I'd maybe sort of definitely been hoping would ask me out. Nobody who'd ended up making me feel so much like a fool.

I'd popped over, probably to fake-complain about him parking his giant truck in my spot, when I stumbled on the private conversation. The guys were behind the counter, their backs to me as Callahan did something to a bike.

"Wren Krause is loud, opinionated, and unavoidable," he'd said. "That woman is too much in every category that matters."

I snuck back out before they could turn around and see me, but I learned enough that day. He thought I was loud and opinionated before? Brother had no idea what was coming for him.

"And that's before the Richard Allred situation," I say.

Hope sighs but doesn't try to argue that one.

Richard Allred, the former Sunshine resident-turned real estate developer came to town not long after I found out what Callahan really thinks of me. Richard was looking for new places to invest his money, and set his sights on Blackbird's Bakery.

Until recently, the bakery was always just me, Mom, and

Tess. We work ungodly hours six days a week to keep everything humming. Even a small outside investment could have meant upgrading our appliances, updating our front-end, or allowed Tess to open her custom cake arm two years earlier than she did.

"Tess doesn't think Maureen would have wanted an investor," Hope points out. "And I doubt you would have enjoyed dating a guy like that."

Maybe. Maybe not. While it lasted, his attention was flattering, if overboard. I've never been much of a flower girl and receiving a dozen bouquets at once tip-toed close to alarming.

But at least he'd been blatant about his interest. I hadn't had to read into anything or second guess or think we had something going only to hear that, no, he actually thought I was a shrew.

But a few dates in, he'd told me he was no longer interested in Blackbird's. He'd heard "local buzz" we weren't doing as well as he'd thought, and he didn't see the point in getting involved in a failing business.

He also didn't see the point in getting involved with me. Someone told him I was a "nightmare" to be around, and he decided I wasn't worth the trouble.

Stunned, I'd asked who had told him that.

Richard's lip had curled as he slicked back his blond hair. "Shepherd Callahan. *He's* the kind of businessman I want to partner with."

A few months later, Get in Gear had new signs out front and a slew of new bikes inside.

So, yeah. Callahan's not my favorite guy. Even if he is, unfortunately, stupidly hot.

"I still think you're wrong about him," Hope says.

"You, my friend, have been blinded by love." Despite what she and Tess and even the ladies in the book group hint at, my opinions about Callahan won't be swayed.

"I tried." She sounds like she's talking more to Griffin than me.

"Anyway. Romance book group was an experience."

"Sounds like it. Do you want to come over tonight? Have some dessert and vent some more?"

It's sweet of her to ask when I know she wants to spend time with her man. They both run small businesses and don't have much free time as it is.

"Not tonight. August's here."

"Don't want to miss out on that." She pauses. "I wanted to tell you in person..."

I sit up straighter. "Oh my gosh, you're pregnant!"

"What?" she shrieks. "No, I'm not pregnant!"

In the background, Griffin has a coughing fit.

"Sorry, it sounded important. Wait—are you dumping me as Maid of Honor?"

They're getting married this winter, but it's going to be so casual, it's practically an elopement. Dropping the Best Man/Maid of Honor stuff would be on brand for them.

"No! Stop guessing!" She takes a big breath. "Griffin and I decided not to get a separate apartment while we're waiting for our house to be built. There's no reason not to just live here until it's ready. But that pushes off your plans to move into my place by a few months."

"Oh." Compared to my guesses, that's a lot more realistic. Even if it kind of sucks for me. "I understand. That makes sense."

"We can go apartment hunting together some weekend, okay?"

"You do not want to see the things I've witnessed." I pull the phone away from my ear to check the time. "I have to go. August's waiting for me so we can start movie night."

"Aww. Give him a hug for me."

"You'd better be talking about August," Griffin says.

"Oh, and August, too," she says with a laugh.

Griffin growls something in the background, and Hope squeals.

"Goodnight, you two." I hang up and toss the phone on my bed. They're so disgusting.

I hate how much I want that kind of disgustingness for myself.

Downstairs, I snuggle August under a fluffy blanket while he pulls up the animated *Robin Hood*. We sink low on the couch, and he rests his head on my shoulder. I almost don't care that I'm stuck in this house with Mom and her boyfriend for the foreseeable future. At least I've got movie nights with my buddy.

I don't need more than this.

FIVE
SHEPHERD

I DON'T OFTEN ADMIT it, but I have an addiction. I would join a support group, but I'd probably punch anyone who wanted to join.

Every week, I buy a pie from Blackbird's. The flavor isn't important to me as long as Wren's the one who made it. She also needs to be the one who sells it to me. There's no point in going to the bakery if she's not there.

She sometimes comes into my shop to argue about whatever, but I can't count on her having a reason to. Not as often as I'd like to see her. So here I am like a puppy with attachment issues, needing to be near her. Talk to her. Eat something she poured her time and attention into.

It's not normal, I know. I also don't care.

The bell over the door jingles as I walk into the bakery. They walled off part of the space and turned it into Hope Parrish's gift shop a while back, but what's left is cheery. Shiny vinyl floor with a subtle purple sunburst pattern, a glimmering white countertop with an extra-large, refrigerated display case, and a couple of pale purple two-top tables in the front windows.

Occasionally, I order a hand pie and eat it here. Wren glares daggers at me the whole time. It lights me up, but I know better than to press my luck too much.

Even if, sometimes, going for broke feels like the only logical conclusion to my addiction.

She's behind the front counter, smiling as she boxes up a pie for an older man. She glances at me, and her smile falters. It only takes her a second to regain her composure, but that brief moment of uncertainty is what I'm here for.

I'm not much of an optimist, but sometimes if I catch her off guard, her first impulse when she sees me is to smile. It used to be, once. Maybe I keep coming in here in the hopes it finally will be again.

A younger guy wearing the dark purple Blackbird's apron moves across from me behind the counter. "Hi there," he enthuses. "How can I help you?"

They've hired on a few new employees in the last couple of months. It makes my visits to the bakery trickier. Unlike her sister, they haven't learned yet I'm only here for Wren. But maybe I can get some information out of the guy whose name tag reads *Jamie*.

"What's new on the menu?" I ask. Lately, Wren's been experimenting with flavors. I'm guessing, since I don't have much to go on, but she's the one who makes the most unusual varieties.

The guy grins wider. "We just added a peanut butter and banana pie, a pear pie, and a cranberry silk pie for fall, in addition to our regular menu flavors."

He waves a hand at the large chalkboard sign on the wall that I already have memorized.

"Those sound hard to make."

Wren side-eyes me from behind the register where she's ringing out her customer. Her lips twitch like she's dying to react. Too bad she's stuck in service mode and can't do it. I come in during lulls to maximize the opportunity to talk with her. And because when this place is packed, I break out into a sweat.

"I'm pretty new here, so I still make basic pies like apple and pumpkin. But our specialty pies are made by the masters." Jamie makes a flourishing gesture at Wren as if she's royalty. "Today, Maureen made the peanut butter and banana pies, and Wren made the cranberry silk pies. I think the pear pie is just like making an apple one, though."

Thank you, Jamie.

As soon as Wren's customer is out the door, her smile drops. She turns toward me in slow motion, her lashes fluttering. The glare she shoots me scrambles my synapses.

It's messed up, but at this point, I want anything she'll give me.

"Why do you want to know how hard it is to make our pies, Callahan?" she asks. "Planning on adding to Get in Gear's offerings?"

I pretend to consider it. "That's not a bad idea. 'Biking with Pies.' I see no issues there."

"You can pair it with your bread."

"Aw, Krause. Still thinking about this weekend and my...bread?"

Her mouth thins. A shame, since her plush lips knock me out. "I'm thinking about how you wormed your way into my romance book club."

She's still big mad about the book club. I expected that. Pretty sure there's nothing I could do that wouldn't have a result like this. Move away, maybe, but what would be the fun in that?

"You guys are in a romance book club?" Jamie's gaze bounces between the two of us. "Cool. What are you reading?"

"Cowboys," Wren says without looking at him. "What's your real angle there, Callahan?"

I affect my most innocent tone. "Isn't it enough to enjoy the wonders of reading with good friends?"

"Not when those sweet ladies could easily be taken advantage of."

She really thinks I'm villain enough to scam them somehow? I drop my teasing and hope she'll hear what I say. "I would never do anything to harm those women. When Rosetta invited me, it sounded like fun. Even I need to be around people sometimes, Wr—"

I catch myself and correct before I say something I'll wish back. "Krause."

Her expression softens minutely. A rare win in these confrontations.

"It's not fair you got in the group while I was still begging to be invited."

She's jealous. Maybe even hurt that she wasn't included when she wanted to be. Her frustration with me is misplaced—I'm just a guest at the party. But I know how to stop her feeling sorry for herself. Not the way I *want* to, but the remedy at my disposal.

I smirk. "I'm sorry I missed that. I'd love to see you beg."

Her eyes narrow, self-pity cast aside. "You don't have anything I'd beg for."

"Are you sure?" Slowly, I move one hand to the opposite cuff of my open flannel shirt and start to loosen the buttons.

Her eyes lock on my movements, pink washing over her cheeks. Yeah. I thought so.

My satisfaction must betray me because she snaps out of her tattooed forearm-fog. Her gaze returns to mine, flustered but stormier than ever.

"What do you want, Callahan?"

"A cranberry silk pie, please."

Her glare stays fixed on me, but her blush deepens. I've

been ordering pies that only *she* makes for weeks on end. Surely, she's figured out my pattern by now.

While Wren boxes up a pie, Jamie leans his palms against the countertop and addresses me. "It's cool that you're not ashamed to read romances."

My attention shifts to him. I don't care what he thinks about me, but for his sake, I hope Wren's new employee isn't judgmental. She'll put a stop to that real fast.

"Why would I be?"

His expression crumples a touch. "I didn't mean that you should be ashamed, just that some guys are. I read them, too. Uh, mostly M/M, but I'm accepting enough to read M/F sometimes."

I laugh at that. "It's always good to be open-minded."

"What was the last one you read about?"

I glance at Wren, but she's still focused on my pie. Might as well shake the hornet's nest a little.

"It's about a man who's secretly obsessed with the woman next door, but she keeps resisting him."

Wren's head snaps up. "You already finished next month's book?"

I hold her gaze. "No."

We play eye contact-chicken over the front counter for a minute. Confusion swirls behind her eyes and I swear she's going to ask me something, but her expression hardens again.

"Sounds like a stalker." She slides the boxed pie to the front of the counter and gives me the total.

I tap my card and take the pie. "She's secretly obsessed with him, too."

Her blue eyes zero in on mine, her mouth set into a pert frown.

Not smart. I just whacked the hornet's nest out of the tree, picked it up with both hands, and made a kissy face at it.

"That's the thing about romance books," she says, acid lacing her tone. "They're full of stuff that would never happen in real life."

"I know what you mean. What was that crazy scene in the last one? The couple got caught in the rain and took shelter in a castle's ruins where they stayed warm by—"

"Callahan!"

Her pink cheeks do something dangerous to me. Worse, they make *me* want to do something dangerous.

"Not in front of the youth." She gestures at Jamie, who's watching us open-mouthed.

I forgot he was here.

"I'm twenty-three," he says.

Wren goes on staring at me like she *needs* me to keep my mouth shut. I'm just not sure which one of us will regret it the most if I don't.

"They lit a fire," I finish.

"Is that...not something people do in real life?" Jamie asks.

I point at her employee. "I think he's right."

She lifts a hand as though shoving an invisible wall between us. "I wasn't thinking about that."

"Oh. What were *you* thinking of?"

Her cheeks flame bright pink. Almost the same shade as the cranberry silk pie I'm going to savor in my cabin tonight like an absolute lunatic.

"Well. I'll see you around, Krause." I've gambled enough for today. Seeing her speechless will have to satisfy. I move to the door and push it open with one hand, the other cradling the pie Wren made. I turn back one last time.

She's frozen, her gaze stuck on me, her expression a mix of anger and something else. The mystery of that *something else* will keep me humming along until the next time we cross paths.

In my shop, I pass Palmer, who's helping a family with bike

rentals, and make my way into the back. I scribble my weekly "Do Not Touch" sticky note and put it on the pie box before carefully tucking it in the mini fridge. My employees know by now not to mess with my pies, but the reminder won't hurt them.

Not the way I will if they touch my pie.

My phone buzzes. It's Leo. His calls are either extra short because he didn't have time to phone in the first place, or he's in a chatty mood, and I have to hang up on him. I've got a few more minutes left on my break, so I answer.

"Hey, Leo."

"What is the protocol for fancy parties?"

I lean against the back counter and chuff a laugh. "You would know."

Leo Dalesandro, former NFL darling, has been to more black-tie events than your average Sunshine resident. My social anxiety keeps my attendance to things like that at zero. Dressed up, all eyes on me, sometimes with a literal spotlight? Hard no.

"Not this one, my man. It's a fancy *lodge* party. I figured you'd have the inside scoop for me."

"There's going to be a party at Moonlight Lodge?" My family owns and runs the resort on the outskirts of town.

"Party's the wrong word. I want to say gala. That's bigger than a party, right?"

"This is the first I've heard." They usually at least give me a cursory invite to things like this.

"Oh, yeah. We're planning a big event next month to celebrate opening up the new wedding venue in the barn. We're raising funds for the children's hospital, and your dad said we should go fancy. So..."

"Are you asking me what you should wear?"

"Yes. I'm going to text you pictures of me modeling different outfits. I need you to give me a thumbs up or thumbs down."

I look around the storage and mechanical section of my shop. Gears, chains, and innards of an electric bicycle's motor litter the workbench. I wear T-shirts seven days a week. The man who won two Super Bowls and three People's Choice awards wants my advice on what to wear?

"I can hear you hyperventilating through the phone," he says. "I'm kidding."

I exhale hard, relaxing my shoulders again.

"I've got some good suits; that's not the issue. I was thinking more..." He fidgets with something in the background, probably a pen tapping a tabletop. "If I should bring a date to this event."

"You're the one planning it."

"Right, right. But like...what's your family's opinion on all that? Do you think?"

He would know more about that, too. He's blended seamlessly into my family since we were kids. More outgoing than I am by a landslide, his energy matches theirs. Now that he's back from playing pro ball, he's pretending Mom and Dad are doing him a favor by letting him work at the lodge while he gets his feet under him again. Really, he's building massive buzz for the resort without having to do a thing.

He's spent more time with them than I have since he's been back. Not sure why he's asking me their opinions.

"Just ask Charlie. I'm sure she's fine with it." My sister probably has a clear vision for this event just like she's known exactly how to turn our grandparents' old lodge into a luxury retreat. But she's not the type to worry about anyone else's dating life.

Thank goodness.

"You don't mind if I ask Charlie?"

"Why would I?" I obviously don't know what's going on at the lodge lately. I didn't even know about this gala, let alone whether or not Leo should find a date for it.

He makes a weird, strangled sound. "Okay. Yeah. That's great. Thanks, man. I appreciate the trust."

"Sounds like you're putting your trust in Charlie."

He laughs. "No kidding. Are we on for Friday?"

I do my best not to sigh. I love this guy like a brother, but our social batteries cap out at drastically different levels. I have to be dragged into a bar, and he has to be dragged out.

Switching up my routine is good, though. To an extent.

"We're still on."

"First round's on you," he says and immediately hangs up.

We both know he's going to ignore everyone's protests and pay for everything, but it's one of his favorite phrases from his pre-NFL days.

Before I head back into the front to finish out the day, I text my sister.

> Shepherd: How's the barn coming along?

> Charlie: Almost done! Stop by some time and see for yourself!

> Shepherd: I didn't know you were planning a big celebration for it

Which shouldn't bother me as much as it does. I haven't worked at the lodge for years. There's no reason to keep me in the loop. But I'm still part of the family. It'd be nice to know about major events out there before the rest of the town.

If nothing else, I'll know to expect traffic on the road home that night.

> Charlie: I thought M&D told you already

This doesn't ease my mind. Mom and Dad don't space out on things. That means they left me out of the loop intentionally.

> Shepherd: Leo did

Charlie: I should have told you

> Shepherd: It's no big deal.

It's still weeks away, apparently. And it's not like I want to go anyway.

Charlie: I've been busy. It takes a LOT of work to convert a barn and wrangle a golden retriever

> Shepherd: You got a dog?

Charlie: I meant Leo

Charlie: I thought you were in a romance book club

I never should have told her that.

Charlie: I read the one you suggested

Charlie: I can't believe you liked it

Charlie: So much pining

Yeah, well. Misery loves company. Even fictional company.

TEXT THREAD

Ada: Just a quick note to welcome Wren into the group

Rosetta: We loved having you join us

Isabel: It was a delight

Barb: I still say we should have an agenda with talking points laid out

Nora: The pie was delicious

Wren: Thanks again!

Fran: Can't wait to see what happens next time [teary emoji]

Nora: What are you crying for?

Fran: I meant to use the winking face [sad emoji]

Nora: That's not it

Fran: I don't have my readers on

Rosetta: Feel free to reach out if you need anything, Wren

Isabel: There's always someone in the group ready to lend a hand

Ada: Some closer than others

Fran: Whatever it might be!

Ada: We're all happy to help

Ada: Isn't that right, Shepherd?
Wren: I'm good, thanks
Shepherd: Whatever it might be

SIX

WREN

SHE'S SECRETLY OBSESSED with him, too?

She's secretly obsessed with him, too?

It's been two days, and I can't get Callahan's smug voice out of my head. I've tried listening to audiobooks, ASMR, and even two-thousands-era boy bands to wash it out. No dice. It's stuck in my brain like baked-on grease on a cookie sheet.

It doesn't help that his voice is pure chocolate, all rich and smooth. Everything would be easier if he had a squeaky, high-pitched voice, not this low monstrosity that would make me crave the sound if it weren't attached to him.

The other part, the part he said first...*that's* easier to forget. He's not obsessed with me. That's just part of what we do. We needle and get under each other's skin and say things that sound like some kind of confession, but it's all leading up to the real punchline: that *I'm* secretly into him.

Obsessed.

Ha.

As though I spend my days thinking about Callahan.

"Are you okay?" Tess asks. "You're wringing out that wash-cloth like you want to tear it in half."

I shove Callahan out of my mind like a woman throwing her ex's belongings out the window. I smooth the rag in my hand and lay it on a shelf behind the counter. In between customers, I've been rage-cleaning the bakery. Countertops, tables, even the mopboards are sparkling.

"I'm fine."

I don't love lying to my sister. The problem is, I know how this goes. The second I bring up Callahan, people start smirking and giving me knowing looks as though they didn't hear a word I said. It's obnoxious.

I've witnessed zero cases of enemies turning into lovers in real life, but everyone thinks the guy I can't stand is my one true love. Make it make sense.

"You'd be a better liar if you fixed one thing." She points at me, her finger inches from my nose. "Your face. It's obvious something's bugging you."

True. And if I tell her, she's going to take a running jump right into Lake Callahan's Not So Bad. Everyone I know loves swimming there. As far as I'm concerned, the waters are infested with brain-eating parasites.

I'm not in the mood to discuss him with Tess. But I can deflect a wee bit.

"Hope isn't moving into an apartment with Griffin." An issue I haven't looked at head-on again since she told me. "They're going to stay where they are until their house is ready. So I'm back to square one on finding my own place to live."

It's disappointing enough that I don't even have to fake extra emotion to go with the fib.

"Oh." Tess's expression falls. "That's a bummer for you. Understandable, but a bummer."

"But, hey! Maybe you and Ian want to move in together? Then I could take your apartment. Or his. I'm not picky."

It's a really nice duplex, and they get it for a steal because

Ian's aunts own it. I wouldn't expect the same hefty discount on rent, but I'd take one of the units in a heartbeat. I would have my own place and be close to August's cuddles again. A win all around.

Tess doesn't break out the "What a great idea!" smile I was hoping for.

"We're not ready to move in together. We've only been dating for a few months. We know where this is going between us, but we don't want to rush anything—for us or August. Plus, I need this time living on my own, even if Ian is right next door."

"Ugh. Why do you have to be so sensible?" The Responsible Oldest Sister Curse, I'm guessing.

"You'll find a place."

"Yup. Just like you found a place—by having one dropped in your lap by a well-meaning friend." Ian's aunts not only *asked* her to live there with reduced rent, they practically threw a boyfriend into the deal. All the rentals I've found want first, last, deposit, an extra fee for my lack of rental history, and my first-born child.

We are not the same.

"You could ask around more," she says.

"Brilliant plan. So many people we know have a sweet apartment they haven't advertised."

She leans a hip against the front counter. "You're being a pill."

I drop my sarcasm. None of this is her fault. "I know. I'm sorry. It's just annoying. Why is rent so expensive?"

Whenever I see the massive total I'll have to shell out for a subpar apartment, my enthusiasm for finally moving out of Mom's house fades a little more.

"You're not exactly broke." She gives me a critical once-over. "Unless you've spent all your money on something crazy."

"Yarn is not crazy."

I go to the fiber goods store at least once a week. I tell myself I'm just going to look, but then I start touching, too. Touching usually results in purchasing. It's a vicious cycle.

"Are you still saving for New Zealand?" she asks, all soft and sympathetic.

Her borderline pity makes me ready to slam the door on this conversation. Just because I've been dreaming about traveling for years and haven't actually done it yet, everybody wants to make it out to be some tragedy.

I raise my voice so I can be heard across the shop. "I'm saving up for the most lavish wedding present for Hope and Griffin."

From her side of the pass-through between our stores comes Hope's, "Woohoo!"

"Diamond-encrusted salad tongs are all the rage."

"I can't wait to use those tongs," she shouts back.

Tess looks unimpressed, but too bad. If we got into a discussion about not doing the things we really want to do, we'd both wind up sad about our choices. She's doing better at going after her goals now, but for a long stretch of years, neither of us followed our dreams.

A few minutes later, I'm spared any more uncomfortable looks from my sister. Rosetta walks into the bakery, and I go into customer service mode.

"Welcome in." Unlike some versions of customer service mode, my big smile is genuine for her. I liked her when I only knew her as Sunshine's head librarian, but now that I know she can throw down about romance, I'm an even bigger fan.

"Wren. I've got a bone to pick with you."

Her stern-mom voice sends a chill through me. "What? Why?"

Have I been kicked out of book group already? I wasn't *that* bad the other day...

"I think you brought those pies to book club to get us hooked." Her faux-frown morphs into a grin. "It's only been a few days, and here I am, needing more."

I put a hand over my racing heart. "Geez. I thought you'd looked through the fine history on my library card or something."

I stopped checking out paperbacks because of the constant late fees. At least ebooks return themselves on the right day.

"Not at all. I'm just here for more of your wonderful desserts." She looks over the selection of pies in the display case. "That pear pie had my eyes rolling back in my head. Ooh. What is the cranberry silk pie like?"

My brain fizzles out as I relive Callahan ordering the same pie. *Because I made it.* He does it every week to get to me. I shouldn't care anymore. But I do. It's our thing, in a twisted way. Some week, he's going to order something I didn't make. Park in a space other than mine. Or he'll stop coming in entirely.

And what will I do then?

"It's, uh..." I need a second. "It's a custard pie that offsets the tart cranberry flavor with the sweetened cream piping and a caramel cookie crust."

"I'll take one of those."

Tess moves to the side so I can grab one to slice and box up.

"I tried to reserve the ebook for next month from the library, but it's got a long waitlist." Best to distract myself with a safe topic. The popular cowboy romance they chose is as good as any. "Paperbacks were the same."

Even though checking out a paperback would result in brand-new late fees.

"Give the waitlist a try," Rosetta says. "The club ladies are the bulk of the current reads. They should finish up in a week or two."

"That's good to hear. I didn't want to go into Bend to find it at a bookstore." Bookstores are worse than yarn stores for impulse buys.

"I have to say, you and Shepherd are already making our group ten times more fun."

Tess stills. She slowly turns toward me like some kind of spooky predator. "Shepherd Callahan is in your romance book club?"

"The very same." Rosetta's got a big old smile on her face.

"I know," I say to Tess. "I'm shocked, too."

"Why?" Rosetta steps closer to the counter. "He's in the library all the time."

Probably researching ways to ruin other people's businesses. There are handbooks for everything these days.

"He's a voracious reader—always paperbacks—and a faithful volunteer." She sounds as proud as if she's talking about her own son.

I freeze mid-slice. "He volunteers at the library?"

"Oh, yes. He started out just shelving books, but we've had a program for the last few years to help middle school boys improve their literacy. Reading with young men like Shepherd makes them feel cool and accepted, and the books boost their vocabulary. It's an informal mentorship situation, too, if the turnaround in Jackson Donaldson's behavior is any indication."

"That's really...something."

I can't say much else. If it were Hope or Tess, I'd think they were making it up just to get a rise out of me. But Rosetta's so earnest in her praise of Callahan, I can't question it.

He volunteers at the library? With kids? He's a voracious reader? What?

I ring her up, still reeling from this new information. It's not like I thought he was a monosyllabic goon, but that and library volunteer are at two very different ends of the spectrum.

She takes the pie, and her smile turns devious. "Who wouldn't want to read with that man, am I right?"

Rosetta walks out, leaving my imagination running wild with scenarios of Callahan reading to *me*. I blame Lila and her Adonis boyfriend. Right after they started seeing each other, she told us how he read to her on the camping trip where they met— and still reads to her practically every night.

A vivid image barrels into my head and parks there: Callahan and me lounging on a couch, his long legs tangled with mine, my head on his chest while he reads a book aloud. My heart pounds a frantic beat, endorsing this imaginary plan.

Tess slides closer to me. "You left a lot out of your description of your new book group."

Yes. I did. I already heard Hope's "I think you've got him all wrong" speech, I didn't need to listen to another.

I take a big step backward. "I think it's time for my break."

Tess's mouth quirks. "That's convenient."

"And mandatory by law. So." I hook a thumb over my shoulder. "I'm just going to..."

Escape, is what I'm going to do.

SEVEN

WREN

I NEED AIR. Something is wrong with me. My lungs refuse to fully commit to their job. I walk through the back of the bakery, past our industrial ovens and massive refrigerators, until I'm out the door and in the alley. I just need a second to process this new information, take a breath, and then forget about it forever.

Except, I can't. How can I when Callahan himself is in the alley, tossing broken-down cardboard boxes into the giant blue recycling bin we share.

No. Our *businesses* share them. *We* don't share anything.

He looks over and catches me staring. Normally, this results in a smirk. Most things I do result in his smirk, but staring especially. He has an uncanny knack for catching me, and it always results in that curl along his lips.

Not this time. Today, he looks stricken, like the sight of me makes him...I don't know what. I'm not a mind-reader. Alarmed, maybe.

He stops chucking cardboard into the bin and stalks closer. "Are you okay?"

Ugh. His deep voice isn't supposed to be all tender and gentle. Not when I'm weirding out over him.

"I'm fine." I cross my arms over my chest. "I just needed some fresh air."

We're going to ignore the fact that I'm standing feet away from the trash bins, and the delicious but powerful smells from the Mexican restaurant farther down the street make the air here anything but pristine.

He takes another, more tentative step closer. "Are you sure? You seem out of sorts."

What is this? Callahan, concerned about me? I must have stepped through a portal into a parallel universe where he's actually a decent guy.

I tilt my chin higher. "This is how I always look."

"No, it isn't. Usually, you've got more spark in your eyes. Today, you look..." He pauses to examine me like I'm a piece of art. Or a crime scene. "You're upset. Confused, maybe. I want to say afraid."

I snort. "I am not afraid of you."

"I know."

His soft smile makes my stomach tumble as easily as if he'd tossed *me* into that stupid bin. We don't do this. We don't get perceptive about each other and go digging around in each other's heads. We don't talk about anything real.

Not anymore.

The fact that we used to spins through my mind so fast I'm dizzy with it. Before I heard what he said about me. Before he stole an investor out from under Blackbird's. We used to be—

"What is that?" He stalks closer, his brows furrowed like a storm cloud descended over us. "Did someone do this to you? Who?"

That "Who?" sends a shiver down my spine.

He gets right into my space and gently takes me by the elbow. It stays warm in the bakery, so I only wear T-shirts at work even through the winter months. His light touch on my skin is pure heat in the chill fall air. That warmth radiates along my arm, raising goosebumps like an electric current.

He's staring at my bare upper arm as if he's ready to go nuclear on someone.

I finally look down to see what he's so worked up about and have to stop myself from laughing. I've had that bruise approximately six hours. "Stop hulking out. Nobody gave that to me. I did it."

His gaze collides with mine, all protective and warm and ready to defend me from unknown assailants, and I don't hate it.

Something is definitely wrong with me.

"I was carrying a tray of pies from the back room, and I slammed into the doorjamb like a klutz. Relax."

He nods, and his worry seems to lessen, but I don't like the fire lingering in his eyes.

Or...I like it too much. I don't know anymore. I need to shut this down. I came out here to stop thinking about Callahan, and now I'm thinking about him more. In worse and worse scenarios.

He ticks his head to the side. "Sorry. The bruise looks like..."

He doesn't explain, but it's easy to guess where his overactive imagination went. It's the right angle for a too-firm grip.

"Trying to be a protective romance book hero, are you?" I ask.

The flames in his eyes burn brighter. "Is that what you want?"

"No." I scoff, but it's weak at best. "Is that what *you* want?"

Why am I even asking? I don't care what he wants. Or, honestly, what *I* want if it has anything to do with Callahan. It's the stupid book club. Intertwining him and romance has turned me upside down. The sky is green, the villain is the hero, and the guy I thought hated me keeps staring at my mouth like he's just waiting for permission.

His fingers are still wrapped around my elbow. I should shake him off. Tell him to get lost. Do anything other than stand here inches away from him, staring into his eyes, and letting him touch me so tenderly.

"You don't want to know what I want." It's not a warning so much as...regret.

Whatever is happening makes no sense. I don't like Callahan. He doesn't like me. The back and forth between us is based on dislike and resentment, not the fire currently coursing through my veins and turning my body into searing lava.

"I'd probably be disgusted." My voice is way too breathy to give that sentence any kick.

His brown eyes darken. "Probably."

He doesn't elaborate. That's unhelpful. I need to know what he wants like I need to draw in my next breath.

"You should tell me. So we can be sure I'd hate it."

His eyes spark, and he takes a step closer. Instinctively, I move a step back, but that puts my shoulders against Blackbird's door. He rests the hand not holding my elbow against the doorframe.

I swallow hard. Might even gulp. He's *leaning*.

"You wouldn't hate it." His voice is so sinfully smooth, I want to drizzle it over my waffles and eat it up.

"I hate everything you do."

His mouth tips up on one side, his gaze taking its time roving over my face like a caress. When it lands on my lips, he locks in. "Do you?"

"So much." The words are barely out before I snap.

I crush myself against him, my hands going around the back of his neck to pull him down so our mouths can crash together. The instant we connect, he's kissing me back, pressing just as hard as I am. *Finally.*

A voice somewhere in my addled brain asks why we haven't

been doing this forever. Didn't we know we were meant to? We should kiss all the time, every day.

His hands course up my back, pinning me to him. Mine have differing goals, one exploring the crest of his shoulder while the other twines in the hair at the back of his neck. It's just long enough for me to get a fistful, holding his head in place.

I love how messy his hair is. I love that I'm messing it up more.

But then we open up to each other, and my thoughts shatter into a million pieces drifting around me like fairy dust. Shockwaves dance along my skin straight up my spine and down to my toes. I want to get closer, mold myself to him. I would fuse myself to Callahan if I could.

Time does this weird thing where it both crawls by so I can savor every moment but flies so fast I can't keep up. I should be memorizing every touch. I should luxuriate in the experience. All I really know is, this kiss should never end.

Callahan slows, losing the frantic energy until he's gently exploring. Caressing. Nipping at my lower lip. His hands splay across my back, locking me to him as if he'll never let me go. This is where we live now. The alley is our home.

I don't have a huge amount of experience in this area, but I've never had a first kiss like this. I've never had *any* kiss like this, altering my brain chemistry like a drug. A delicious, free, highly addictive drug. Sign me up for a lifetime supply.

He starts to pull away, but he's not in charge. I growl like a tiny animal, drawing him to me again. I bite him back for his insolence. As if we're ever stopping.

I slide my tongue against his, desperate to drive him just as crazy as he makes me. He groans, and I silently cheer for my success. Except, him going crazy just makes me lose control that much more. A victory for us both, then.

He cradles my face in his hands, his soft kisses turning feather-light.

Incidentally, those are just as capable of devastating me as the frenzied ones. On a multiple-choice survey of Callahan's kisses, I want *All of the above.*

His mouth leaves mine, but he presses one last, lingering kiss there as if he doesn't want to stop, after all. The chill air in the alley sweeps over my lips. I sigh, wishing I could hit *Snooze* and get five more minutes. When I finally open my eyes, it's to find his staring down at me.

Callahan looks like he's ready to dive back in for round two. Hard same.

But then I catch the smirk teasing along the edges of his mouth. I know that smirk too well.

"Did you hate that?" he asks.

The curl of his lips and the smack of pride in his voice snap me back to my senses. I drop my hands from him, knocking his away from where they were holding me in the process. He takes a step back, probably out of self-preservation.

This is the same guy who said all those rude things about me. Who turned an investor away from my family's business only to go work with him, himself. Who gets off on riling me up and leaving me feeling like a fool.

Just like right now.

From the romance book hero lean to the kiss that left me legitimately mindless, was this all just a way to one-up me? I think I might be sick.

I want to respond in a totally mature way and scream, "I hate *you!*" in his face. Instead, a pathetic sound comes out of me like a wounded animal. I find the door handle and barrel back inside before I can discover the depths of humiliation in store for me when it comes to this man.

I'm pretty sure the limit doesn't exist.

TEXT THREAD

Ada: The enemies to lovers in this book is just perfection

Rosetta: No spoilers!

Ada: It's not a spoiler when we knew it would be enemies to lovers from the beginning

Fran: So much delicious tension between these two

Isabel: Wouldn't it be fun to see that play out in real life?

Nora: Who has an enemy in real life?

Fran: Who has a castle in real life?

Barb: Gary and I rented a castle when we went to Scotland five years ago

Barb: Haggis is much better than the rumors say

Fran: Cowboys are real

Nora: Do you know any?

Rosetta: I read once that the reason we read enemies to lovers is because we like the idea of someone seeing us at our worst and loving us anyway

Isabel: How romantic

Barb: I never caught on to the bagpipes, though

EIGHT

SHEPHERD

I DON'T LOVE GOING to The Stumpjumper with Leo on my best nights. The bar is noisy, crowded, and smells like stale beer and old fries. But tonight? When my mind is full of the kiss I shared with Wren? My body still singing from the feel of her? When her taste is still on my lips? I should have skipped social hour.

I'll be lucky if it's only an hour.

"The interior designer brought in six pieces of white fabric for us to choose from for the tablecloths. I thought they were all exactly the same, but Charlie knew the right one to pick."

Leo's been monologuing about the work he's doing at the lodge with my sister for a while now. It's part of our dynamic—he talks, I listen. Tonight, I'm barely doing my share.

Mentally, I'm back in the alley with Wren in my arms. Wondering when we'll have a moment like that again. *If* we will.

That "if" kills me.

He takes a drink of his beer. "The changes she's made at the lodge are unbelievable. She's so impressive. She could make this her whole career. Just travel around the country rehabbing resorts and making them upscale."

"Mmm." I can't imagine my sister with this much ambition for anyone else's property. She's dedicated to ours because she wants to live up to our grandparents' legacy. More than is healthy, in my opinion, but I can't deny her vision for the place has made it a success.

The megawatt grin on his face turns up a notch. "It should be a TV show. 'Changes with Charlie.'"

"Sounds like an After School Special about puberty."

He grimaces. "We can workshop it."

I can't tell how serious Leo is. He has connections in the entertainment industry—pitching a reality show for my sister is extreme but not out of the realm of possibility for him.

He fiddles with the coaster beneath his beer glass. "On second thought, that might be a bad idea. She's overworked as it is."

"True." Charlie's been heading one project after another out there for the last few years. She's overseen renovating the main lodge, building new guest cabins, and expanding their activity offerings. If she thought a TV show would help the lodge, she'd do it even if it ran her into the ground.

Leo looks me over. "You're kind of off tonight."

"More than my usual?" I am, I'm just trying to hold up my side of the conversation.

"You're distracted." A sneaky smile curls his mouth. "I'd almost guess you're thinking about a woman."

Guilty, but I'm not in the mood to confess anything. Leo's the one who rhapsodizes about the latest woman he's into, not me. Divulging information about my private life makes me antsy even without the precarious dynamic between me and Wren in the mix.

"Worry about yourself. Which of the three women who dropped their numbers in your lap tonight are you going to call?"

It's part of the package of being friends with someone famous, but all the attention makes my skin crawl. People stare like he's a chimp in a zoo and they're waiting for him to do a trick. They pretend to take selfies, but they're actually sneaking photos of him. The boldest ones come over to meet him. The shameless ones leave their numbers on napkins alongside lipstick kisses.

The smile drops off his face. "I'm not going to call any of those women."

"That's right. I heard you're dating that fitness influencer who's staying at the lodge." He's not. Leo is my opposite in this, too. He's incapable of keeping things to himself. If he was dating her, I would already have heard way too many details.

He groans. "How did you find out about that?"

"Palmer. After singletrack, gossip is his favorite subject." He asked me to confirm or deny the rumors, but I told him in no uncertain terms he won't get information about Leo out of me. Nothing Leo doesn't share himself, anyway.

"There was a blind item about it. 'Fitness influencer and former NFL center getting cozy at Oregon resort.'" He drags his palm down his face before resting his chin in his hand. "Charlie heard about it."

"She's probably happy for the free publicity for the lodge."

He shakes his head, his usual cheer turned morose. "It's one more reason she doesn't take me seriously. I took your advice and straight up asked her to be my date to the gala, but she said no."

I stare at him, his words jangling around in my skull. "I didn't tell you to ask Charlie on a date."

He stares back. "Yes, you did. Those were your exact words. 'Ask Charlie.'"

"No. I meant you should ask her if you could *have* a date, not to *be* your date. Wait. You're..." I look around the bar as if I'll find answers at someone else's table. "You're actually interested in my sister?"

Leo's a good guy, or we wouldn't be as close as we are. I trust him implicitly and know in my gut he would never hurt anyone in our family. I still have a small but powerful urge to fight him.

"We've always teased and joked around. We were friends. But ever since she kissed me a year ago—"

"She *kissed* you?" That doesn't sound like Charlie at all. She's sensible and smart. Impulsiveness isn't her style.

Which means it wouldn't have been a spur-of-the-moment thing.

I'm going to need another beer for this.

At least he looks sheepish. "I'm doing this all wrong. Charlie is awesome. She's talented and capable and makes my manager look like a chump. She's beautiful and funny and..." He splays his hands. "I care about her. A lot."

I exhale hard. I've never had to deal with the hypothetical of a friend being into my sister before. Especially not my closest friend. The football hero. Who's also working with her. And living next door to her—in the house *I* set him up with.

No part of that's reassuring me.

He flashes a small smile. "If it makes you feel any better, she thinks I'm an idiot."

"That helps."

"But maybe you could—"

"Nope. Whatever you're thinking, the answer is no. I'm not going to be your wingman or give you advice or be your Cyrano de Bergerac for my sister's hand." First, I would be lousy at giving anyone dating advice. Second, I can't think of anything that would make me more uncomfortable.

"But you'd be such a good Cyrano."

"I regret even knowing this much about it." I finish off the last of my beer. "What happened to that Dalesandro charm all the TV hosts love to go on about?"

"My Dalesandro charm only annoys her."

Sounds like Charlie.

If that's the case though, why did she kiss him a year ago? I rake a hand through my hair. It's none of my business, and I don't want to know.

A few feet away, four middle-aged women have their phones out. They're fluffing their hair like they're taking selfies, but their phones are pointed at Leo. Sneaky, they are not.

"You've got some adoring fans at eight o'clock," I tell him.

He sags against his chair. "Can't I just lie low for the evening?"

"You and 'lying low' don't go together." He's an attention hound through-and-through. Avoiding the spotlight isn't his style, even if he claims it's why he came back to Sunshine.

Or...did he come back for Charlie? This is bad. I was better off not knowing about his interest. Crush. Whatever you call it, I need a mental *Delete* button.

He huffs laughter. "You're probably right. Hey, Grant and Griffin are over there. Let's go say hello."

Proving my point about his inability to lay low.

I look over my shoulder and spot Grant Irwin with Griffin McBride at a big table in the corner, along with their girlfriends and another man. I don't bother asking where Leo met Grant, who's opening a branch of his family's outdoor stores down-town. Best to just assume if they're in the vicinity, Leo's going to meet them.

"Lead the way."

He grabs his beer, and we walk over to their table. They get up and greet him like he's late to the party instead of a gate crasher. Griffin invites us to join them, and we take a couple of empty seats.

My internal clock counting down to an acceptable time to leave just reset.

The third man at the table is introduced as one of Grant's brothers, but I lose track of the conversation. My attention snags on Wren standing at the crowded bar across the room. Our kiss flashes through my memory like a lightning strike. I've relived that kiss a thousand times in the hours since it happened, turned over every moment again and again. Her taste, the feel of her, the utter perfection of us together at last.

Followed by confusion when she'd gone back inside, mad at me all over again. I should have known one unbelievable kiss wouldn't undo years of biting back-and-forth. A guy can dream, though.

I focus on Hope, who's seated next to me with Griffin's arm slung across her shoulders. "Is Wren with you?"

She cranes her neck to spot her friend at the bar. "Yeah. She didn't want the beer we're drinking, so she left to order a cider."

Wren probably won't be happy when she comes back to her table and finds me here waiting. I could make an excuse to leave. Find another time to talk to her when we can have more privacy than sitting at an eight-top surrounded by half-drunk people.

Across the room, a man sidles up to her. I don't recognize him, but he's standing way too close to her for my comfort. Apparently for hers, too. She takes a step to the side, but he drifts nearer again, chatting her up.

Déjà vu hits me like a slap to the face. Right when I think stars are aligning with Wren, someone else steps in. Not this time.

"I think I'll get a cider, too." I stand and stalk toward the bar.

I shouldn't get involved. She's a grown woman who can handle herself. Stepping in will probably give her one more reason to be ticked with me.

The guy crowds her, practically caging her against the bar.

I shouldn't get involved, but I'm going to, anyway.

NINE
WREN

I JUST WANTED to have a relaxing girls' night. Go out with my friends and distract myself from *that* moment in the alley I can't get out of my head. Instead, my girls' night wound up including several guys, and now a dude at the bar who won't take no for an answer.

He's trying to be flirty, but the undertone of *or else* ruins the good-guy vibe.

"Come on, what's your name? Is it so hard to give me that?"

I hold my body rigid so I don't accidentally touch the hipster in the vintage shirt. If looking him in the eye brought this on, I hate to think what he'd do if we made contact. "I'm just waiting to order a drink."

"It's on me. All I want is your name."

Yeah, right. I'm positive this guy wants more from me than just my name.

Suddenly, a body wedges between us. I'm ready to throw an elbow at all this crowding when I look up and realize it's Callahan.

"Sorry I'm late, kitten."

Sometimes in romance novels, the hero's voice is described as a "purr." I've always thought it a flowery and borderline impossible illustration. Men don't make sounds like that, I'm sorry. But there's no better word for the way Callahan's deep voice rolls across my skin. He *purrs*.

He's gazing down, eyes dark and warm, and the tension drains out of me. I'm *relieved* to have him here. I'm borderline giddy, like I'm filled with champagne bubbles, all because he showed up.

What. Is. Happening?

He turns slightly as though just now noticing the guy who'd been pushing for my name. "Are you waiting for the bartender?"

His question is casual, but carries an undercurrent to it that says the dude had better not be waiting for anything else.

The guy grimaces. "No. I'm all set."

He walks away, blending into the chaos of The Stumpjumper.

Which, by the way, I plan to point out to Hope and Lila was a terrible place for a girls' night. I much prefer eating my weight in loaded fries at Delish than fending off pushy guys in a bar.

Now that the jerk's gone, Callahan gives me an inch of space. I instantly wish we were still touching.

I must be coming down with something. A weird sickness that makes me crave Callahan? There'd better be a cure.

"Are you okay?"

He's concerned for me, but there's a layer of protectiveness to the way he's watching me, too. He's hulking out again, just like those heroes in the monster romances Lila keeps talking about. I didn't think actual guys did that, but here we are.

It's confusing. Almost as much as my visceral reaction to him.

"I'm fine. I know a few self-defense moves if he'd pushed his luck."

This just deepens Callahan's scowl. He turns and looks across the bar as if searching for the guy to make sure he's keeping his distance.

I mean, I don't know that. I'm making it all up in my head. But when his gaze meets mine again, the fiery look in his eyes makes me think he'd gladly confront that jerk.

We go to one romance book club together, and suddenly, he's my hero?

I'm going to ignore the elephant-sized kiss in the room. It was just the hottest kiss of my life. Totally unrelated. No need to bring it up.

The bartender finally takes my order. Callahan adds a second cider to mine, and the gal behind the bar whisks away again.

It's time to pull myself together and get this under control. I shift my hands to my hips in a power stance, my arm brushing his.

"I would never accept the nickname kitten, by the way."

"What should I call you?" He needs to stop using his deep, intoxicating voice on me. It's distracting. I hate it.

I hate how much I don't hate it.

I think for a minute. Nobody's ever given me a romantic nickname before. Right now, hearing him say my name would be enough, but I can't blurt that out at a bar.

"Goddess." What I'd intended for snark comes out closer to a plea. This evening is sliding right off the rails. Should we go in the back and make out again?

I mean...should we?

"Done."

He touches his hand to the small of my back. It's featherlight but rocks through me like the whole-body shudder right before you fall asleep. This isn't okay. I'm not thinking like myself. Whatever magic he's weaving, I need to find a spell to block it.

"What are you doing here, Callahan?"

"Leo dragged me out."

There's another one of Callahan's mysteries. He's best friends with Leo Dalesandro, former NFL star center and whirlwind of down-to-earth friendliness. From what I've heard, they've been buddies since they were kids. It has to be a case of an extrovert taking an introvert under his wing, I just can't figure out why. Callahan is broody, sarcastic, and doesn't seem to really *enjoy* people. Peak lone wolf stuff.

Leo is definitely a pack animal.

"He's assimilated into your group, FYI."

I turn back to our table and spot Leo sitting between Grant and his brother, talking while gesturing broadly with his hands. A sigh gusts out of me. "Girls' night is officially out the window."

"Were you trying to have a night to yourselves?"

"*I* was. Hope and Lila had their own plans. We hardly ever get a night out now that everyone's hooked up. I just wanted some bonding time with my girls." I sound way too disappointed over a simple thing like adding a few extras to our evening out. "I need to make more single friends."

What a sad sack. All my friends have boyfriends, woe is me. Pathetic.

Even more pathetic? *Callahan* is the one I'm confiding in.

"I'm sure Fran would be happy to have a night on the town with you."

I laugh in spite of myself. Then I imagine how a night out with the flirty seventy-something might actually go and laugh even harder. Things could get wild. "I don't know if I'm ready for that much excitement."

I pause, staring at him mid-laugh. Callahan actually cheered me up. He took my frown and turned it upside down. Just like the rest of me, apparently.

The bartender finally returns with our frothy glasses of cider. Callahan pays for both before I can get my cash out.

"I owe you a drink," I tell him as we head back to the table.

"You don't."

"Mr. Vintage Bowling shirt insisted on buying me a drink, too."

He scowls. "Fine. You can buy me a drink."

"Fine."

At the table, I take my seat next to Hope. Callahan sits at the last open space at the opposite end. I'm not disappointed. This is good. The best, probably, since I need some room to clear my head. Shake out all these Callahan-related cobwebs.

It's hard to do when our kiss still lives in my bones, sending out shockwaves every time I think about it. Which, obviously, I don't. That would be crazy. I'm trying to forget it.

But nobody's ever kissed me like that. Like I'm the oxygen he needs to survive. Like nothing else exists in the world beyond us. Like he's been holding himself back and is finally set free.

I take a big gulp of my cider. I can't wax rhapsodic about Callahan in a bar. *You're better than this, Wren.*

Conversations move around the table, but I barely participate. Every time I look his way, Callahan's watching me. The creeper. Except, that means I'm looking at him just as often. We must both be creeps.

I need to rise above him and not take his bait. Keep my eyes on my half of the table. Definitely not look at his mouth from six feet away like a weirdo. Focus.

Grant's brother turns to me. Rhett is several years younger than him, so about my age. Despite the age gap, they're obviously related—his hair's a little lighter, but they share the same blue eyes and mega-watt smile. He's built similarly, too, if a few inches shorter. Unlike Grant, Baby Adonis is a shameless flirt.

"What do you do for nightlife around here, Wren?" He flashes his big smile at me as if he's already charmed by the answer I haven't given yet.

"You're doing it." I raise my glass to toast him, but my gaze darts to Callahan like a little psycho.

He's leaning back in the uncomfortable bar chair as if he doesn't have a care in the world. His casual confidence is mildly aspirational and majorly irritating. Nothing's bothering him right now? Like, I don't know, that crazy kiss in the alley?

Because he doesn't care, Wren. It was all part of his twisted mind games. Probably.

"We've got the same amount of nightlife here as you do back home," Grant points out.

"I thought you were trying to get me to visit *more*," Rhett shoots back.

"When whitewater rafting season starts up again, you'll have a lot of reasons to visit." Lila's switched over into tourism mode, her eyes overly bright. "We've got a dozen rivers across the state with all classes of rapids for you to explore."

Grant kisses her temple. "Nicely done, princess."

She gestures at Callahan. "And if you like biking, Shepherd can point you to all the best paths."

"Oh, yeah?" Rhett acknowledges him at the far end of the table. "What kind of paths?"

"A lot of old doubletrack where they're phasing out ATVs. Some newer singletrack trails."

I don't know what any of those words mean, but he's got the table's interest.

"And Shepherd's working on getting some of our fire roads converted into biking paths, too." Lila's not ready to give up her

Callahan praise. "He's got a plan to link them up to existing paths in town."

"It's not just me."

Lila rejects his attempt to brush her off. "That's not what the people on your team say. They're working on the fundraising, but the trails are your vision."

He ticks his head to the side as if even that small acknowledgement pains him.

It makes total sense that Callahan's planning some big bike path expansion. More bike trails means more bike sales and rentals for Get in Gear. He's already proved he puts his business first in everything.

Except...watching Lila's efforts to pull in more tourism and business opportunities for Sunshine, I've learned that nobody gets involved in stuff like that totally for themselves. There has to be some positive community spirit at the heart of it. A little shimmer of altruism hiding in Callahan's bleak heart.

Gross.

I sip at my cider, trying to force even more new information about him into the small box where I've kept him the last couple of years. It's getting crowded in there. I'm just not sure which parts to toss out.

Rhett turns back to me. "What would you be doing right now if you weren't partaking of Sunshine's extensive nightlife?"

Easy. "Crocheting my weirdos."

His brow furrows, but a smile curves along his mouth. "I don't understand that sentence."

"I crochet," I explain. His smile doesn't budge, but he looks just as mystified. "It's a yarn craft like knitting, but with a hook. I make stuffed animals. Well...they're not animals. They're just blobby little guys."

And I adore every single one.

"Granny crafts are popular right now." Callahan's mouth has a curl to it. Smile? Or smirk?

I love my granny craft, but now I kind of wish he didn't know about it. I need a cool girl hobby, like blacksmithing or glassblowing.

"The tight end on the Hornets knits himself a sweater every season," Leo says. "Claims it helps him focus."

"It must work," Rhett says. "He plays like a beast."

"Do they look good?" Griffin wants to know.

Leo shakes his head slowly. "Like a JoAnn's barfed on him every time."

Hope squeezes my elbow. "I want your weirdos for my store."

"I love you, but I'm not meant for that side hustle life." If I tried to perfect and sell my projects, it'd suck the fun out of making them, and I'd lose my outlet for stress relief.

Do I have an army of them in my room? Possibly. Will I give up any of them? Never. Except gifts to August, of course.

She coos as if somebody smuggled a dog in here. "They're so cute and ugly."

Leo raises his glass. "To cute and ugly."

Rhett slides his elbow closer to mine on the table. "I'm in town for a few more days. Maybe you can show me what else there is to do in Sunshine tomorrow night? Other than visit this illustrious bar and indulge in granny crafts, I mean."

His giant smile momentarily disarms me, but before I can answer, someone else does.

"I thought you had plans tomorrow night, Krause," Callahan says.

I blink at him. "Plans?"

His mouth tips up. "With someone from your book group."

Is that a dig about my pathetic social life? I'm so inept, my only options are Fran and the romance club ladies? Granny crafts with my granny friends. I told him that out of loneliness and desperation. I should have known he'd throw it back in my face.

I shoot him a scowl and turn to Rhett. "I'd love to show you around Sunshine tomorrow."

He beams like he's on his way to pick up his prize for Best Smile. "Can't wait."

I glance at Callahan because yes, that did just happen, but my triumph crumples like wadded-up paper. He doesn't look sour, like I one-upped him in one of our verbal battles. He looks *hurt*. Two deep lines cut between his dark eyebrows, his mouth thin and flat beneath his beard. Something like betrayal darkens his eyes until I have to look away.

My cider tastes bitter the rest of the evening. I make half-hearted attempts to keep conversation going, even if Griffin, Grant, and Rhett mostly discuss hikes and lakes and altitude sickness. Lila talks about her idea for a summer concert series in a local park. Leo praises some high school grunge band he heard playing downtown. Hope shares about other granny crafts taking off in her store right now.

Callahan doesn't say a word.

I can't look his way again. My stomach churns with guilt and regret like a demented cement mixer. I don't kiss one guy and make plans with another a few hours later. Even if the first guy has me so confused I don't know which way's up.

But what else was I supposed to do? Say "Oh, no thank you, Rhett. I'm currently hung up on the guy who kissed my face off this afternoon and then had the audacity to make fun of my lack of a social life this evening."

When our group finally breaks up for the night, Rhett and I exchange numbers. He leaves with Grant and Lila, lobbing one last Baby Adonis smile my way before they take off down the street. Leo says loud goodbyes to everyone, only to look around and realize Callahan already disappeared.

I refuse to think about *why* he slunk away without a word.

Hope and I hug on the sidewalk while Griffin waits by his truck.

"I hope you know what you're doing," she whispers in my ear.

Truly, I do not.

TEN
SHEPHERD

WHEN I WAS A KID, before we lived there, too, my family would often visit my grandparents at the lodge. No matter what we originally came for, I'd eventually make my way to one of the garages to tinker on an ATV or dirt bike. Grandpa would find me wrist-deep in something mechanical, covered in grease, happily shut away from the people coming and going on the property.

He used to tease me that I liked machines better than people.

I don't dislike people. I just don't understand them sometimes.

I replace the brake pads on a Specialized Rockhopper, trying to lose myself in the routine task. Shunning customer service, I've taken on all the repair duties today. I've had my hands on one bike after another, but it's not enough to clear my head. Nothing ever is when it comes to Wren.

I've enjoyed the bite in our exchanges over the years, but I never felt we were out to draw blood before. Never looked down and realized I was the one bleeding. Never had the sinking sensation that maybe I'd had her wrong from the beginning.

No. Not from the beginning. When I first got to know Wren, our banter was purely teasing. Flirtatious, even. We sometimes ate lunch together at the picnic table in the alley, gradually opening up to each other on a more personal level.

I admire her drive in her family's bakery. I appreciate how she refuses to take crap from anyone. And I adore her sharp intelligence. Six months of lunches together and conversations over pie orders, and I was lost.

I'm not a fast mover, romantically. Occasionally, I've accepted date invitations from women I don't know well, but typically, I prefer to take my time getting to know someone first. I don't like casual dating—I want to be sure we're on the same wavelength before I ask them out.

With Wren, I'd thought we were of the same mind.

Until her banter turned into snark. She took several giant steps back and walled off our connection. Whatever was building between us stalled out.

But it was too late for me. I was already in the thick of it with her. And I've spent most of the last two years hoping to recapture that initial spark between us.

I guess I'm an optimist, after all.

My phone buzzes on the front counter. I glance at the message but can't swipe to answer. Not sure what I'd say if I did.

> Rosetta: I heard Wren hasn't found a copy of this month's book yet

> Rosetta: Perhaps someone with a paperback could share?

> Rosetta: Perhaps someone with high quality forearms?

At least she's messaging me personally and not in the group

thread. Reading about fictional romance isn't enough for these women. They're trying to manufacture it in real life, too.

Another text comes through.

> Leo: How bad is it if I've been accidentally feeding a skunk cat food on the porch?

> Leo: Accidentally

I huff a breath at my ridiculous friend. If he's trying to win over Charlie, luring skunks onto lodge property isn't the way.

The bell over the door chimes—a feature it took me almost a year to add, after one too many jump scares from quiet customers lurking in the shop. I look up from the bike behind the front counter to see *her*. I'd say my thoughts summoned her, but if that were true, she'd be with me every moment of the day.

Her hair is slicked back into a neat ponytail, I assume to keep it out of the way in the bakery. She wears the purple Blackbird's apron over a pale pink T-shirt and jeans, black Converse padding across the cement floor. Her dark blue eyes bore into mine, a line already between her eyebrows as if *she's* upset with me.

I don't know why she would be, but what else is new?

"We got some of your mail by mistake." She moves closer, holding up a large white envelope.

I return my focus to the bike. "Leave it on the counter."

She slides it over but doesn't walk away. If she's here to gloat about her date, I'm not in the mood. She won. I surrender.

I tighten the brake cable tension and test the lever, making sure the brakes catch properly. The hum and slide of the wheel spinning and stopping isn't enough to mask the sound of Wren's long inhale.

"You didn't park in my spot today," she says. She's been

complaining when I do for ages, but today, it sounds like a question.

"I thought I'd let you have it." It was supposed to give her one less reason to come in here to talk to me. Turns out, she wants to battle me even when she gets her way.

"You're not *letting* me," she says. "I parked in that spot long before you showed up."

"So I've heard."

I finish up with the brakes and wipe my hands on a rag, still avoiding looking at her. A note taped to the back of the counter reads, *Be yourself.* I left that reminder for Laurel, who can struggle with customer interactions.

Today, it feels like a personal triple-dog dare.

"Shouldn't you be getting ready for your date with Rex?" Not that I really want to remind her.

"Rhett," she says absently.

"Did you decide where you're taking him?" I ask through gritted teeth. I want to know what she'd like to do on a first date but never in this context.

Dinner out? Or prepared together? Watch a movie on the couch? Or drive to watch the sunset? Something entirely different? I know what I would choose, but what does she want?

That's always been the question.

I wipe down the bike, the silence in the shop deafening.

"I don't understand you," Wren finally says. It's more accusation than anything else.

"The feeling's mutual."

"You're so...infuriating."

"You read my mind."

"You're acting like what happened in the alley—"

My gaze snaps up to hers. "You mean when you kissed me?"

She jolts back, her eyes wide. "*You* kissed *me!*"

I force a laugh. She can regret it if she wants, but she can't pretend she didn't instigate every second of what happened between us. "Keep telling yourself that."

Cracks appear in her sassy façade, showing glimmers of heat underneath. Her cheeks bloom with a touch of embarrassment, too. No need for that when I'd kiss her again in a heartbeat.

I toss the greasy rag aside. I'm tired of dancing around.

Resting both hands on the front counter, I lean a fraction toward her. "You kissed me, Krause. So hard, I saw stars. The best kiss of my life."

Her blue eyes darken, dropping their focus to my mouth. "The best?"

"Hands down." I always knew it would be, when we got there. The rest... "I can't say I'm flattered you agreed to go out with another guy a few hours later."

She throws her hands on her hips, stepping closer to the counter between us, the spark back in her eyes. "What was I supposed to do when you were acting like my social life's so pathetic I've only got elderly ladies for company?"

A growl of frustration rushes out of me. "I was asking you out. You were supposed to go out with *me*."

She stares, her mouth working, but no sound comes out. How could she have no idea? I didn't think anyone could be worse at picking up on romantic signals than I am. Unless she's been actively rejecting them this entire time.

"You didn't—" Wren stares like she's seeing me for the first time. She gives her head a firm shake, then crosses her arms. "That was a terrible way to ask someone out."

"Apparently."

In hindsight, I agree. My impulse was to step right in like I did with the guy at the bar and tell Rhett to back off. Make it clear Wren's spoken for. Beat my fists on my chest, hoot like a gorilla, and shout, "Mine."

Whatever Wren thinks of me, I'm not actually that prehistoric.

And, despite that phenomenal kiss in the alley, she's not actually mine.

"Do you really—"

Wren cuts herself off when a man pushes through the door and heads for our selection of road bikes. She looks from him to me as if remembering where we are. The man slides his hand over seats and handles, clueless that he's interrupted anything.

Wren and I stare at each other for another full minute. I've made myself pretty clear, but her confusion might as well come with a giant neon sign attached.

"I guess I should go." Her brow furrows deeper along with her frown, as if she's not sure she should go at all.

"See you, Krause." I keep my voice gentle. This isn't a dismissal. If I didn't have a customer—and she didn't have a date tonight—I would have so much more to say.

"Yeah. I'll...see you." She turns like she's moving through molasses, heading for the door. Before she pushes through, she looks back one last time, that stunned expression still on her face.

I'll be thinking about that look all night.

"Do you have any more of these carbon fiber gravel bikes?" the customer asks once she's gone.

"Yeah." Inconvenient interruption or not, I can't be mad at the guy for coming into my store. "Let me help you with that."

I slide past the bike I've been working on and glance down at the piece of mail Wren brought over. It's labeled *To Resident*.

ELEVEN

WREN

I'VE SUSPECTED BEFORE, and occasionally been accused, but now it's official. I am a terrible date.

Rhett is cute, funny, and friendly to everyone. He's got a soft, Texas accent that makes everything he says sound vaguely complimentary. He's engaging and interesting and close with my closest friends. This would be a great evening if I could just stop thinking about Callahan.

The best kiss of his life? What? Who even says something like that out loud? I mean, yes, I was thinking it, but he really just went and *said* it.

"Is this a safe space, Wren?" Rhett levels me a serious look. "Can I tell you something in confidence?"

We're at a small booth in the new ramen restaurant, waiting for our orders. It's reasonably crowded for a Saturday night in Sunshine, so I'm not sure it's really the best location for an ultra-private conversation. I'm probably not the best pick for one, either, as distracted as I am.

But I gesture for him to proceed. "Sure."

His smile lights up. "When Leo Dalesandro came over to

our table last night, I played it cool, but inwardly I was screaming like a six-year-old on a waterslide."

I laugh at the vivid imagery. "It takes some getting used to."

He visited once or twice a year when he was in the NFL, but it's a totally different ballgame when he's here full time. Pun intended. We've got a handful of sleazy guys who hang around hoping to take a picture of him doing just about anything they can sell. Getting coffee. Picking up his mail at the post office. Having a throw down make-out session with another big-name celebrity.

I mean, I assume that's what they're hoping for.

"I've been glued to his career since he signed with the Austin Hornets." Rhett's doing an admirable job of keeping his enthusiasm at a reasonable level, but the light in his eyes is awfully bright. "We've been to a bunch of games over the years —Magnolia Ridge isn't that far outside of Austin. I could have brought merch for him to sign if it wouldn't have made me look like a total nut job fanatic."

"Don't tell me you sleep with his trading card under your pillow."

He slips an index finger in front of his mouth. "Shh."

"Grant didn't give you the heads-up about our homegrown celebrity?" Grant doesn't really seem like he's into that kind of stuff, but it'd at least be worth a mention.

"Grant's too busy praising Lila to talk about anybody else." He shakes his head, looking around the restaurant as if Leo might show up again. "I knew Dalesandro had retired to Oregon, but I had no idea it was to *here*."

"Lila's probably adding it to her spreadsheet of reasons you should move here when the store opens up in the spring."

His eyes sparkle. "Caught onto that, did you?"

"Is that a possibility?" I'm curious, but I don't want to sound eager, like I'm trying to get him to move to my hometown on the first date.

Especially when I wish this wasn't a date.

"I never thought about it. I'll be back when the store opens, for sure. Maybe even before then, who knows. Right now, I'm just getting a feel for how the social media and promo stuff for the new store should go. It's a totally different vibe out here than Magnolia Ridge."

"Examples, please."

"Easier access to different sports and activities, like mountaineering and whitewater rafting. The store will have a slightly different focus for what we sell based on what people are most likely to do here. We try to carry a bit of everything, but make sure products make sense for the area."

I've never really thought about what Grant's store will sell. Since it's outdoor stuff, the details sort of slide out of my head. But now, I'm questioning how the new store will affect other businesses in town. Whether or not there will be overlap. If it will cause problems.

"Do your stores sell bikes?" I ask.

"No."

"That's good." I exhale a squeaky laugh. "I mean, that's too bad. That you don't sell bikes."

"Are you in the market for one?"

"*No.* No way. Bikes and I don't go together. Don't want one, don't need one. I don't even know the first thing about them or where I would ride one. I know they say you never forget, but I bet I can't ride a bike anymore. That's how little they mean to me." I take a sip of water to stop myself from talking any more about how I definitely don't bike.

He watches me with an amused tilt to his mouth. "Huh. I kind of thought everyone was a biker around here with the way Lila and that guy—"

"Callahan." I bite my lips between my teeth.

"I thought his name was Shepherd."

"Shepherd Callahan." Shut up, Wren. Just shut it.

"Right. They made it sound like biking's a big deal here. But not for you?"

Our waiter appears and sets two steaming bowls in front of us before ducking away again. The spicy fragrance wafting up from the noodles, chicken, and soft-boiled eggs smells amazing. We both grab our ramen spoons and chopsticks and set to work.

"I'm not really outdoorsy," I say, wrangling noodles.

Rhett *tsks*. "Are you trying to break my heart?"

"I'm pretty sure you're the heartbreaker here."

"Maybe sometimes. Unintentionally." He lifts a shoulder. "Things happen."

"Uh-huh." Neither of us is trying all that hard on this date. From his extremely laid-back attitude about most things tonight, I don't get the impression he's on the hunt for his one true love. Which doesn't mean he couldn't stumble onto someone, but Rhett seems like the type to fend off love with holy water and garlic.

"But enough about my fear of commitment. Tell me more about your granny crafts."

I blow on my soup. "I really only have the one granny craft. Crocheting my little guys is it for me."

"Do you have any pictures of them? I'm not picturing 'weirdos' in my head."

I fish my phone out of my purse and pull up my camera roll. I've been sending pictures to Hope when I finish them. I like the validation.

I scroll through to find my most recent creation. He's dark purple, with floppy ears and a tail. "Not quite a bunny, not quite a fish."

I show him a couple more mashups. They're goofy little guys, but I love them.

"Cute. Is the truck yours, too?"

"Uh, no." I close the app and tuck my phone away.

I may or may not collect photographic evidence of Callahan parking in my spot behind our businesses. Most days, he can't. My work in the bakery starts hours before Get in Gear opens its doors. But those days when I have a late start? He always takes my space.

Until today.

The weird ache in my chest when I saw his truck parked two spots over made no sense. Reminding myself that he stole Blackbird's investor isn't the healing salve it used to be.

"That's it for my granny crafts," I say a little too brightly. "But I do have some granny friends, and those are pretty close."

"You run with a wild crowd."

"So crazy. Their favorite topics are the weather forecast and Callahan's forearms."

The only explanation for my continual Callahan-vomit is that he's messed with my brainwaves this week. I normally never talk about him, but here I am, yapping away and dropping his name like I'm getting paid for it.

But your honor, "You were supposed to go out with me" is a hard line to recover from.

"Your grannies spend a lot of time around Callahan's fore-arms, do they?"

At least Rhett doesn't seem annoyed that I keep bringing up another man. Not as annoyed as I am.

"Uh, we're all in the same book group."

"Yeah? What kind of books?"

I hunch over and slowly slurp up my ramen broth. This conversation is all downhill from here, I can tell already.

"Romance."

He mirrors my action, his eyes practically dancing. "Tell me more."

"That's probably a bad idea all around."

He smiles even wider. "I'll take 'Incriminating Subjects' for one thousand, Alex."

I raise a hand to stop his train of thought. "No. No way. That's not it. It's more that..."

Yeah. I've got nothing. I drop my hand.

Rhett just chuckles over his soup, unbothered.

"I'm really sorry." For accepting his invitation when I knew I was a mess, for bringing up Callahan all night, for being a general wreck of a person.

I should be delighted to be on a date with a guy who by all accounts is excellent at his job, smells nice, and is fun to talk to. Rhett is so cute, he almost hurts to look at. And he seems to be interested in me at least a little, which is all kinds of flattering.

And yet...no spark.

"Don't be sorry. I'm having a good time learning about Sunshine and making a friend." He seems to really mean it, at least.

And I did say I wanted more single friends. I just didn't specify a gender.

"When you come back to town, I'll give you names and numbers of half a dozen single women."

He holds his hand out over the table. "Done deal."

I shake his hand, relieved he's not offended.

He releases me. "Did you want to talk about Cal—"

"*No.*"

"Oh, thank God. I'd make a terrible therapist, but I figured I should at least offer."

TWELVE

WREN

MY GIRLS' night was a bust. My date with Rhett was a bust. It's time for a dose of the best self-care around: August cuddles.

I fire off a text to Tess before I leave the restaurant. She claims I'm welcome anytime, but not even I'm obnoxious enough to drop in without any warning. There's already a car in the second parking spot on Tess's side of the duplex when I get there, so I park in front of Ian's half.

I check my phone, but she gave my text a heart. Thank goodness her guest doesn't mean I can't visit. I'd hate to go three for three with spoiled evening plans.

I don't even manage to knock on the door before it's pulled open and a little someone launches himself at me.

August squeezes me around the waist, his chin tipped all the way up. "Wren! Did you come to say goodnight?"

I heft him onto my hip. "Oof, you're getting big, kiddo."

"I ate a lot for dinner."

His big blue eyes are so earnest and full of innocent, boundless love. Hugging him makes everything better.

"That must be it." I set him back down and walk inside but have to stop short.

Charlie's here. Everything in my life's coming up Callahan lately.

She waves at me from Tess's couch. I wave back with a shaky hand, sure she can tell just from looking that I kissed her brother yesterday. Maybe he left imperceptible flannel particles on me. Or...what if I *smell* like him now?

I wouldn't hate it, but she might recognize the scent.

Ignore the woman having a mental breakdown, please.

"We're sort of having a casual work meeting," Tess explains. "Wedding stuff."

Charlie's in the process of converting one of the buildings at her family's lodge into a dedicated wedding venue. Her offer to have Tess be their primary wedding cake vendor is part of what spurred my sister to finally go all-in with custom cakes at Blackbird's.

I'm grateful to her. I like her. I just kind of wish she was anywhere else right now. If my evening with Rhett is any indication, I'm going to bring up Callahan in about three-point-five seconds. I don't think my current audience will be quite so chill about a mistake like that.

"I just came over for some nephew time. I thought maybe I could read stories and put him to bed." Weird how those sweet little routines you don't even think about leave such a hole when they're gone.

"I don't mind giving up my privileges."

I spin around to find Ian standing in the short hallway that leads to the two bedrooms. He's wearing a long-sleeve henley and athletic shorts that reveal his prosthetic leg. Just like randomly finding Daniel in my house, it's still a little strange to discover a vision of manliness in a space that I expect to be mostly feminine.

Also, I'm continually impressed that Tess pulled in the burly redheaded pirate hottie. Go, sis.

"You can both read me stories," August offers. Always finding solutions, this one.

Ian grins down at him. "How about you read to Wren tonight, and read to me and Dutch tomorrow?"

August beams his gap-toothed approval.

"I just want to point out that it takes a man and a dog to replace me," I say to the room at large.

"I'll tell you goodnight now, though." Ian drops to one knee and holds out his arms. August trots over to hug him tight.

Seeing a guy with a man bun and thick beard hold a child like he's precious to him makes my heart turn to goo. No wonder Tess fell so freaking hard for the man.

After, August leads me into his bedroom. Tess does his nightly blood sugar checks, kisses his cheek, and tells him goodnight, too. Then, it's just me and my little man.

We read about cars and trucks having adventures. Pigs and worms with the worst luck. Chickens staging a revolt against their farmer. All the while, his head rests against my shoulder, getting heavier and heavier. He's got the stuffy I made for him tucked under one arm, its dual tails peeking out from beneath the coverlet.

"Are we going to have Wren Wednesday this week?" he asks in his sleepy voice.

I smile over that. "You bet."

His school has early release on Wednesdays. Sometimes he goes to daycare early, but other weeks, we cycle through who gets to pick him up and have special time with him. This week's mine. And I can't wait.

"Can we go to the park?"

"Sure."

"Can I ride my bike?"

"Of course."

"Maybe you can bring your bike, too."

I laugh, picturing it. "My bike isn't safe to ride."

The old bike I got in middle school is still in the garage at home. The frame's rusty, and both tires are flat and probably unusable. I'm sure it has more dangerous defects I can't even recognize. But it's sweet August wants to include me in his fun.

"You could fix it up," he says.

I refuse to imagine the look on Callahan's face if I were to roll that thing into his shop. He'd laugh me right back out the door.

"For now, I'll be happy to watch you ride your bike," I tell August.

"I'm good at riding." His mouth opens wide in a big yawn. "I hardly use the training wheels anymore."

"That's because you're awesome." I kiss his forehead. "Love you, buddy."

"Love you, too, Wren."

I wish I could say the moment clears my mind, but it soothes my heart, and that's more than enough.

I join the others in the living room, hopefully betraying nothing of my tumultuous thoughts.

"Rough day?" Tess gestures for me to take the empty armchair across from Ian. She and Charlie are on the couch, a tablet between them with a gallery of wedding cakes on the screen.

"I don't want to interrupt your meeting." I drop into the chair anyway.

"You're not." Charlie sets the tablet on the coffee table. "I'm venting about Leo more than we're talking about venue business."

"You and Leo?" I didn't think I was so out of the loop with town gossip I would have missed that nugget.

"No. No way. Not like that." Charlie's got both hands up, the perfect definition of denial.

I'm getting a weird sense of déjà vu right now.

"He's working at the lodge with me," she explains. "My parents asked him to help with some marketing as we get the venue off the ground."

"Yeah. A retired NFL player marketing a wedding venue. I can see that." Not that Leo wouldn't do it. Ego doesn't seem to be a big problem for him.

"I know. But he's like a second son to them, and they love having him around. He's practically my brother." Her nose wrinkles on the last word. "But he's constantly underfoot and has way more energy than I know what to do with. The man needs a hobby."

Tess laughs. "As a retired NFL player, I'm pretty sure this is his hobby."

"It's got to be hard for him to adjust to a life without football," Ian says. He knows a thing or two about starting over. After he lost his leg, he had to reevaluate his whole career, too.

"I'm sure his millions of dollars will help him adjust." Leo's a great guy, but I don't know how sad I can be about him not getting paid big bucks to play his favorite game anymore. Plus, he doesn't seem all that distraught.

But looks can be deceiving, can't they?

For example, when the broody, unassuming guy kisses you like he's on death row and you're his last meal. Didn't see that one coming.

"That's not very kind of you, Wren." Leave it to Tess to mother me a little.

"No, she's right," Charlie says with a laugh. "He's going to be fine. He's got a lot of ideas for what he wants to do next. I'm sure he'll land on something that makes sense. Until then..." She gusts out a sigh. "I get to be his boss."

"Lila's trying to get the two of us to do some kind of local promo for the new Irwin's store when it launches." Ian shakes his head as if this is just as ridiculous as Leo marketing the wedding venue.

Except, in his case, he actually is a world-famous mountain climber. From all I've heard, Grant actually fanboys over *him*. He'll fit right in at the outdoor store.

"Prepare yourself to be Lila's new best friend." Tess smiles over at her man. "Sunshine doesn't have a lot of famous residents. You and Leo just might be the entire club."

"What about that hotdog-eating contest winner?" I ask. "Nobody ever talks about her."

Tess tucks her feet beneath her on the couch. "I think she moved to Arizona."

"There's that guy who came in last on that obstacle course game show a few years ago."

I thought my week's been embarrassing—that guy went down a thirty-foot slide and landed in a pool of Spaghetti-Os on national television wearing nothing but a Speedo and goggles. Things can always get worse.

"I don't know if that counts as famous."

"Richard Allred's from here," Charlie points out. "But I'm sure Lila doesn't want to associate him with Sunshine with all those scandals going on."

My entire body goes still. "What scandals?"

"Tax fraud and embezzlement, mainly. But he dabbled in sexual harassment, too."

Tess shoots me a pointed look. She knows all about what happened with Richard—every last detail.

"Shepherd saw it coming," Charlie goes on, unaware of the silent conversation going on next to her. "He told me to steer clear of the guy years ago."

Callahan told her? I'm breathing so hard, I'm convinced everyone in the room can hear my lungs working.

"Did he say why?" Tess, sweetheart that she is, must sense I'm spiraling.

Charlie's mouth takes a sour slant. "He said Richard was sniffing around a local businesswoman, and Shep overheard him saying some nasty things about her. Stuff right in line with a guy who has four sexual harassment lawsuits against him in the works."

An invisible knife twists deep in my chest, pinning me to my chair. I gulp on air, my mouth desperately dry. "Did he say who it was?"

"He didn't tell me, but I've never seen him so angry. He said he was super close to beating the crap out of the guy right then. Probably would have wound up in jail, but it would have been worth it." She grins like she's proud of him, but her smiles slips away the longer she looks at me.

I don't want to know what my face is doing. I'm horrified by her story, but not for the reasons she must think.

"Shep's not a violent guy, normally," she rushes to add. "He's just protective. He wouldn't hurt anyone who didn't have it coming."

I'm smashed flat like that cartoon coyote after a run-in with a boulder. I am paper thin, liable to drift away on a breeze.

I try to pull myself together and behave like a normal person, exhaling a weak imitation of a laugh. "No. He's not like that."

I can feel Tess's gaze on me, but I don't have the heart to look at her. I need three to five business days to process this. I've been dealing with so much new Callahan information, my brain can only take so much before it cracks right down the middle.

"It sounds like Shepherd saved that business a lot of headaches," Tess says gently. "And that woman a lot of heartache."

"I thought—" My attempt at total casualness dies when I

can't make my tongue work. I swallow and try again. "I thought he made some kind of deal with Allred, though. A while back."

Richard told me he did. It was his parting shot. But now that he's been labeled a fraud, it's hard to take that at face value.

"Shepherd never worked with him. His business funds came from the inheritance we got from our grandparents." Charlie glances around at us. "They didn't leave us a lot, but you know it doesn't take much to help a small business."

I nod like a bobblehead, my world flipping upside down yet again. I thought Callahan turned Allred against Blackbird's, and me in the process. And ever since, I've been...

My stomach clenches. I've been horrible. I've sniped at him and been rude and generally awful to be around. I thought his terrible behavior justified mine.

But if Callahan's the hero of the story, then it turns out...I'm the villain.

THIRTEEN
SHEPHERD

DESPITE WHAT SOME PEOPLE THINK, I am not a hermit. I just like living in the woods.

A few years back, when Charlie started adding more cabins to the lodge, I built one on a secluded section of my family's property. It's less than a mile from the houses where my parents and sister live, but we don't share access roads. Nobody comes to my little slice of the forest by accident.

So the sound of a car crawling up my gravel drive is hard to miss.

I glance out the front window expecting to find Leo's SUV rolling up. He sometimes drops in with food and the excuse of whatever game is on TV. But I have to blink my eyes a couple of times when I see Wren's tiny sedan stop out front next to my truck.

She gets out, gazing at my cabin. It isn't as upscale as the ones Charlie's been adding to the resort, but it's a solid, comfortable A-frame. Wren's looking at it like she expected to find a ramshackle lean-to with my underwear hanging on a clothesline right out front.

I open the door, catching her with her fist up to knock. She startles, her eyes flying wide.

"Oh. Hi."

It took her some effort to get out here to see me, so the confusion in her greeting doesn't make much sense. But like most things between us, I roll with it.

"Hey."

She opens her mouth but then swallows down whatever she wants to say. Her gaze darts to where my hand rests on the doorframe.

The lean wasn't intentional, I swear. I appreciate the color rising in her cheeks, though.

I drop my hand and wait for...whatever it is she came to say.

Nerves seem to wrap around her like a too-tight sweater. I've been frustrated with both of us since she accepted that date, and agitated for the last twenty-four hours, trying not to think about her *on* it. But I don't want her feeling small and anxious around me, like she has to be careful with her words. I'd rather have her fire.

I step back, opening the door wider. "Do you want to come in?"

"Um. Sure. Thanks." She steps in over the threshold, the scent of soil after a rainstorm following her in. "I came by to—"

A strangled sound escapes her. If she was surprised by my cabin's exterior, she's gobsmacked by the interior.

"You have a rolling ladder." She drifts across the room as if under its spell.

My cabin's bigger than the guest lodging, but it's still just one room down here, with two small bedrooms upstairs. To maximize space, I built floor to ceiling bookshelves on one wall. A rolling ladder made the most sense for accessing the uppermost shelves.

Plus, it looks cool.

She walks past the sofa and the reading lamp to reach the bookshelves, staring open-mouthed. She grabs the rolling ladder in one hand, seemingly tempted to climb it.

"They're not displays, right? You've read them? Or plan to?" She runs her fingertips along spines as if she can't stop herself from touching the books.

"No. They're movie props. I bought them on eBay to give the cabin some ambience."

She grabs a book, pulls it out, and flips through the pages. "It's real. And...annotated."

Well. She went straight for my Greek mythology collection.

"You don't think much of me if you have to ask if my books are real." Who would put up a wall of fake books in the first place?

To be fair, I haven't read them all. But I have good intentions for tackling the ones I haven't gotten around to yet.

"I don't know what I think anymore." She speaks so softly, I'm not sure she means for me to hear it.

Fair enough.

She puts the book back but continues browsing, pausing now and then to read titles. If I'm not mistaken, she deeply inhales, smelling them before stopping to admire one of the black and white photos on display. "This is pretty."

"Thanks. That waterfall's not far from here."

Wren spins to face me. "You took the picture?"

I nod. She goes on staring.

"You seem surprised." An understatement, since her face is the textbook definition of "screaming internally."

"I wasn't expecting..." She waves a hand around to take in my mini library. "*This* when I pulled up to your murder cabin."

"I assure you, no one has died here." My heart stopped when I saw her pull up out front, but I've fully recovered.

Almost fully recovered.

"That's what they all say."

"It's not as remote as it looks. My parents and Charlie live down a path just to the east."

"And I would get an axe in the back before I could ever get them to rescue me."

She's so ridiculous. "I would never axe you, Krause."

"No. You'd use your hands. You'd want to get dirty."

She stares at me across the small space, her gaze heating until her eyes are tiny blue flames. I could be wrong, but I don't think she's imagining me *murdering* her.

After a minute, she shakes away whatever mysterious thing she's contemplating. "This is a really nice place."

I'll let it go that she's so surprised. The few people I've invited out here have had similar reactions.

"Thank you. I used to live right next door to my parents and Charlie, but I needed more space than that." Living within fifty yards of my entire family is more togetherness than I'm cut out for. "This is my sanctuary."

It's a lofty descriptor, but it's apt. I need time alone to recharge, and it's easier to do that here than it ever was with all of us so close together.

"Must be nice." Wren runs her hands along the back of the couch. "I've always lived in the same house with Mom and Tess. And now that Tess is gone, Mom's got a new boyfriend, and he's always around. I'm starting to feel like an outsider in my own house."

She stops abruptly, as if she never meant to confide something in me. I appreciate the trust, even if it's accidental.

"Anyway," she says with a forced little laugh, "you've definitely got space out here. I was sure I took a wrong turn when I got off the main road."

It's not all that far from the turnoff, but if you've never been out here, the lack of *anything* can be alarming.

"How did you know how to find my murder cabin?"

"I asked Charlie. I hope that's okay. I could have texted you, but in-person seemed best. I figured I could back out of a text a lot easier than I could an actual conversation."

Her gaze snags on something on the other side of the couch. "Do you play the guitar?"

"Yes." She's still staring at the acoustic guitar, but I need her to reverse course. "What conversation did you want to have in person?"

This could go so many ways, I'm not sure what outcome to hope for.

Well. I do know. I'm always hoping for one, specific outcome when it comes to Wren. But I have no idea what's realistic anymore.

She moves a step closer. Several feet still separate us, but after how often she's run from me literally and figuratively, the small gesture gives me a thrilling kind of hope.

"I want to apologize for the other day."

She doesn't clarify, but I need more than this. Her vague apology could encompass too many things I would never want her to regret. "For the kiss? Or for accepting a date with the other guy?"

She glances away again, pink washing over her cheeks. "For the second part."

Something inside me frees like a chain that'd been snagged and finally spins smoothly again. The fear she might retreat from me entirely has been gnawing at me.

"I appreciate it, but you don't owe me anything." Especially not after the way I fumbled my date invitation. What could I honestly have expected?

"Right. Yeah. I get it. I'll just—" She moves to step past me like she's going to leave.

I grab her hand to stop her. She gazes up at me, a fresh wave of embarrassment shining in her eyes. It's clear my response to her apology didn't land the way I intended it to. If we're trying to meet in the middle, we keep getting it wrong.

"Do you want to have dinner?" I ask.

"I—what? With you?"

"Yes. With me." I gently squeeze her hand. "I barbecued shoyu chicken right before you got here, and I've got steamed rice and broccoli to go with it. It's not my 'marry me' bread—"

She huffs a breath and rolls her eyes but miraculously, doesn't let go of my hand.

"But it's pretty good. If you'd like to stay." I tilt my head a touch closer to hers. "I'd like you to stay."

My intentions should be clearer this time. I can almost see the wheels spinning in her head as she stares up at me. The longer it takes for her to answer, the more I steel myself to her inevitable rejection.

"Okay." She squeezes my hand back. "I'll stay."

Relief rushes through me like I'm coasting down a mountain path. "Good. Come sit down."

My cabin's main floor is a great room setup: the kitchen bleeds into the dining area and merges with the living room. You can stand anywhere down here and see every other part of the room. But I keep checking over my shoulder as I plate up dinner, making sure Wren doesn't disappear on me.

She might have accepted my invitation, but the tiny line between her eyebrows says there's still a good chance she'll come up with a reason to bolt. I want to soothe her uncertainties, but that will take more than a simple dinner together to accomplish. It's a start, though.

I serve our meals and join her at my small table. As soon as she takes her first bite of chicken, she puts one hand over her mouth and groans.

"This is so unfair."

Smug satisfaction puffs out my chest. "Does that mean you like it?"

She finishes chewing and points her fork at her face. "Uh, yeah. From the obscene sound I just made, you know I like it."

I refuse to indulge in thoughts of her saying that same sentence in any other context.

"Seems pretty fair to me. I've been eating delicious food you made for years."

"That's different." She doesn't hide her glow of pride, though. "That's my job. This is about you having unexpected life skills."

"Cooking is an unexpected life skill?" I don't dare point out how basic this dish is. "Did you imagine me living off of squirrel meat here in my murder cabin?"

Her mouth tips to one side. "You add variety by foraging for questionable mushrooms."

"A gourmand. Nice."

She rolls her eyes, but she's still smiling. "Have you been doing photography a long time?"

"A while now. It's become an extension of my time in nature."

She shifts her attention to her food.

"What's that face for?" I can't miss the way her nose wrinkles. The chicken's too sweet for her sour response.

"Nothing. Just...the whole outdoorsy scene is not for me."

"That's right. You're looking for an indoor cat." I sort of thought that was a jab aimed at me, not an actual aversion. "What don't you like about it?"

"Bugs, for one. And there's a lot of sweating, which isn't my favorite way to spend a day. My friends have dragged me on a couple of hikes with their boyfriends, and it mostly seems like an excuse to make out in fresh air."

"And you're opposed to making out in fresh air?"

Her gaze locks on mine, her thoughts performing a vivid dance behind her eyes. "No...not *opposed*, I guess. It's never been an option."

"And if it was an option?" Do I sound eager? Hell, yes, I do.

"I mentioned the bug issue."

"We can slather you with eucalyptus oil."

She goes on staring at me until her gaze drops to my mouth. She quickly refocuses on her plate. "I'm giving it a solid maybe."

I can handle a maybe when it comes with that tiny smirk attached.

My thoughts stray to a hike with Wren that's mostly making out. I have to pull off my hoodie and cool down. I drape the sweatshirt over one of the empty chairs and take my seat again. Her attention snaps to my tattoos, her gaze moving up one arm and then the other.

"You can ask whatever you want," I tell her. This is true about everything.

Her gaze eats up the images inked on my skin. "Does it hurt to get them?"

"Yes." I rub the elbow closest to her. "Going over the bone is probably the worst. The inner biceps come in second."

She cringes but doesn't look away. "How long did these take?"

"I started five years ago. My artist and I had a vision for the entire piece, and I added to it whenever I had time and money." It was slow going at first, when extra money was scarce. Now that Get in Gear is doing well, time is the harder factor to come by, since it requires a trip up to Portland and back.

"Do they have meaning, or do they just look cool?"

I can't help my smirk. "You think they look cool?"

She doesn't meet my eyes. She's too busy cataloguing my tattoos. "Shut up. You know they do."

"They all have meaning. Some more than others. But they're not random."

Just like she was drawn to my rolling ladder and the books, she slowly reaches out a hand as if she's under a spell. Her fingertips lightly trace over the pine trees on my forearm, moving up over the mountain peaks that stretch along my biceps. I breathe slowly, her gentle touches as difficult to sit through as the original tattoos.

"What do they mean?" she asks softly. "Or is that private?"

"It's not private." Not from her. "The trees are for the time I spend outdoors. Bugs and all. The mountains are for my grandfather Callahan, who was my rock."

I turn my hand over to reveal my inner arm.

"Lupines?" she asks.

It squeezes something in my chest that she recognizes them. "For my grandma."

I stretch out my other arm. "Another forest scene over here. The river running along my inner arm is for my parents. The little cabin in the woods there is for Charlie."

Wren meets my eyes. "Because of the lodge?"

"We spent a lot of our childhood playing out here. And she loves it so much, it seemed to fit."

"These are beautiful. I've never really looked at them before."

She's certainly never touched them before. She slides her palms over my skin, admiring the tattoo artist's work as if it's somehow separate from my body. As if she's not lighting up my nerve endings one by one. Her fingertips graze beneath my short shirt sleeve like she wants to sweep it out of the way to see the uppermost reaches of my shoulder.

"You have bugs in here." She taps a finger on my outer biceps. "A beetle?"

"My other grandma. She never killed insects if she could

avoid it. Always trapped them in a glass and set them free." She would have loved the shiny beetle on my arm in her honor.

"You're such a secret softie." Wren's both teasing and approving at once. I'm immediately hooked on the affection in her voice.

"I didn't know it was a secret."

"It's sure not common knowledge." She moves her attention to my left arm, drawing it closer to her across my body. She traces the river from my inner elbow down to where it foams on rocks above my wrist. "You're kind of a brooder. You don't really blend with a crowd. But here you are, walking around with your heart literally on your sleeve."

Not the way I would have described it, but I see her point.

She leans in closer. "What's this?"

Her thumb grazes over a tattoo I got a year ago on my inner left biceps. I probably should have kept the hoodie on, but maybe I wanted this risk. I've played it safe with her for too long.

"What does it look like?" I ask softly.

She stares at the small bird nestled among the trees on my arm. "It looks like a—"

Her pause drags out, inflating between us like a balloon pressing us apart. She meets my gaze, her question repeated in her eyes. But whatever she finds in mine must not be enough to reassure her. She sits back in her chair, dropping her hands from my arm.

"I don't know," she says with affected indifference. "I guess it's a generic, chubby little bird."

It's true, chubby little birds are popular among botanical tattoo enthusiasts. I've seen a few around town. But surely Wren recognizes her namesake. She just doesn't want to admit it. Or doesn't want to risk being wrong.

Understandable. I've walked that line enough myself tonight as it is.

"Does that one mean something?" she asks carefully. "The...bird?"

I nod. "I'll tell you when you tell me what type of bird it is."

A risk for a risk.

A line forms between her eyebrows, and her mouth takes on an unimpressed slant. "I didn't realize there would be a test at the end."

There's the Wren who calls to me.

"It's all open book."

We finish dinner, and she helps me clear the dishes away even though I tell her she doesn't need to. She wipes down the table, too, despite my frowns. Pretty sure she cleans the countertop just to make sure I stay in my grumpy mood. Afterward, we face off in the kitchen.

"Thanks for dinner," she says. "It was surprisingly nice."

"I'm going to ignore the 'surprisingly.'"

Her smile tugs at something deep in my chest. "I had a good time."

"Me, too."

This feels like an end-of-evening goodnight kiss moment. The kind of moment where we make up for our awkwardness over dinner by kissing until I've got her pressed up against the door.

She must sense it, too. Instead of moving closer, she takes a step backward. "I should probably go."

I can't be disappointed when we've made this much progress tonight. Still. I want that goodnight kiss.

"Be careful on your drive back to town. There's a lot of deer out this time of night." Probably shouldn't have put the idea of her swerving to avoid a deer into my head. I've had a few close calls, but never an actual accident. There's a first time for everything, though, and her car is tiny. "Text me when you get home."

"I'm sure I can get to my house just fine."

"I'm sure you can, too, but I'd like the confirmation."

"It's not that far." She turns to look out the window, but it's already dark out. "The weather's not even bad."

Not going to think about her little car trying to navigate these roads in the winter. Not thinking about her sliding off the road and into a ditch. Nope. "Krause. Don't argue. I'm asking for a simple text."

Her wry smile appears, as if she's discovered a treasure trove of leverage. "Are you a *worrier*, Callahan?"

She says the word like it's a bright red label she's slapped on my chest. She's not wrong, but we're not getting into this right now. I would love to verbally spar with her some more, but my anxiety's cranking up and making it hard for me to think.

I level her with a hard look. "Just text me, please."

She relaxes, but her smile widens like I just handed her a secret. I suppose I did. Of all the things I've revealed tonight, this is the one she wants to spend her energy on?

"Okay. Sheesh. I will text you when I get home." She pulls open the front door. "If you wanted a goodnight text so badly, all you had to do was say so."

With that, she walks out, snapping the door shut behind her. I watch out the window until her taillights disappear down the drive.

Refusing to pace, I sit on the couch, my phone on the cushion beside me. If I thought I was lost before, having her here in my space has sealed my fate. I hope the stormy petrichor of her perfume lingers for days.

Fifteen minutes of heroically keeping my stray thoughts in line later, my phone finally buzzes.

Wren: I made it!

Shepherd: Glad to hear it

Wren: That road is kind of spooky in the dark

Shepherd: Not helping

Wren: But I'm fine!

Wren: Even tucked myself safely into bed already

That's not helping, either.

Wren: Thanks for inviting me tonight

Shepherd: Thanks for staying

Wren: Goodnight, Callahan

Shepherd: Goodnight, Krause

TEXT THREAD

Isabel: Did anyone else get to the part with the cowboy hat yet?

Rosetta: If you start dropping spoilers, I will leave the chat

Isabel: It's not a spoiler

Isabel: I just don't understand it

Fran: If she wears the cowboy's hat, she belongs to the cowboy

Fran: I can't say more, or Rosetta will leave the chat

Barb: Do you think that works with other types of hats?

Ada: What do you say to a movie night?

Ada: We can borrow my son's in-home theater while he's out of town

Ada: Plenty of seating

Ada: We'll watch something appropriate for our group

Nora: I don't watch movies appropriate for this group

Fran: I have some suggestions

Barb: Would hardhats be the same situation?

Ada: Maybe we should stick with Jane Austen so we don't see anything we're unprepared for

Ada: Friday night. I'll send the address if everyone's interested

Nora: As long as clothes stay on in the movie

Barb: A policeman's hat

Isabel: We can bring sweet treats for our sweet movie night

Ada: Sounds like a hint for Wren

Nora: What about a wizard's hat?

Ada: I want to make sure everyone's on board

Barb: What do you call the hat men wear in the Army?

Barb: When they're all kitted up in their gear?

Fran: That's the one. I can get behind that hat

Shepherd: I'm in for movie night

Shepherd: I don't have a hat, though

Fran: Might be disappointing for some of us

Ada: Hats aren't mandatory

Nora: Unless you think you might get cold

Wren: I'll be there

Wren: With sweets

Ada: A night of romance it is!

FOURTEEN
WREN

IT WAS DEFINITELY a mistake to give those women my phone number. As if the group chat wasn't bad enough, they've started messaging me directly, too.

Fran: What kind of sweet treats do you think Shepherd will bring?

Fran: He's so talented in the kitchen, isn't he?

Wren: I really don't know

Fran: Maybe you should message him and find out

Fran: So we don't have duplicates

Wren: I'll be okay if people bring the same kind of treat

Fran: You could always go in together on a dessert. We wouldn't mind

Fran: Maybe something with chocolate kisses, hmm?

Not half an hour later, my phone's shimmying in my pocket again.

> Ada: My son's house is on a gravel road

> Ada: Will your car be able to handle that okay?

> Ada: You can always carpool with someone who has a sturdier vehicle if you need to

> Wren: My car won't fall apart on a gravel road

> Ada: We don't have to make that common knowledge

> Ada: I can ask around for a ride for you

> Wren: I promise you, I can drive it just fine

"These ladies are a menace." I hit *Send* and stuff my phone back in my pocket.

"Did you find people who match your energy?" Tess walks into the front of the bakery with a tray of pies to refill the refrigerated case. She's gradually shifting her hours to mid-days to accommodate her custom cake orders, but she still works out here with the pie peons part-time.

"Har har. I'm not this bad."

She shoots me an incredulous look. Well-deserved, too, but I don't have to acknowledge it. Or that I have a shirt with *Certified Menace* written in glitter tucked away in my closet.

"It's sweet that they keep in touch between meetings."

"Oh, Tess, you innocent flower. 'Sweet' is not the word for it. They're casually leaving spoilers in the chat every other day, and I haven't even found a copy of the book yet. Now, they're planning a movie night for this weekend and practically begging me to bring more pies. Next, they'll want to have a spa day together."

I wouldn't hate that plan, actually. A spa day sounds kind of nice.

"A movie night, huh?" The tiniest smile curls along Tess's mouth. "Is everyone included in that invitation?"

I help her slide pies into the case. "Don't give me that look. Yes, everyone's invited. Yes, we're all going. It's no big deal."

We're just going to watch a romantic movie that may or may not include a hand flex. There's nothing to get worked up about. As I keep telling my frantic little heart every time it flutters around in my chest.

After we restock the case for the afternoon, Tess leans a hip against the counter, watching me like a detective looking for clues. "Are you going to keep pretending that what Charlie told us the other night doesn't mean anything?"

"I never said that." Sure, I left at the same time Charlie did to avoid this very conversation, but I didn't *say* it didn't mean something. I've been careful not to say anything to Tess about it at all.

I haven't confided what I've done with Callahan to my sister. Not on any level. She doesn't know about that brain-melting kiss in the alley, or my misguided revenge date, or the way I sought him out at his cabin. I didn't tell her about his dinner invitation or that I stayed and manhandled his arms as I committed his tattoos to memory.

I didn't tell her how he's honored the people he loves in beautiful scenes up and down his arms, or how that glimpse into his heart made mine go as soft as a marshmallow over high heat. I for sure didn't tell her about the little bird he's got tucked away among the trees. I'm trying to block that one from my mind. It won't budge, though. It's right there in my head every time I close my eyes.

It can't be what it looked like. There was probably a special on fat little birds at the tattoo studio that day. It doesn't mean anything. He just happened to get a random bird on the second-most painful spot on his arm. Nothing to see here.

"Shepherd was protecting you, Wren." She drops her voice as if this is a Very Important Observation. "He didn't betray you."

"I connected those dots, too." And promptly had a nervous breakdown about it, thank you.

She goes on staring at me, but I don't meet her eye. Getting other people to spill their guts is where I shine. But blabbing about *my* big emotions? I'd rather not.

Her sigh lets me know what a massive disappointment I am. "Fine. I've got cakes to make this afternoon. If you decide you want to talk, you know I'm always here for you."

Guilt lurches through my stomach like Frankenstein's monster, huge and unwieldy. "I know."

She's never been the problem.

Tess takes the empty tray into the back where she's carved out a dedicated space for making and assembling her cakes. In a few more minutes, she'll be lost in decorating and immune to anything that goes on out here.

I trust my sister with anything I could tell her. I just don't trust myself. If I start talking about my feelings and going soft, that's when everything crumbles beneath my feet. Emotions are like the ocean: dangers lurk in the deep. Nameless creatures that will pull you under, squeeze you tight, and suck your face right off. Safest to cruise along at sea level. What happens in the deep is none of my business.

Customers wander in and out of the shop, and I wish I could say it's a nice distraction from Callahan, but it'd be a big fat lie. I can't stop thinking about what I've learned *really* happened between him and Richard Allred. The way he held my hand during his impromptu dinner invitation. That mystery bird on his arm.

His freaking rolling ladder.

As if I didn't have enough torment in my life, in walks Rose Rainey. She's got long, dark hair that falls in perfect, beachy curls. She's wearing a bohemian, flowing dress like she's on her way to wander wildflower fields. If Sunshine did superlatives for residents, she'd get voted in as the "Nicest Person in Town" every year.

She also happens to be Callahan's ex-girlfriend.

No. Big. Deal.

"Hi, Wren." Rose's ever-present smile is so bright, I want to shield my eyes.

I'm in customer service—I'm deeply familiar with fake smiles. But Rose's smiles never strain at the edges or look flimsy and glued on. They're bestowed on everyone equally and without hesitation. They always make her eyes crinkle, too, like she's the happiest she's ever been right this minute.

I'm not even sure I'm smiling now. I subtly slide my mouth around. Nope.

"Hey, Rose."

"It's such a lovely day out, isn't it? I hope the weather stays like this a little longer." A sunbeam shines through the transom window over our door specifically to give her brown hair a honey glow.

Even the sun is against me.

I don't know how long she and Callahan were together or how serious things were between them. She was around a lot when he first took over the space next door, but by the time his shop opened, she didn't come by anymore. I never asked him about it because I didn't really want to know the details.

Now, I regret not digging around and prying for more information when I had the chance. Even though I'm still not sure I really want to know the details.

"It's surprisingly warm." I haven't been out in it except to take trash to the bins in the alley.

Which I did *not* do in the hopes I would run into Callahan. I also didn't linger out there longer than usual, standing around like a fangirl waiting to catch a glimpse of her favorite boy band member after a show. Totally wasn't worth Tess's dirty looks for my lateness when I came back in, either.

"It's my boss's birthday today. He said he didn't want anything, but I know he's coming in later, so..." She gestures at the case of pies. "Might as well surprise him with a little something."

She buys birthday gifts for her boss, too. Is this woman even real?

"Do you know what flavor he likes?"

Rose stoops to peer into the case. Did I mention she's supermodel tall? She's lithe and gorgeous and soft and billowy and I should definitely stop taking notes before I hurt my own feelings.

I'm not ignorant of my own looks, but I'm firmly on the *cute* end of the spectrum. Not an Amazonian goddess like some people.

"Ooh, he likes bananas. How about one of the banana cream pies?"

I pull out one of the pies and slice it, trying not to come up with reasons why Callahan would have broken up with the sweetest human being on the planet. I don't really care to think about why she would have dumped him, either. Maybe it was a mutual dumping and nothing personal on either side. That happens, right?

No matter what, definitely not my business.

"Your bakery is so cute," she says, looking around the shop. "I love how cheerful it is. Like a welcome from an old friend."

"Thank you." I get basically zero credit for the remodel we did years ago, but I try to match her energy. I'm not a menace one hundred percent of the time. "Hopefully it has a happy vibe for the pie-loving people of Sunshine."

Matching her energy was a terrible idea. I sound like a dork.

"The Painted Daisy next door is *the* most adorable," she says, craning her neck that direction.

No argument there. Hope's shop is bright and sunny and filled with the cutest little handmade goods imaginable. Rose would fit right in on the shelves.

"I keep encouraging Reed to add more color to Perk Me Up," she says. "Give it a little pop of something. He says it's colorful enough as it is."

I pause, picturing the coffee shop's crisp white walls and shiny concrete floor. "Where's the color?"

She leans forward, her eyes lit up. "He means the wooden tables and chairs. *Brown* is too much color for Reed Bridger."

Even Callahan's shop has more color in it than that.

I finish up with the pie, fighting the urge to ask her what happened between her and Callahan like a psychopath. Just go straight to the source to get the inside scoop. But I do have some limits to my crazy. I press my lips tightly together and slide over the pie.

"Thanks so much, Wren. Reed is going to love this." She swipes her card. "In his own, subdued way."

I doubt very much her boss who thinks brown is too colorful and specifically told her not to do anything for his birthday is going to *love* her kind gesture. But I wave her on her way with her delusions, her skirts swirling as she leaves the shop.

If this is the kind of woman Callahan is into, I would make a poor replacement. Rose is sunshine and happiness and hugs that go on a little too long. I'm full of snark and sarcasm and have to fight the impulse to flip him off. Rose is cotton candy, and I'm a sour gummy worm. We're not even in the same realm.

Callahan's long-ago comments to his employee barge through a wall in my brain like the Kool-Aid Man.

"Wren Krause is loud, opinionated, and unavoidable. That woman is too much in every category that matters."

It'd hurt when I first heard it. Not going to lie, it hurt for a long time after, too. I know my own faults, so the description wasn't surprising. But for a while, I'd thought he didn't mind my faults. Maybe even liked my nonsense. But compared to his ex? I can see why he would have said it.

I can't even be mad at Rose. She's too sweet for that kind of resentment to make sense. Then again, I've done plenty of things that don't make sense in my life.

Like kiss Callahan. Which I really need to stop thinking about. The problem is, I don't think I can.

"She's obsessed with him, too."

Why does he have to be right all the time?

FIFTEEN

WREN

I AM SUCH A SUCKER.

August didn't want to walk to the small park by our house for his Wren Wednesday. Nope, he wanted to go to the bigger park on the other side of town. The one with miles of paved paths, two big play structures, and a disc golf course. He also asked for a picnic lunch and unlimited rounds of hide and seek.

The hide and seek was pushing it, but I'm terrible at saying no to him. Naturally, I loaded his bike into the back of my car, got him buckled into his car seat, and headed across town after school.

"Look at me, Wren!" He's carefully balancing on his bike so both training wheels hover over the path. There's not a lot of wiggle room, but if he gets it just right, he's really riding on his own.

Ian says they might as well take the training wheels off now, but Tess isn't on board yet. She still wants to be a mama bear hovering over him.

"You're doing great, buddy."

He stands to pedal, shifting from side to side with each push. "I'm good at bike riding."

"You sure are. Do you want to go to the playground?"

We're following the path that loops around the park, but it branches off not far ahead. That path splits through the middle of the park, taking us to both playgrounds, with the disc golf course spread out in between.

"No. I go this way with Ian." He pedals along, nodding his dinosaur-covered helmet. "I want to watch the BMX guys."

My stomach does a completely unnecessary flip. "Are you sure you don't want to do the monkey bars? I bet you can get all the way across now."

"No. I like to watch them go—" He makes a series of hoots and screeches that somehow exactly match the idea of people racing up and down the BMX trail. "I want to do it when I get big."

"That will be so fun." I don't have much enthusiasm, but he doesn't notice.

We loop around the perimeter until we reach the BMX trail at the rear of the park. Several kids ride the dirt hills, whooping and hollering just like August's demonstration. They're also wearing heavier-duty helmets than his, along with knee and elbow pads. If August really wants to do this when he's bigger, Tess is going to have a stroke.

My eyes are apparently Callahan-seeking missiles. I spot him near the trail as if that was my goal in coming out here all along. I should have known if it was bike-related, he would be here. He's standing by the gate in the chain-link fence that surrounds the BMX park, talking with another man.

My best hope is to play it cool and pretend I'm not here. I lay out the blanket I brought in the grass beneath a shade tree and sit down to watch August ride the paved paths. With any luck, Callahan will leave in the opposite direction. He probably won't even turn my way.

August shoots past me, pedaling like he's trying to reach hyper speed. "Look how fast I can go, Wren!"

This is why I can't have nice things.

Callahan spins around, and his gaze lands on me, squeezing the breath from my lungs. He's at least twenty feet away, but I shiver as if I'm close enough to see the flecks of gold in his brown eyes. I swear his beard twitches. Probably a smirk. That seems to be his default around me. He says something to the other man before heading my way.

That's just perfect. It's not enough for me to show up at his work whenever I please, I'm dropping by his home unannounced and uninvited, and now—well, whatever this is, there's a clear correlation here. Bikes lead to Callahan. Don't mind me, I'm just casually stalking the man.

He stops a few feet from my picnic blanket.

"I didn't know you'd be here." Yes. That's a good and normal thing for me to blurt out.

"I didn't know you'd be here, either." He seems to find the coincidence a lot funnier than I do. His mouth slips into a loose smile that unclasps something deep in my chest.

August stops his bike level with us. "Hi, Shepherd! I'm riding my bike today."

"I see that. You're doing really well. I can tell you've been practicing."

I'm not sure I've ever heard Callahan talk to August before. The fact that August remembers his name at all means they've run into him several times. Callahan's sweet, soft encouragement does bad things to my ovaries.

I was starting to think my ovaries were myths. Aside from the less pleasant monthly reminders of their mostly unremarkable existence.

"Yeah. I'm with my aunt Wren. She says I'm the best bike rider in town."

"You're the most enthusiastic pedaler I've seen."

August grins at him, then shifts his attention to me. "Can I ride all the way around the BMX part?"

I look at the section of paved paths where he's pointing. Because of the hills on the BMX trail, August won't be visible the whole time as he loops behind it. I'm usually pretty chill with him, but I should probably have a line somewhere. Or so Tess keeps telling me.

"Ian lets me." His big, pleading eyes prove he knows exactly what he's doing.

Unfair of him to pit me against his new favorite person in the world. I like being in the top spot.

"Okay, but be careful. If you pass someone, make sure they know you're there." He doesn't get going super fast, but he's still figuring out how to brake appropriately. I'd hate for him to crash into someone in his eagerness.

"I will." He turns his bike around on the path before careening away.

Callahan gazes down at me. "Do you want me to follow him and make sure he's okay?"

I scan August's route again. It's not a busy day at the park, and he'll only be out of sight for seconds at a time. I'm over-reacting.

Oh, no. I'm turning into Tess. I can't let that happen.

"That's not necessary. Thanks, though."

He goes on standing there, alternating between watching me and watching August. Not that long ago, I would have said something snarky to encourage him to move along. He would have bantered back, and I would have glared as he walked away after getting in a parting shot.

Now...

"You can sit down. If you want." There's more bite to my

offer than I intend, but Callahan's mouth tips up as if I issued him a fancy invitation complete with wax seal.

He sits next to me, stretches out his lanky legs while keeping his sneakers off my blanket, and leans back on his hands. He scans the park as if he's not even seeing what's in front of him, peak Callahan nonchalance on display.

But then his gaze collides with mine, and nothing about this feels nonchalant. It's giving off deeply chalant vibes. A week ago, I didn't even want to share the same air with him. But look at us now, sitting two feet apart on a picnic blanket, gazing into each other's eyes like we're acting out some romance book trope.

Again.

"Checking up on your business interests?" I ask, tilting my head toward the BMX trail.

August's pedaling for all he's worth, his attention divided between the path in front of him and the kids on the track. A crash is definitely in that kid's future. I just hope it's not on my watch. Ian can have that bonding moment.

"The pump track is maintained by a team of volunteers," Callahan says. "We come out regularly to inspect it and see what needs to be done next time."

"The pump track?"

His mouth tips up beneath his short beard. I should not be thinking about how surprisingly soft that beard feels when it scratches over my skin. Or that I want it there again, ASAP.

"You don't pedal to get around it. You use your body weight to 'pump' the bike over the rollers." He nods toward the course. "Watch."

I rip my gaze away from his beard to observe the kids on the track. I've never paid much attention before, but he's right. They're not pedaling most of the time. They're standing out of their seats and leaning from their shoulders to get the bike over the humps, using that momentum to carry them through the valleys.

"And that's fun?"

His soft chuckle brings my focus back to him. "Some people think so."

"It's biking without the actual biking."

"Does that mean you're interested in trying it?"

"*No.*" He doesn't need to know just how many years it's been since I rode a bicycle. Or how many times the word *bicycle* has flitted through my mind in the last two weeks.

More than average, that's all I'm willing to say.

"I heard you need a ride to movie night."

I spin to face him so fast, my neck cracks like a chiropractor's ASMR video. "What?"

"Ada said you're concerned about your car getting out there in one piece. She said I'd better offer, since you're too shy to ask me to pick you up."

"I didn't—I never said—those devious little sneaks." I should have known they would never be satisfied just dropping their hints to *me*. I hate to think what they've said behind my back. What I know now is more than enough.

He chuckles again, the low sound warm and cozy. "I figured as much. Nothing about you is shy."

Nope. Loud and opinionated, that's me. Unease crackles through me like a burst of static electricity. But he's not watching me like he's thinking about how obnoxious I am. It's more like...admiration. Affection. Attr—

A jazzy, electronic tune cuts through the air between us.

"Son of a bus." I pull out the phone that has August's continuous glucose monitor app on it and check the notifications. "Crap."

I kneel up on the blanket and wave at August, who's luckily on the nearest part of the loop around the BMX trail for the second time already. He spots me and pedals faster, heading our way. Thank the patron saint of little kids he's not going to make me chase him down.

It's happened. It's not a good look for anybody.

"Everything okay?" Callahan asks as I sit back down.

"Yeah. He just needs a snack." It's not an emergency, but it's still something I would have had at the front of my mind if it weren't for the six-foot-three distraction at my side. Good Wren would have caught the downward trend in his blood sugar levels before the alarm even sounded. Bad Wren's been too busy staring into deep brown eyes to calculate how long August's been riding his bike.

"'Son of a bus?'" Callahan repeats, amusement layering his voice.

"Shut it. I'm trying to be a good influence on my nephew." Casual swearing used to be one of my favorite outlets for colorful self-expression before he came along.

"Did you guys see me?" August rides off the path and straight into the grass, stopping just before he reaches the tote bag I've got at my feet. "I rode and rode."

"You did awesome. It's time for a snack, though."

"Okay." He unbuckles his helmet and drops it in the grass before flopping down between Callahan and me. "What did you bring?"

I pull the insulated lunchbox from my tote bag, spilling my yarn, crochet hook, and weirdo work in progress across the blanket in the process. August isn't the only one who had grand plans for our afternoon in the park. I hand him a juice box and a wrapped sandwich. It won't take much to counteract his activity out here, but he needs a little something.

He happily eats the food, still watching the bikers on the BMX trail. Or "pump track," I guess it's called. I pop open a small bag of spicy corn chips and tip it Callahan's way.

He sits straighter so he can take one. "Thanks."

"Ian said I can try the track as soon as I'm done with training wheels." August nods over his plans for world domination by way of unfettered bicycling.

"It won't be long now," Callahan tells him.

August grins wider. "I'll ride so fast when they're gone."

"Is it hard to learn?" I ask Callahan. "The pump track, I mean. Is it safe for little guys to ride it?"

Most of the kids in there look well out of elementary school.

August shoots me a wounded look. "I'm not so little."

I slip an arm around him for a quick hug. "I know, buddy."

"There are informal times for beginners to ride the track every week," Callahan says. "As long as he goes when it's not busy, he'll be fine."

"Mama wants me to get a helmet that covers my whole face!" August seems thrilled by this step up in protective gear. I bet my sister's less enthusiastic. Or rather, ready to enthusiastically cocoon him in bubble wrap.

"That's not a bad idea," Callahan says. "Maybe some gloves and knee pads, too."

"Yeah." August's gone all dreamy, clearly zoning out imagining himself kitted up to tackle the track. "Can I go watch them ride?"

I check the app on his phone. The little line indicating his blood glucose levels has stopped its downward trend. "Sure. Don't go inside the fence, though. Sit on the bench outside to watch."

"Okay!" He scrambles up, finishing the last bite of his sandwich before trotting over to the bench.

Callahan watches me with a wry smile. Some might even call it a smirk. I don't hate it as much as I used to.

"What?" I ask.

"You're worried about him."

I roll my eyes. "If this is a reference to me poking fun at your grave concerns over my ability to get home the other night, it's totally off base. It's not like I asked him to text me when he gets to the bench."

"It's sweet."

"Sweet. Yuck." Going to ignore how those words in Callahan's mouth make my stomach dip. "It's normal to worry at least a little over the people you..."

The rest of that sentence dies out on my tongue. *Care about.* I can't connect those words between Callahan and me right here in the middle of this park. Even if my traitorous gaze goes straight to his left arm, currently covered by—wonder of wonders—a red flannel shirt.

"He's diabetic," I say instead of finishing my thought. "So there's extra stuff to think about beyond the usual little kid scrapes and tumbles."

"That's what the app is for?"

"Yeah." I flip it back on so he can see the graph making its way back to normal range. "The urgent alarms are a lot more grating than this one was."

"He seems to be handling it well."

"He's a little champ." I can't help the surge of affection as I look over at August kicking his feet on the bench and watching the teens run the BMX track. "He doesn't let anything stop him."

After a minute of silence, I glance back at Callahan again. He's got that heady mix of admiration, *etcetera,* in his eyes once more. "What?"

"It's sweet," he says again, so softly, it wraps around me like a hug.

I'm not the "sweet" type. I've given him plenty of proof that's not my default setting. But when he calls me that, I almost believe it could be.

A breeze drifts over us, making me wish I'd brought a second blanket. Or that Callahan's figurative hug were a literal one. But honestly, the warmth in his gaze does a pretty solid job of staving off the chill on its own.

"I have to get back to the shop," he says after another minute. "I'm glad I ran into you."

"Me, too." That small admission makes my face heat as if I confessed my undying devotion. But after the way I've talked to him for so long, any little concession feels huge. Being *glad* to see him reveals plenty.

He shifts to lean closer to me. I have the insane thought he's moving in for a kiss—followed by the even more insane impulse to meet him halfway. But he doesn't get that far.

"Are you sure you don't want that ride on Friday?" he asks.

I open my mouth to shoot down the offer, but...it's not a horrible plan. Carpooling is good for the environment and all. It would save wear and tear on my car's shock absorption system. Something along those lines.

His brown eyes sparkle, and I realize just how obvious I'm being. Can't have that.

"I can drive by myself." Factual. And neatly avoids answering his actual question.

He nods as if he expected this. "Then I'll save you a seat for when you get there."

Why does that not sound like any less of a date than him picking me up and driving me there himself?

Callahan stands and gazes down at me. "Thanks for letting me share your picnic."

I wave my hand, brushing off his thanks for the chips I shared. Next time, I'll be prepared with an actual picnic for both of us, not just August.

Wait, next time? I'm making plans to prepare a *picnic* for the guy? I've completely lost it.

"Bye," I say before my thoughts get totally out of hand.

He walks away, pausing to say goodbye to August at the BMX track. I watch him stride up the path that leads to the parking lot back there, eating up the casual way he shoves his hands in his jeans pockets. There's something so confident and unconcerned about him that's massively intriguing.

Just before he reaches the edge of the park, he turns back and catches me staring after him. He lifts a hand, and mine automatically raises in return. Then he continues on, disappearing into the parking lot.

I thought I was playing it cool with Callahan, but the warmth washing through me from his low-key goodbye says I am anything but.

SIXTEEN

SHEPHERD

SUPPOSEDLY, the customer is always right. In this case, the customer has the word *Wrong* glaring over his head in bright neon.

"I like this bike, Daddy." A little girl has a mountain bike out of its slot, hands clutching the seat and handlebar like she's ready to ride it home. Her eyes rake over it as if the bike is better than Christmas and Hanukkah combined.

"I think this one is meant for you, honey." Her dad's at the other end of the rack next to a pink bike that's at least a size smaller than the girl needs, with white streamers and a wicker basket on the front.

It's nowhere close to the bike meant for off-roading that his daughter's claimed. She's got to be eight or nine, and he's trying to get her onto a bike we typically sell to four- and five-year-olds.

She frowns at the kiddie bike her dad's showing her. "I like green."

Palmer and I share a look behind the front counter. We've seen this scenario play out dozens of times before. Sometimes it's about girl/boy color preferences. Sometimes it's about a parent who wants their kid to off-road when they just want to ride around town on a cruiser bike. At its core, it's always about an adult trying to push what they think is best onto a kid who's just trying to have fun.

I try not to insert myself into conversations like this. I *try*. I generally fail.

The bell over the door chimes, and I momentarily forget the man ignoring his daughter's interests. Wren walks in, scanning the shop as if it's all new to her. The purple of her apron might be my favorite color, second to the blue of her eyes. When her gaze lands on me, a hook lodges behind my ribs, reeling me closer.

I cross the room to meet her, even though I usually stay behind the front counter when she comes in. Then again, she usually looks at me like I might need the buffer of a few extra feet between us.

Today, her mouth twists, fighting a smile. I'd rather she lay me out flat with the real thing, but I'll take the progress.

"Hey." I leave more space between us than I want to, but I'm trying to be both a gentleman and a good business owner. I can't very well crush her to me and hope to maintain either description.

"Do you have bike bells?"

Not where I thought this was going, but I can adapt. "Sure, we've got a few. They're over here."

I lead her to the display rack. We've usually got a mix of plain, practical models and ones with fun patterns. To be clear, our bells are neither gendered nor age-specific. I've seen burly guys get the rainbow-printed ones with the chiming bells, and petite, older women opt for the air horns.

She looks over the selection, but then side-eyes me. "Also, hi."

"Hi." That afterthought greeting shouldn't give me the hope that it does. "Is the bell for you?"

I would never try to force her into biking if she had no interest, but the image of us on a ride together is appealing. Maybe because I'm still stuck on that "making out in fresh air" thing she mentioned the other day.

"Ha. No way. It's for August. I'll feel better when people have warning that he's coming."

"If I know little kids with bells, he'll ring it full time."

The glimpse of her smile kills me. "A noisy child is a safe child."

Another adage for her shirts.

"Any of these will fit on his bike. It just depends on the style you want to get him."

Her eyes light up, and she grabs a box off its hook. "'The loudest bike horn in the world.' Tess would never forgive me."

"It's usually meant for commuters riding through traffic and competing with car horns, just as an FYI."

Doesn't seem to be a deterrent for Wren.

She clutches the box to her chest. "How bad is it I'm tempted to get this for him?"

"It would make you a very good aunt but a terrible sister."

"That's all I ever aim for."

The dad and daughter's conversation carries to us from the other side of the room.

"I like this one, Daddy." The little girl's voice breaks. "I don't like pink."

"That's a boys' bike, honey. Let's get you a cute one that's meant for little girls."

The man's patronizing tone grates even at this distance.

Wren shoots mental fireballs at the guy. "Did he just—?"

"Yup. Excuse me for a minute." I slip past her, needlessly brushing one hand across her lower back as I go.

Behind the front counter, Palmer gives me a thumbs-up in solidarity. He knows the drill.

When I reach the man, his daughter is on the verge of tears. I hate this part of my job. Ordinarily, I'm not a fan of confrontation, but somebody needs to speak up. Here in my shop, that's going to be me.

"Do you need any help over here?" On my best days, my customer service voice isn't much gentler than my normal one. Intervening on this conversation, I probably sound accusatory. That fits.

The man looks like he's been caught red-handed. Good. Means this should be easy.

"We're just trying to settle on a bike for my daughter. I've been showing her these girls' bikes, but she wants the same kind her brother has." He shoots me a look as if I'm going to commiserate with him over how foolish she is.

Tough luck, guy.

"Do you know how to ride already?" I ask her. I'm gentler with her than I was with her father.

She nods. "I learned on my brother's bike. It's like this one but blue."

I figured as much. I turn back to her dad.

"Based on her height, that pink bike is too small for your daughter. I wouldn't recommend that size because she won't be able to ride comfortably." I gesture at the one she's still clutching. "This brand's kids' bikes are all unisex. They're good for paved or dirt paths, with a comfort seat. If she already rides a bike like this, it might be the best option."

"I thought there was a difference between girls' and boys' bikes. You know." He leans closer to me, and I catch a whiff of cologne. "Anatomically."

I kind of wish Laurel was here to laugh in this man's face. I'm tempted to ask him to explain what he means just to hear him sputter over made-up nonsense.

"Women's bikes typically have shorter stems and shorter

reach, due to women generally being shorter than men. But the best bike for a woman is any bike that fits her. The same is true for men. There's no *anatomical* reason not to go with the bike your daughter wants."

He stares at me for a few seconds like he's waiting for me to get to the punchline. When I don't, his resistance slumps along with his shoulders.

"Oh. Well." He looks at the bike his daughter's holding. "I guess we can go with that one, then. If it doesn't make a difference."

I don't know if it's the information I gave him or simply the fact that I'm a man that ultimately convinced him, but I'll take it as a win for his daughter. And her happy smile is a win for me. "Palmer will help you two with that."

I return to Wren, who doesn't hide how she's been following along.

"Is that a common thing?" she asks.

"Not really, but it does happen." More often than I'd like. At least the man gave in and is willing to get her the bike she wants. I've seen more than a few kids leave disappointed because their parents only focused on making themselves happy with their purchase for their child.

She glares at the man across the room. "Maybe *she* needs the loudest bike horn in the world to drown out her dad."

"Did you choose violence, then?"

Her brief laugh pings through my chest like a firework, lighting me up. "No. August would probably rather have this normal-sounding bell that has dinosaurs on it."

"Good choice." I bring her to the front counter and ring up the bell. At the other end of the counter, Palmer's writing up paperwork for the girl's new bike.

Wren looks over at the little girl, who's still holding onto the bike's seat like she's afraid it might get snatched away.

"I like your new bike," Wren says. "That dark green is a really cool color."

The girl beams at her. "Green is my favorite."

"I bet you're going to have so much fun riding it."

She nods, making her curly blond hair bounce. "I can't wait to get it home."

Wren turns back to me. She looks me over, no doubt examining whatever incriminating thing my face is doing. "What?"

I lean slightly over the counter, tipping my head down toward her. "It's sweet."

She rolls her eyes but doesn't hide her smile. I'll tell her as many times as it takes for it to stick. Wren isn't all sunshine and rainbows, and I would never want her to be. But just like yesterday at the park with her nephew, this glimpse of her softness makes me crave more.

Lila Parrish walks in as I'm finishing up Wren's purchase. She comes straight to the counter and turns to her friend. "What are you doing here?"

It's an innocent enough question, but Wren's cheeks take on a hint of pink. Her gaze darts from Lila to me and back again. "Getting a bell for August's bike."

Am I imagining the higher pitch in her voice?

"Aww." Lila flips her attention to me. "Do you have a minute, Shepherd?"

Not when I'd rather spend all of them on Wren, but I'm not at liberty to say that yet.

"Sure."

Lila clasps her hands in front of her chest, grinning up a storm. "The town council wants to hear your presentation about the bike trails expansion at a special town hall meeting next month. Open it up to discussion and get interest building for it. Isn't that great news?"

I pass the dinosaur bell to Wren along with her receipt, alarms clanging in my head. "A town hall meeting?"

Lila's thrown herself into her new job drumming up tourism for Sunshine. She's organized all our major events this year and spearheaded new ways to both draw in visitors and boost community involvement. She's been pushing for my trails expansion project since she first heard about it over the summer, but somehow, I assumed she would take over convincing the town council on her own.

"It's the perfect way to help us get backing from the community," she says. "The more residents we have invested in this, the easier it will be to get approval."

We've already got one resident invested—Wren's not shy about listening in.

"Is this about the trail expansion you were talking about the other night?" she asks.

Lila nods, both of them watching me with wide, expectant eyes.

"What, uh..." I swallow hard and try to keep my thoughts together before they slip through my fingers. "What kind of presentation do they want?"

"We need to create a slideshow that includes everything from your plans for the trail connections, data on other towns that have made similar conversions to their fire roads, a loose estimate of the cost breakdown." She waves a hand in the air. "And, you know, something about how fun it will be."

From all I've seen, Lila is about as outdoorsy as Wren. Maybe a little more now that she's dating the guy opening the outdoor store a couple of blocks down. But she's willing to be eager about anything if it will help out local businesses.

I just figured she would turn that eagerness on the town council.

"I have a lot of that information already. I can send all the docs to you."

Please let me send the docs to you.

She smiles even wider. "We can work on it together. I'm thinking I'll do a five-minute intro and hand it over to you for a twenty to twenty-five-minute presentation to hit all the major points. That's how much time they're giving us, so we might as well use it all and hit them hard."

I clench and unclench my clammy hands, imagining myself on stage. Everybody's eyes on me. While I choke. "What kind of attendance are you expecting?"

"Meetings like this tend to get fifty to a hundred community members involved. I'll aim for more to really drive enthusiasm."

She's currently doing the opposite.

"Uh-huh." A cold sweat breaks out beneath my double-layered shirts. A staccato beat thumps in my chest. "I'll think about it."

Lila's eyebrows tug down. "It's not really optional."

Wren keeps glancing from me to Lila, probably trying to make sense of the weirdness that has to be emanating from me like a toxic cloud.

"It would be better if you handle it all," I tell Lila. "Isn't this your area of expertise?"

She laughs lightly. "Not exactly. This will go better with *actual* expert testimony. That's you. You'll be able to explain about the trails firsthand and what it will mean for your business, the community, and Sunshine's tourism. They don't want to hear from me. They want to be wowed by your compelling presentation."

They won't want to hear from me, either. I'm pretty sure I'll fall short on the *compelling presentation* part. Especially if I'm trying not to throw up the entire time I'm on stage.

My stomach sinks as though that's a distinct possibility

already. Logically, I know I'm not going to throw up. It's my body's physiological response to the anxiety coursing through my system like a typhoon. But in this moment, I can't shake the idea I'm going vomit in the middle of my store, in front of Lila and the woman I—

My stomach lurches.

I take a big step backward. "I'll help you with the details, but someone else can give the presentation. Maybe Palmer."

Lila's gaze shifts to my employee who's still working with the man and his daughter, before landing back on me. "We'll have the best shot if it's you, though. I thought you'd want to take the lead after coming up with the whole concept and drawing up the plans. You're the one who's most invested."

I can't address the question she's delicately avoiding. *Why won't I do it?* Blood pounds in my ears, drowning out everything else. "I have to take care of something in the back. We can talk more about this later."

Ignoring Lila's soft sound of protest and Wren's rapt stare, I escape into the back. I cross the room, shaking out my hands and willing my body to knock it off. I'm not being chased by a predator—I'm just imagining myself giving a twenty-minute presentation in front of a hundred people.

I'd rather take my chances with the predator.

I should have known just passing along information wouldn't be enough to get these trails built. I thought I could serve as a consultant or something, not be the guy up on stage trying to win over a crowd.

There's a reason I largely work alone, and it's not because I'm a control freak. Mix too many people with too much attention and say goodbye to my rational brain. My fight-or-flight mode takes over, and I freeze up. Panic. Lose every last ounce of calm.

No matter what Lila thinks, I can't give the presentation.

Even if I managed to keep my body in line, my brain will power down and I'll lose the interest of everyone in the room. Become a public spectacle *and* a public failure. My worst nightmare on every level.

"Shepherd?"

I stop with my back to her, closing my eyes to bask in the sound of my name on her lips. I always knew the woman played dirty. *Now* she wants to go all soft and gentle on me?

I turn around, hoping I at least look like I've got a handle on this, but Wren's already right in front of me, barely a foot away. She looks me over, taking in my hands still opening and closing, pausing on my chest rising and falling with shallow breaths, and ending by staring into my eyes.

I've waited a long time for her to truly see me, but I never wanted her to witness this.

She draws closer until we're toe to toe. Still watching me carefully, she takes both of my hands in hers. "Breathe with me. In for three." She inhales slowly. "Hold for three. Out for three."

I follow her lead, taking the slow breaths I should have resorted to in the first place. Never breaking eye contact, she guides my breathing, draining the tension out of me as expertly as if she's shifting my anxiety into a lower gear. After several minutes, my hands become loose again, and my heart rate slows to normal.

She goes on looking up at me, her deep blue eyes piercing straight through my heart. "You really don't want to give that presentation."

I exhale a soft laugh. "No, I do not. How did you know to do this?"

She's still holding my hands, her fingers lightly moving over my skin in time with our slow breaths. I'd like to stand here with her touching me forever, despite the light scent of grease and rubber all around us.

"When August was first diagnosed with diabetes, he had a few emergency trips to the hospital. They triggered panic attacks in Tess."

Her thumbs work soft circles over the backs of my hands. I've never felt anything more soothing.

"Not you, though."

She tips up her nose. "I'm a rock. But it was scary to see him like that. He was such a tiny thing to be so sick. We felt so helpless, all we could do was watch and hope."

There's so much genuine love radiating from her, her fear for him hurts, no matter how long ago it happened. She's devoted to her nephew, and it's obvious she would do anything for her family. Including learn how to recognize and quiet her sister's panic attacks.

My dragon treasure hoard is overflowing.

"Tess's response was understandable." Her child was in an actual life-or-death situation. Any parent could have had a similar reaction. She wasn't simply contemplating a brief foray into public speaking.

Wren's small smile tells me she sees right through that comment. "Anxiety doesn't always have to make sense, though."

I appreciate that she's encouraging me to open that door to her, but I'm still coming down from a panic rush. I can't get into it right now. I will—just not today.

When it's obvious I'm not going to say more, she gently squeezes my hands. "I should get back to work. I've left Mom alone for a long time already. Do you need anything?"

You. Always and only.

"I'm good. Thanks for worrying about me."

She slowly drags her hands over mine as she lets go, simultaneously moving a step back. Her gentle smile takes on a devious tilt. "Don't get used to it, Callahan."

Oh, kitten. I'm already addicted.

Ada: Don't forget about movie night tonight!

Fran: I've been looking forward to it all week

Fran: Watching people fall in love right before our eyes

Fran: What could be more exciting than that?

Isabel: Does your son still keep it chilly in his house?

Ada: He says it helps his metabolism

Barb: The last time I saw a movie in the theater, I wish I'd brought a blanket

Ada: Good idea. Bring extra blankets if you want one

Fran: Ooh, it's getting cozy tonight

Nora: Did we ever decide on the movie?

Rosetta: I'm bringing my Jane Austen collection

Nora: I vote for Pride and Prejudice with Colin Firth

Rosetta: That's almost six hours long

Nora: Firth makes it worth it

Barb: Some of us are going to struggle to stay awake as it is

Fran: But at least we'll all have friendly movie companions to fall asleep on

Barb: If I get that tired, I'm just going home

Ada: Everyone has a ride, correct?

Isabel: If anyone's uncertain about getting there, we can work out a way to ride share

Wren: We're all certain

Shepherd: If anyone's uncertain, they can let me know

Fran: I'm uncertain

Nora: I don't think you're the target for the question

SEVENTEEN

WREN

IT'S JUST a movie night with a group of friends. Acquaintances, when you get right down to it. People I barely know. I should not be nervous. I should not have butterflies fluttering around in my chest like they're trying to organize a prison break.

I definitely shouldn't be this feverish when I lock eyes with Callahan across the room of the swankiest house I've ever been in.

"Everybody's in the kitchen." Ada swings the front door shut behind me, needlessly gesturing at the crowd on the other side of the great room. Then she ducks her head closer toward me. "I was starting to wonder if you needed that ride, after all."

"Nope. I'm here." Last to arrive, apparently, but here. At least I'm consistent.

Ada leads me to where the rest of the group is gathered around the gleaming white kitchen island. I keep staring at Callahan, which is nothing new. My racing heartbeat and dipping stomach *are*, though.

"What did you bring for us, Wren?" Barb zooms over to take the big plastic food container from me.

"Cookies." One of my favorite recipes using fancy chocolate mints instead of chocolate chips, but from the way Barb's face falls, she was hoping for something else.

"Oh." She takes the container like I passed her a used tissue. "No pies this time?"

"Nope." I pop the *P*, ignoring a couple of other disappointed looks. I could have easily grabbed a pie or two after my shift, but I made cookies at home instead. If they only invited me to their club for my pies, I'd rather know now.

I'd still keep coming to book group, mind you. But at least I'd know where I stand.

"Are these mints?" Rosetta asks, inspecting my cookies.

"Yup."

"You are heaven-sent. I love mint anything."

Ada guides me around the women filling their plates, conveniently leading us closer to Callahan. "Your cookies sound delightful."

"How did your son afford this house?" Barb asks Ada with zero finesse.

Granted, it's a magnificent house. Huge and modern, with sleek lines and shimmering glass accents everywhere. It also looks like nobody actually lives here. Where are the water glasses forgotten on the coffee table? The throw blankets crumpled on the floor? The subtle divots on the couch cushions that say people read there for hours at a time on snowy days?

Surely, I'm not the only one who lives like that.

"He makes movie trailers." Ada pauses for the impressed *oohs* and *aahs* to die down. "He lived in L.A. for almost twenty years, but now he does all that from his home studio. He goes back once in a while, though, and I make good use of his theater when he does."

"You must be eager for him to finally settle down," Nora says, nibbling on a brownie.

"I wish." Ada exhales the long-suffering sigh of a mother with a confirmed bachelor for a son.

I finally reach Callahan. I'm probably standing too close, but I blame the crowd around the food. "What did you bring?"

He nods at the table. "Wouldn't you rather guess?"

I glance over the assorted offerings. Cream cheese brownies, sugar cookies with sprinkles, a store-bought tiramisu. Snickerdoodles dusted with cinnamon, a peach poke cake, and molasses crinkle cookies. I feel like Indiana Jones picking from a hundred versions of the Holy Grail.

"The napkins?" I suggest.

His mouth tips up. "You got me."

My stomach dips again like it's on a Callahan-powered rollercoaster. I told myself I wouldn't get all hot and bothered over him tonight. Or...*more* hot and bothered. My body isn't listening.

Honestly, neither is my brain. Callahan's seemingly unflappable calm has both annoyed me and brought out mild admiration over the years. But seeing behind the curtain to his panic attack yesterday put him in a whole new light. I can't help wondering if that's part of the reason he stopped working with his family at their fancy lodge. More importantly, I worry over what it will mean for the trails he's been working so hard to get built. If he really can't give the presentation, what will happen then?

Am I feeling sympathy for Shepherd Callahan? So weird.

But I can't deny, talking him down from his anxiety-fueled hyperventilation session reminded me there's a genuine human underneath all that flannel.

One who's currently watching me like he wishes we were alone in an alley somewhere.

"Shepherd, these chocolate chip cookies are perfect." Fran

has sidled close to both of us, a half-eaten cookie in one hand. "How do you get them to keep so much height?"

"I chill the dough before baking them." This man should guard his secrets better. At least four sets of eyes light up over that info, no doubt ready to steal the move.

"I'll guess... You brought the chocolate chip cookies," I tell him, grabbing one from the tray.

"Well done, Sherlock." He watches me take a bite, eyes narrowing as I make an involuntary yummy sound.

Okay, *mostly* involuntary.

"Good?" he asks.

They're delicious. Chewy but not too soft, a bit of crunch but not over-baked. I eat the cookie in three indelicate bites and pop the end of my thumb in my mouth to get a spot of melted chocolate.

Callahan's eyes lock on the move, and it's like the world tilts, shifting me his direction.

"They're okay," I tell him. "I won't know for sure until I've tried another."

"Always good to do a thorough taste-test."

Heat crawls up my spine as if the temperature in here just spiked.

For the record, it's stupid cold. You'd think being so super rich, Ada's son could heat his house to a decent level.

"All right, ladies and gentleman," Ada says from the other side of the kitchen island. "We've got *Pride and Prejudice* queued up and ready to go. Grab your snacks and drinks and come to the last door on the right down the hall and around the corner."

"I thought we were going to vote," Barb says, stacking cookies on a small plate.

"I haven't seen *Northanger Abbey* in a long time," Nora says.

Barb's mouth drops open. "How is that your choice?"

"It's better than the cousins in love in *Mansfield Park*." Rosetta makes a sour face I feel one hundred percent. "I always preferred *Persuasion*."

"Captain Wentworth's love letter is so dreamy." I have to get my point in before they move on. "Top-tier pining from that man."

"You like a smitten man, do you?" Ada asks, lifting her eyebrows in a cheeky move.

Nora harrumphs. "Nobody beats Colonel Brandon's pining."

"My favorite is Mr. Rochester." Fran loads her plate as though she didn't bring the conversation to a screeching halt.

"That's not Jane Austen," Isabel says after a minute. "And deeply troubling, to boot."

"He's not a shy violet like a lot of Austen heroes." Fran inspects a tray of cookies. "He's passionate. Stormy. You know he's got fire."

Rosetta laughs. "Pun intended?"

"He also dresses up like a gypsy woman to try to trick Jane into confessing her love," I add. "Like any totally normal and not at all wacko guy would do."

Don't even get me started on the fake relationship with Blanche Ingram. Fake dating only makes sense when the love interests are the ones doing the faking. Rochester's way was just cruel.

"Whatever it takes to get a woman to admit how she feels. Right Shepherd?" Fran asks. "I've got some long skirts and patterned scarves you can borrow."

She winks at him and heads out of the kitchen with a couple of the other ladies in tow.

"Menaces," I mutter under my breath.

"Trickery's not on your list of preferred qualities in a man?" Callahan asks.

I snort. "Neither is bigamy, so if you've got a wife hidden away in your cabin, tell me now."

I freeze as the sassy smile falls off my face. Staring at the food on the table and not the man standing at my side, I'm tempted to toss the blanket I've got rolled under one arm straight over my head. Just pretend I'm an overstimulated bird and avoid looking at him for the rest of the night.

He tilts his head closer to mine. Why does he have to smell like a forest right now? "No wife or girlfriend, in my cabin or otherwise."

The remaining ladies around the island giggle, shooting us obvious looks and bobbing their eyebrows. Between their flirty pushing and my stupid mouth, we've already conspired to make the evening into a steaming bowl of awkward soup. Teamwork makes the dream work.

"Nobody's surprised you're single, Callahan." I'm reaching for my classic snark, but to my horror, I sound *happy* about this information. And the way he's smiling down at me, he heard it, too.

"I'd be willing to change that, Krause."

I swallow hard, my poor brain completely blank. It's all fun and games until somebody's making heart eyes in the middle of romance book group.

"Are you two joining us? If we don't start the movie soon, half of us will be asleep before the credits roll."

Turning to Ada, I try to snap out of my brain fog. "Yup. We're ready."

I follow her down the hall, refusing to look back to see if Callahan's behind me. Obviously, he is. No need to check.

But I peek anyway, catching him trailing me with a plate of

treats in one hand and a glass of water in the other. The amused tilt to his mouth confirms I shouldn't have looked back.

We reach the movie room, and Holy Batcave, my guy. It's a mini movie theater with four risers, each with a full-size leather sofa on it that has small tables for snacks and drinks at either end. As I watch, Nora fully reclines her seat. The projection screen takes up one massive wall. Mr. Darcy will be taller than me on this.

A quick glance at the sofas confirms that not only did the ladies give Callahan and me no other option than to sit together, but we're in the back row. They might as well have tacked a sign over the sofa that says, "Now kiss."

It's terrible that I'm considering it, right?

I put my snacks on the side table and arrange my throw blanket over my legs. I sink into the cushions, snug and comfortable despite the chilly temperature in here. The cozy couch reminds me just how long it's been since I really relaxed today. When Ada dims the lights, I can't hold back my ear-popping yawn.

"Are you going to make it through the movie?" Callahan asks.

"Possibly. I've been up since five."

I don't usually go out on days I open at the bakery, but I made an exception for tonight. No need to question why, thank you.

He leans closer. "Feel free to fall asleep on me if you need to."

It's pretty dark in here, but I can hear the smirk in his voice. No way will I admit just how nice snuggling up to him sounds right now. Best if I avoid temptation altogether. I lay out in the opposite direction, resting my head on the plush armrest and tucking my legs up, pressing my feet against his thigh. "Thanks."

It's wrong of me to admire how firm his thigh is, yes?

He chuckles, taking my socked feet into his lap as the *Pride and Prejudice* intro music starts over the rising sun on the screen. He lays one warm hand on my toes, the other on my exposed calves. This...is objectively worse than simply sitting side by side through a romantic movie. Do my feet stink? Maybe they're shaped funny, and I never knew. Ada said it's a shoes-off house, and I had no problem going along, but now I realize I should have stayed as fully dressed as possible.

Callahan's eyes stay on the movie, but he traces the image on my socks with his thumb. It's a green trash bin with flames coming out of the top, *Everything is fine* printed above. I don't pay attention to Mrs. Bennett's grand plans for Mr. Bingley for even a moment. I'm too busy furtively watching Callahan.

When he starts rubbing my feet, I simply perish.

Maybe worse, I make an embarrassing sound as he kneads into my arch. Apparently, I'm a mush for physical touch. Or... ugh...maybe I'm just mush for Callahan.

"Okay?" he asks softly, his fingers gently pressing into the soles of my feet. Instead of watching the movie, now he's focused on me, his face glowing gold in the dim light.

This is my chance. I can tell him to knock it off. Say I was trying to shove him away, not offer an invitation. Pull my feet back onto my side of the sofa and remove the temptation entirely.

Instead, I nod, mumble, "Mm-hmm," and burrow deeper into my blanket.

I'm in danger.

EIGHTEEN

SHEPHERD

IT'S impossible to concentrate on the movie with Wren laid out next to me. I'm not sure anything could pull my attention away from the vision on the other half of the couch. She's tucked under her blanket, the only parts of her visible her feet in my lap and her heart-shaped face. Her blond hair trails over the sofa arm in a waterfall I want to run my fingers through.

Sometime around the second dancing scene, her eyes drift closed. It's a testament to how tired she is from her early hours in the bakery. And maybe the extra-plush sofa. She's never been this soft and peaceful around me before. My mind fills with images of us in similar scenarios on my couch at home.

Minus the eager audience. Despite specifically arranging this movie night so Wren and I would have maximum privacy, the ladies can't stop turning around to check whether we're making use of it. Some are subtle and look our direction as part of an elaborate stretch. Fran, though, sets her chin on her couch's back rest, watching us with a grin that's disconcerting in the darkness.

Wren, sadly, misses the scene that makes the other women swoon. After learning how much they like rolled shirtsleeves and leaning in doorways, I shouldn't be surprised the key scene in a historical romance is a two-second flex of a man's hand. Whatever it takes, I guess. I'm still filing that info away for later.

Eventually, the end credits roll, and soft lighting comes on. The other ladies stand and talk among themselves but send volley after volley of smug looks in my direction. Wren wakes slowly, stretching her arms over her head like a cat, her legs straightening across my lap. Her eyes open, gaze landing on me.

Her sleepy smile hits my heart so hard it hurts. Affectionate and easy, as if nothing could be more natural. And now I'm imagining us in *other* similar scenarios. Heat blooms from my chest and up my spine. I'm a greedy man—I want the first smile when she wakes every day.

"Movie night was a *great* idea," Fran says too loudly. "Just what some of us needed, hmm?"

Wren's eyes widen, fully awake now. She pulls her legs from my lap, sitting bolt upright as if an alarm's going off. One probably is, somewhere in her mind.

I rake a hand through my hair, wishing these women had an ounce of delicacy.

"That was unintentional." Wren doesn't give much bite to her words, but she's not looking at me, either. She's too consumed with folding and smoothing her blanket to glance my way.

"I offered." I pictured something with my arms around her, but I have no regrets about the way the evening played out.

Except maybe all the eager women who chronicled every moment. I won't be surprised if one of them took photos. If they post them to our group chat, we'll be having words.

We follow them out of the movie room, Wren combing her fingers through her hair. She's never looked better to me, but as fast as she's walking, I don't think she's ready to hear me say it.

In the kitchen, Ada boxes up desserts and hands them out. "Everyone gets a variety of what's left."

"I just wish I had a slice of pie to bring home to Gary," Barb says.

Wren frowns but doesn't respond to the lament. I can understand why she'd want to draw a line somewhere. The number of casual acquaintances who have asked me to "take a look" at their bike is astronomical.

"Well," Isabel says, shooting a pointed look at me, "tonight was quite a success."

"Even more so than expected," Rosetta adds.

"So sorry you missed so much of the movie, Wren." Fran doesn't sound sorry at all. "But you already know how enemies to lovers goes, don't you?"

Wren snatches her plastic container from Ada. "Yes, well, I'd better get going so I don't fall asleep and crash my car in the ditch on the way home."

Do not even think it.

Her gaze locks on mine like she heard me. Something apologetic flashes there, warming my already overheated heart. She doesn't want me to worry.

As if remembering the other sets of eyes in the house ready to analyze her expression, she turns her back to me.

"Maybe Shepherd should drive you home tonight," Ada tells her. "You can get your car tomorrow when you're rested."

"I'm just kidding. Fully awake." Wren points at her face. "Bright-eyed, even."

"At least let him walk you to your car."

Wren takes a step backward, apparently fleeing Ada. Instead, she collides with my chest. I steady her with a hand at her hip until she regains her footing. Six sets of eyes gobble up the interaction.

Wren's shrill laugh is entirely fake. "I'm good."

"I'm serious." Ada's using her stern voice I remember from second grade. "My son has seen bears out here, and I hate to think what else could be lurking in the dark. You're not going out there alone."

"Oh. Um. Okay."

Not the enthusiastic consent I'd like to hear from her, but understandable given our audience. After a few quick goodbyes, we exit the house, the crisp air a shock to the system after the warmth of our evening on the couch.

We cross the home's extensive gravel parking lot like we're stuck in first gear. If something is out here, we're not doing a good job of trying to avoid it.

Wren side-eyes me. "I don't need a bodyguard."

"Depends on what's out here."

"Do you really think there are bears?"

"We see black bears sometimes at the lodge." Rarely, but I'm still not letting her leave my sight in a place this secluded. Anything could be out here, including the worst threat of all—other people.

"Have you seen them at your cabin?"

I grin in the darkness. "What answer is more likely to get you to visit again?"

She scoffs. "As if I want to tangle with a big, hairy beast."

"Are you talking about me or the bear?"

Her mouth falls open and she stumbles in the gravel. I take her elbow with my free hand, helping her right herself.

"Even I have motion-activated lights at my house," she mutters.

"If there's a lot of wildlife out here, they might never turn off."

She looks around, but it's too dark to see anything. The

home's porch light provides a dim glow, but it doesn't reach the trees surrounding the clearing. It's pitch-black out there, and if you're not used to it, more than a little unnerving.

We get to her car, the last in the row of eight vehicles. We really should have carpooled. What a waste. She's parked next to my truck, so I toss my leftovers in the passenger side while she does the same at hers. We meet between the cars, pausing as if intentionally delaying our goodbye.

I certainly am.

"What are you doing after this?" Terrible small talk, but I don't want her to drive away yet.

She laughs. "You mean besides going back to sleep?"

"Besides that."

"I'm probably going to read in bed and ignore my mom and her boyfriend."

"You don't like him?" She mentioned him the other day, too.

"I'm starting to feel like an outsider in my own house."

She rests her back against her car door, her face barely illuminated. "I like him. He's a nice guy. It's just that I always feel like I'm in the way. It's weird enough being twenty-nine and living with my mom, but now I'm basically living with my mom and her new man."

She lifts a hand between us as if to cut off my nonexistent commentary. "I'm going to move out ASAP. I've been looking. It's just...awkward right now. Instead of relaxing at home, I'm intruding on them."

I know a thing or two about too much family togetherness. "I'm usually home after seven-thirty. If you need a place to hang out."

I have no idea what I'm offering and would hate to try to quantify if she asked. All I know is, she's welcome. To anything. Anytime.

"Wouldn't that ruin your lone wolf persona?"

Her teasing works through me like whiskey, loosening me up and priming me to make poor decisions. Or maybe just long-awaited ones.

I take a step closer to her. "I'm not a lone wolf."

She sways forward, her gaze never leaving mine. "You sure seem like one. I don't want to intrude on your personal space." She scrunches her nose. "Again."

I crowd closer, the scent of cut grass drifting up from her, fresh and intoxicating. Never thought the smell of grass did it for me. Probably, it's that everything about Wren does it for me.

"Maybe I want you in my personal space."

Her lips part as she processes that confession. I'd give her a whole bucketful of them if I didn't think it would send her running. She stares at me so long, her denial must be coming. My gorgeous flight risk.

She surprises me by resting her hands on my chest. Gingerly, as if I have broken ribs she's afraid of touching too much, but it counts. Does it ever. Her soft, tentative touches are an inferno across my skin.

"If I did come by," she says slowly, "it would only be to catalog all your books. For research purposes."

I rest one hand on the side of her car, caging her in. "I'd be honored to be your research subject."

Her mouth tips up. I want to trace the lines of those lips with my thumb. Lean in and put an abrupt end to this conversation. Now that I know what she tastes like, it takes everything in my power to resist.

"And obviously, I would eat your food."

"I'll cook for you any time."

I move my free hand to her waist, marveling I'm allowed to touch her after longing to for endless months. Her fingers splay across my chest, running over the buttons on my shirt pockets.

All the while, we stare at each other in the darkness like we're tucked away in bed beneath a comforter.

We breathe in time, sharing space. My heart races beneath her fingers. The pulse in her throat jumps.

"Are you going to kiss me or what?"

I love the edge of urgency in her whisper. I slide my hand from her waist to the middle of her back, the other carding into her hair. A sigh escapes her, and I'm tempted to capture it with my mouth. We're so close, it would only take the smallest tilt of my head to reach her. Or her sliding onto her tiptoes. Maybe I'm a masochist, but I love the anticipation. I've waited for her this long. I don't mind drawing it out.

"You want me to kiss you?" My question is loose and languid. I'm in no rush, but I need her to admit it. To stop this one step forward, two steps back dance and meet me in the middle.

She hesitates as if looking for loopholes in a trick question.

"Just...one more time." Her voice cracks as I lean in. I glide my cheek against the shell of her ear, and she shivers beneath my hands. "Just to get this out of our systems."

"It will never be out of my system." I run my nose along her neck, down to her collar bone, breathing in the fading smell of grass. I love the way she rotates through perfumes, every scent a new secret to discover. "You're in my system for good."

"We still don't like each other...right?" She's breathy and restless, but it's the uncertainty that stops my dazed exploration.

I pull back until I can look her in the eyes. It's dark, but we see each other well enough. "What kind of bird do I have tattooed on my arm?"

She blinks hard, her fingers tensing on my chest. "What?"

I repeat the question, inching her closer to me with my hands, willing her to say the words and admit what she already knows.

"I—" Her eyes dance between each of mine, searching for something. She swallows, and even this soft light is enough to show me that she's steeling herself. Closing herself off to the truth. "I don't know. I'm not a bird watcher."

This beautiful, stubborn, infuriating woman.

I tighten my hold on her hair to tip her face up, and she sucks in a breath. This close to her, I almost give in. But I relax my hand, leaning in to press a kiss to her forehead. I linger, breathing her in, her fingers gripping my shirt so tight I'm surprised she doesn't rip the fabric.

She wants a kiss, desperately, but can't bring herself to confront how either of us actually feels. That's okay. I can be patient. I've had practice.

I draw back, easing my hold on her. "Goodnight, Krause."

Confusion bleeds into frustration, and her gaze shutters. She releases my shirt, her hands slowly falling to her sides.

"Text me when you get home."

She glares, huffing a humorless laugh. "What happens if I don't?"

I shrug. "I'll drive by your house and make sure you're home safe."

"My mom's boyfriend is the sheriff, you know. He could arrest you for stalking."

"Then you'd better send me that text."

That earns an eye roll, but I don't think she's as annoyed as she's letting on. She pulls herself from my arms, though, and I step back, watching her climb into her car. She slams the door like she wishes I was closer to it, practically peeling out on the gravel drive a moment later.

I round my truck to the driver's side, glancing over the row of cars in front of the house. The entire book group was preparing to leave when we walked out, and Wren and I were out here for at least fifteen minutes. Surprising that none of the women opted to leave during our protracted goodbye.

Most likely, the absolute silence out here means they've been watching us from inside the house so they wouldn't interrupt.

Sighing, I climb into my truck and echo Wren's sentiment. "Menaces."

NINETEEN
WREN

"I NEED the plate of fries to be as big as my face." I pass Delish's menu to Amy Ellison. It was only ever a formality. "Bring me all the potatoes you have."

Drowning myself in salty carbs seems appropriate.

Amy marks my order on her notepad. "Burger with cheese and avocado and a whole mess of fries. Need dessert tonight?"

"Probably not." I should show some restraint. Goodness knows, I don't have much of it in the rest of my life.

"Are you going to kiss me or what?" Pathetic. Proven by the fact that he went with "or what."

"Jodi made dulce de leche cheesecake," Amy adds.

"I'll take a slice of that, too, please." I long ago decided calories only count if I'm the one who prepared them. I will gladly eat treats made by someone else.

She makes another mark. "Everything okay, honey?"

Amy owns and runs Delish with her wife, Jodi. Beyond serving the best food in town, they're generous with listening ears and impartial advice. They're close with my mom, and from all the times we've blabbed to them, they've become unofficial aunts for me and Hope. Since they're Ian's actual aunts, we're practically in-laws. They're awesome. But I can only handle spilling my guts to one person tonight.

I gesture at Hope, who's sitting across from me and already ordered a more reasonably sized platter of fries. "I'm here for therapy."

Amy nods. "Holler if you need anything else."

"I will." She walks away, and I shift my attention to my best friend. "So."

Hope waits, eyes wide. "So?"

I asked her to come out with me tonight alone. I was very specific about the last word. I'm not ready for Tess and Lila to know all my sordid secrets, and there's no way I could say anything in front of Griffin. But I didn't give her much to go on —just asked for an emergency girls' night as soon as she closed up her shop.

She delivered on her part. She's here, ready and willing. Now, I just have to follow through on mine.

Easier said than done. Well, in this case, the *saying* is actually the hard part. Easier done than said.

I'm terrible at mushy stuff. I'm meant to push my feelings down until they're a hard lump of coal in the pit of my stomach. I don't whip them out and pass them around like a baby at a family reunion. But if I keep swinging between anger and confusion, I'm going to do something stupid.

Stupid*er*.

I barely functioned today at work. My eyes were so glued to the bakery's front door, you'd think I was eagerly waiting for an online order to arrive. Every time someone passed the windows, I glanced up, *hoping*.

It's that hope I'm not sure what to do with.

I suck in a deep breath. "There have been some...changes... on the Callahan front."

Hope smiles. My stomach twists. This was a mistake. I can just carry on like I've been doing, without any clarity from my friend. Sure, I'm pretty much flailing wildly in the dark, like I've been shoved into a wet paper bag and am trying to punch my way to safety. Half the time, I'm pretty sure I'm only hurting myself.

But I've become really good at swinging those punches.

Hope doesn't move, but I can practically see her questions bubbling to the surface behind her eyes. "Changes such as...?"

I do a quick scan of the diner. There's nobody in here that I'm worried about, but it never hurts to double check in a town like Sunshine. Then again, six nosy women already have their fingers in my personal life like raccoons with a tub of peanut butter. Why not broadcast it to the whole diner?

I clasp my hands on the shiny tabletop. "We might not be as nemesis-y as we used to be."

The slo-mo excited face Hope makes is exactly why I wanted to meet somewhere public. Yes, I needed a massive intake of fries, but with a crowd, she won't be able to squeal and jump up and down and whatever else she might do in these kinds of situations.

It's weird that I haven't had many of these situations, isn't it? I've dated, of course, but I've never really *cared* that much before now. And even that feels like a lot to admit. Caring? What's that?

"Specifically, what changed?" She drops her voice for the delicate conversation.

"Specifically, everything."

"Please give me more information."

And I do. I spill all the details about what's happened between Callahan and me from the moment I first walked into book group and saw him surrounded by all those cardigan-wearing grandmas. I tiptoe around his anxiety and panic attack, but I lay out everything else. The kiss. His cabin. His confusing restraint last night. All of it.

By the time I catch up to today, we're halfway through our burgers.

"Why wouldn't he kiss me again?" That's the question that kept me up half the night. Was it me? My breath? Is he a massive control freak who masks it with indifference? What?

His refusal to kiss me could be more proof this is all mind games to him. A way to get me to look dumb and weak. It's worked pretty well so far, too. First I mauled him in the alley, and then I begged him to kiss me last night. So embarrassing.

That doesn't really track with everything I've learned about Callahan these last couple of weeks. But if it's not mind games, his rejection leaves me even more confused.

I slump my chin in my hand, toying with a fry. "If he's just trying to work past this tension between us or something, shouldn't he go for it?"

Ahem. Like I did.

"Is that what you think is happening?"

Hope's being all sweet and gentle with me, like she's talking to August. That's how much of a mess I am. She has to pull out the little kid voice.

"You think this is just a one-time thing?" she asks when I don't answer right away.

"*It will never be out of my system.*" If I hadn't been so drunk on his *everything*, I might have processed that little declaration more last night. In the stark light of day, the words are like a grenade, blowing my excuses to rubble.

But then I come back to the same question: why not kiss me?

"Is that what *you* think is happening?" I toss back. Yes, I've reverted to begging again already. Please, I have no answers.

Hope lifts a delicate brown eyebrow. "Are you sure you want to know what I think?"

Probably not. She's swung hints and insinuations about Callahan my way for literal years. I've ducked and dodged every last one, pretending they've never touched me even when they dug right under my skin. Pretty sure this time, she's aiming for the bullseye over my confused little heart.

I brace myself against the booth. "Hit me with it."

"I think you've liked each other for a long time. *Mutually*." She puts special emphasis on the word along with an arch look.

I snort, even as my traitorous brain pictures that little bird on his arm.

"Yes, you had reasons to dislike him that you now know are wrong...but he's basically your ideal man. Think about the guys you've dated that went nowhere. What were they like?"

"Not the best. My college boyfriend was too clingy and had no ambition for his life. The next guy was so emotional, I never knew which version of him to expect." I think back. "I guess the last guy I dated was just kind of bland."

And that brings us up to three years ago. Roughly the time a certain Shepherd Callahan started remodeling the store next door to the bakery.

Hope points a fry at me. "Exactly. Shepherd's their exact opposite."

"No, he's..." But I've got nothing else. She's right.

"Shepherd is independent and does his own thing, just like you. He's a dedicated business owner, so same. You live for his visits to the bakery because you like how he challenges you. He's funny, too, when you're not going at each other's throats."

It's wrong to think about how he dragged his nose along my neck last night. So. Very. Wrong. But oh, I need a repeat of that move.

She levels me with a serious look. "And we can't ignore that you've been thinking about how handsome he is since he opened up his shop."

"Handsome." I stick out my tongue as if the description is all wrong.

It *is* all wrong. Sexy. Devastating. Makes my stomach swoop and my toes curl from twenty feet away. Those fit Callahan better.

"Now, something's shifted between you two," Hope goes on. "It's delicate, and you're both trying to sort it out. Maybe he wants to make sure this fragile thing between you isn't going to immediately shift back. You have to admit, you've been giving him crap for the last two years."

The truth of this makes me squirm. "Your successful relationship has really turned you into a guru."

"I'm speculating, obviously. But what guy wouldn't want to make sure his feelings are reciprocated?"

"You think he has feelings for me?" Man, I sound so pathetic. Begging my friend to tell me if a guy likes me. *Check yes or no.* But also, I really need an outside source to confirm.

"If the tattoo you described on his arm is any indication—"

I shush her. I should have kept that information to myself. "We don't know for sure what it is."

It could be anything. A goldfinch. A sparrow. A thrush. For all I know, it's a totally random bird. On his tattoo sleeve dedicated to people he cares about. That he wants me to name because...he's a creepy dude with low-key control issues? Something.

The dubious smile she gives me quiets my internal denials. "Fine. We'll ignore the tattoo for now. The real question is, do you have feelings for him?"

I take a huge bite out of my burger. Hope laughs at my obvious stalling tactic but waits patiently while I chew. My thoughts aren't any clearer once I swallow the bite down.

These last couple of weeks have been emotional chaos, one new thing about Callahan flying at me after another. But each new thing has been surprisingly great. I like and admire him more than ever. Every interaction with him makes me want another.

That's always been true, even when I thought it was spite drawing me to him.

"I might have things going on in the heart area." I sound like exactly as big of an idiot as I feel. "For Callahan."

Hope grins wide. "Did that hurt to say?"

"A little."

"Does he know you have heart things going on?"

"Like I can tell him that." I'm not sure I fully realized it until right this moment. How was I supposed to barf all that on him before I knew it myself?

"You could try."

"I knew telling you would be a problem. You're in love, and Griffin loves you back. You think that's the answer to everything." I bite a ketchup-covered fry, looking around at the diner patrons. "Where are all the bitter and jaded people when I need them? Someone come give me cynical advice about my love life."

I shiver. I can't believe I'm claiming spending time with Callahan as a *love life*. Or how right it feels to call it that.

"I'm not saying you have to tell him everything. But maybe you could try telling him *something*."

It's a reasonable suggestion. Anyone not already hardened to being vulnerable with their feelings would do it. But actually trying it is more terrifying than swimming in the ocean and seeing a shark fin.

"Being soft and vulnerable gets your heart broken." Ask me how I know. "It's much better to be cool and aloof and full of snarky sayings."

She reaches out to take my hand on the tabletop. My heart squeezes at that sweet gesture. I'm tempted to call it a night, lay twenty bucks on the table, and scram. This evening is all kinds of too much, and I've reached my limit.

Hope is undeterred. She holds on like she knows I'm considering an escape. "But sometimes, being soft and vulnerable gets your heart cared for, too."

"So sappy." I refuse to admit how much I want that. "You're the worst."

She grins at me, reveling in my faux outrage. "I know. What are you going to do?"

I shrug. "Freak out, I guess."

And maybe drive into the woods.

TWENTY

WREN

THIS IS PROBABLY A BAD IDEA. Probably definitely a really bad idea. Just because things turned out okay for Hope, I'm going to take her advice about romance?

No. I cannot be thinking the word *romance* when I'm standing on Callahan's porch again like a woman obsessed. I could have called. Added a text to our goodnight messages from last night. Something normal like, "Hey, are you home? I thought I'd drop by because it turns out I'm feeling ways about you and I can't process them alone and also I think I kind of miss you for some reason?"

Would have been easier than trying to say it.

I ring the bell, refusing to think about the crazy look in my eyes the attached camera must be recording right now. It's so quiet out here. Last time, he opened the door before I could even knock, but tonight, I count the minutes that go by while I wait.

He could be asleep already. His truck is here, but that doesn't mean he's around. He said his family lives close, maybe he's over there. He could be somewhere in the forest chopping wood in one of his ubiquitous flannels for all I know.

Probably best if I don't picture myself stumbling across that idyllic scene.

I've just turned to leave when the door opens behind me. I spin back around, only to squeak out the most pathetic sound of my entire existence.

Callahan's in his doorway, wet and naked with only a towel around his waist. I don't stare. That would be so rude. But I do note the water droplets that slowly track down his nicely formed chest, over his flat stomach, to finally get absorbed by the fluffy white terrycloth at his middle.

His tattoos do, in fact, stop at his shoulders. They curl around his deltoids like clouds capping off each nature scene. My gaze zeroes in on the little bird on his inner arm. He doesn't have tattoos on his chest, but the light dusting of dark hair there is revelation enough.

I should probably not know what his belly button looks like. That's too much, right? But there it is, kind of flat and weirdly appealing.

It would be absurd to say I've never seen a man shirtless. I'm no stranger to lakes and rivers in the summertime. I have eyes. But the way I'm goggling at him, you'd think I lived in a convent and just discovered abs. The thing is, I've never seen *this* man shirtless. He's tall and lean, lightly muscled, and so very, very...

Swallowing hard, I drag my gaze up to meet his. Please let that detailed ogling have been instantaneous instead of several minutes long. "I thought you'd be dressed."

He runs the hand not clutching his towel through his wet hair, making it curl at the ends. "I can't be decent all the time."

Strangely, he doesn't seem embarrassed. I, on the other hand, am slowly melting into a puddle on his front porch.

"You said I could come by."

"I'm not turning you away. Come in." He opens the door wider, moving to let me pass.

I walk through, searching for anything to focus on other than that stark white towel. Anything.

"Are you naked under there?"

I should just cut my losses now. Run out the front door and try this again another time. Or never. If he's going to open the door in the nude, it'd be best to stay away from his cabin entirely, right?

Right?

"Do you want a peek?" He shoots me a devilish grin, his hands moving to open the towel.

I spin to put my back to him. "No! I don't want to see that."

My eyes have other ideas. I look over my shoulder anyway.

He laughs, flashing the towel open to reveal solid blue swim trunks. "I'm not naked."

"Oh." I should not sound so disappointed.

"Interesting that you looked, though."

I'm going to ignore that. "What are you doing in a swimsuit? Do you have a hot tub?"

Lila's told me that all the cabins at the lodge have them. I heard way too much about how she shared one with Grant back when he stayed there.

"The opposite. I've got a cold plunge tub on my deck."

"I don't know what that is."

He tilts his head toward the back of the house. "I'll show you."

Still dripping, he leads me through the living room, and I touch the rolling ladder as I pass. *One day, friend.* He pulls open the back door, revealing a big deck with an unobstructed view of the woods, two Adirondack chairs, and what looks like a tiny black hot tub except it's topped with ice cubes.

Just looking at it makes me want a blanket and a hot tea.

"I don't believe you fit in that." He's got to be way too tall for that thing. It looks like it could barely hold August.

"I fit just fine."

My already overtaxed brain fizzles out in a puff of smoke. I grasp for an ounce of coherence, my fingers finding nothing. "With the ice, though? Sounds like torture."

As if to prove my point, a breeze blows over the deck and straight through the open door. He shivers, an image that etches itself on my brain for future playback. He shuts out the cold, but we don't leave the small alcove. I look around, trying not to stare at any part of him. He's got a couple of coats hanging by the door and a pair of boots at the ready.

Big, big boots.

"It's to help with anxiety." He gazes down at me, no shame in admitting his vulnerability now. "Theoretically, it regulates my nervous system."

"Does it work?"

"In my experience, it does."

"I thought cold showers were supposed to distract you from sex and stuff." Nice, Wren. Never been smoother.

Especially when I'm trying to focus on anything but the mostly naked man in front of me.

"In my experience, it doesn't." He indicates I should go into the main part of the house. "I'll get dressed. Make yourself at home."

He climbs up the staircase, leaving wet footprints as he goes. My brain whirls with questions about what's up there. What his bedroom looks like. If the ceiling is sloped, and if it is, how he gets around. What he's putting on.

I shake my head, moving toward the best distraction at my disposal: his library. He's got a little bit of everything here. Technical books about bike mechanics. Books about hiking trails and campsites in Oregon. Several shelves of classics like Dickens, Fitzgerald, and Hawthorne. Contemporaries covering horror, sci-fi, and mysteries.

Everything Rick Riordan has ever written.

He's got Austen and Brontë tucked away in here, too, along with some modern rom-coms whose bright covers add a nice pop of color to the otherwise drab assortment.

There's also a vinyl record collection on one shelf. Was not expecting yacht rock, but I can see that kind of laid-back classic rock for Callahan.

I'd noticed the photographs when I was here last time but didn't really examine them. I do now. No surprise, all the photos are of scenery or use nature as the backdrop. He's got a family photo. One of him and Charlie at a lake somewhere. A snapshot of him and what must be Leo when they were kids in a treehouse.

A picture of him with an elderly man catches my eye. I can't resist picking up the frame to get a better look. It's more recent than the others, maybe a couple of years old. The two men have their arms slung around each other, the older one wrinkled and frail but smiling just as bright as Callahan.

"That's my grandpa."

I spin so fast, I clutch the frame to my chest so I don't drop it. His hair's still damp, but he's put on a navy blue henley that clings to his arms, and gray sweatpants. I *know* he chose that combo just to spite me. It's like the man wants me to be tongue-tied twenty-four-seven.

"I'm sorry. I was just—" I replace the picture where it was. "I was snooping."

"I gave you permission." He steps closer, seemingly to get a better look at the photograph, moving in until his arm brushes mine. "He passed away about three years ago."

"I'm sorry." It's been longer than that since my grandma died, and her loss still hurts my soul sometimes.

"Don't be. He had a good life."

Callahan gazes down at me. Waiting. I did come all the way out here to see him again, but...ugh. Why are words so hard?

"You've got a lot of different kinds of books." I'm not deflecting at all.

"I like some of everything. Nice shirt."

"Thanks." I tug at the hem of my long-sleeve tee. It's got an illustration of a woebegone frog with the quote, *I have a serious case of mood poisoning.*

"Do you want to sit down?"

"Yes. No." I squeeze my eyes shut for a moment. When I open them, he's still standing there looking like the coziest snack. The jerk. "I'm probably distracted enough as it is."

The smirk that touches his mouth sets off a brush fire in my chest. I take a big step backward. It's better if I keep my cool for this. He glances me over, the smirk fading as he takes in the extra space between us. He stays calm and collected, though. His easygoing nature throws me off. At least when we're snarking, I know what he's thinking.

Or I thought I did. Maybe I've never known.

"You're in my system for good."

Unhelpful.

I should have planned what to say before I came over here. My brain has been mostly making static noises since my conversation with Hope. A thought or two in my head would have been nice.

"I might possibly owe you an apology. Probably." I exhale hard. Maybe I should practice some breathing exercises while I'm at it. Anything to get a sense of calm going instead of this worrying adrenaline rush.

Is this how Callahan feels when he's on the spot? Like he wants to barf and run away and sit with his head between his knees all at the same time?

"For what?"

I can't tell if he genuinely isn't sure or if his list of grievances is so long, he needs me to narrow it down.

"For..." I wave a hand in the air. "How I act with you, I guess. What a brat I've been, mostly."

He doesn't ask questions, but his placid reaction makes me want to explain anyway.

"I was led to believe some things about you that I recently discovered weren't accurate."

Why do I sound like a baroness making a non-apology to the servant she let go?

"What things were you led to believe? And by whom?"

This is the hard part about apologizing. You have to actually confront all the stupid stuff you've done.

"Is that relevant?" I ask.

"Seems pretty relevant."

I sigh, but...I want to get past this. I owe him the truth. "Richard Allred."

Callahan's gaze darkens, and not in the good way. More like he's thinking about how many times he can throat-punch the guy before Allred's lawyers step in.

"He told me you convinced him not to invest in Blackbird's." I tick my head to the side, not liking the rest. "And that you said I was a nightmare. I thought you said all that because you hated me. For some reason."

At least those things were only ever secondhand news. I can't repeat the things I actually heard him say, even if he's changed his mind in the years since.

"How did you discover that's not accurate?"

He doesn't specify if he means the story about him thwarting our business or that he hated me. Hopefully that means all of it was inaccurate.

"Charlie said something about how much you couldn't stand the guy. Something about how you wanted to beat him up because he was such a jerk to...someone in town." I can't look at him. This is the worst. I thought he tried to ruin me, and he actually did the exact opposite. "And I guess he's been revealed to be a fraud now."

"Now that you know he's a fraud, it's easier to believe I'm not the bad guy?"

I hate how his voice drops. My confession wasn't supposed to make him sad. But he's not wrong. I refused to entertain the idea Callahan could be a good guy until the truth of it slapped me across the face.

"It's not just that. Rosetta told me about your volunteer work in the library, and I've seen how much you're doing for Sunshine with the bike trails. And the romance book group ladies love you. They can be menaces, but they have good hearts. You're sweet to August, and that counts for a lot. It's all made me realize how unfair I've been to you."

He just watches calmly while I spew out my feelings. Or most of them.

I exhale a huge sigh. Time for the big reveal. "I like you, okay? Against my better judgment."

His mouth tips up. "Don't go all Mr. Darcy on me. I might swoon dead away at your feet."

My instinct is to laugh along with him, but I shoot him a dirty look. "Be nice. I don't know how to do this."

"Apologize?"

"That, too. But also..." I gesture between the two of us. "This."

"You can't tell me you've never dated." It's flattering how incredulous he sounds.

"I have. I've just never tried very hard before. Having feelings isn't really my strong suit."

The rundown of my exes with Hope earlier was a bit of an eye-opener. I picked crummy guys and then was surprised I never got invested? Play stupid games, I guess. I don't want stupid prizes anymore.

"And now?" Callahan sure is calm when he's tormenting me.

"Now...I want to try." I suck in the most steadying breath I can. "With you."

His mouth pulls into the slowest, widest smile. I can't even call it a smirk. He's *loving* his front-row seat to the Awkward Wren Show.

"Don't make it weird," I add.

"I'm glad you want to try. Because I'm already there."

I cannot with this man. Doesn't he know those are inside thoughts?

My gaze sweeps over his living room until I spot the distinct retro-cowboy cover of next month's romance group pick. I wave vaguely at it. "Where did you find that? I haven't been able to snag a copy yet."

Distraction to the rescue. The Awkward Wren Show is now on hiatus.

"We could read it together."

My heart leaps at how casually he suggests it, no matter how impractical the idea is. "Reading over each other's shoulders? Doesn't seem like that would work very well."

I might read faster than he does. Plus, we'd have to be super close to make that work. Practically plastered against each other. Like at the first book group meeting, but with zero space between us.

Reading together is growing on me.

"I could read out loud," he says.

Did this man just offer one of my secret fantasies to me on a platter? I should have some self-control. This evening has already had enough strange moments. I should tell him I'll read it after he's finished. Reading one at a time, that's the logical thing to do.

"Let's do that," I say instead.

TWENTY-ONE
SHEPHERD

SUGGESTING I could read our romance book out loud to Wren was a terrible idea. Giving voice to all this attraction and barely-contained longing is torture, even if it's fictional. She sits at the opposite end of my couch, her feet tucked up beneath her, listening as I read the couple's flirty banter, heated arguments, and endless poetic descriptions of cowboys.

It would be awkward if she weren't smiling so hard. She's not taking it very seriously. Probably because I just read the phrase *glistening sea-blue orbs* regarding the heroine's eyes.

She stretches, shifting the smallest centimeter closer along the couch. At this rate, it will take her all night to get to my side, but I'm prepared to wait.

Frustration roared through me when she admitted why things stalled out between us. I should have known I'd have fallout from confronting a wealthy narcissist like Richard Allred. I just had no idea he'd retaliate with *her*. Of all the options at his disposal, he found my weakest spot.

Although, I probably revealed my intentions loud and clear when I got in his face after overhearing what he said about her. Even all this time later, his plans for her make my blood boil. He was confident enough to go into vivid detail at Stumpjumper where anyone could hear him—I have no doubt he intended to follow through. Use and discard was the gist of it.

I should have punched him when I had the chance.

"Do you have a blanket?" Wren says as I turn a page.

"In the basket at your end of the couch."

She twists to look. "You have a blanket basket? Are you a real adult or something?"

"Or something."

She stands to collect the blanket. When she sits back down, she's erased most of the space between us. I fight a smirk and read on. Shifting the open paperback to the arm of the couch so I can turn pages one-handed, I rest my other hand between us, palm up.

I keep reading, waiting for movement in my peripheral vision. I swear, she stares at my hand like she's examining it for booby traps. I'm not sure what nefarious motives she thinks I have in the offer, but she seems to sift through them all. Finally, she slips her palm against mine, the echoes of her small touch radiating up my arm.

If she were to look, she would see the smuggest, most satisfied smile on my face. But she goes on watching my hand like it's a marvel. We kissed until we were both breathless and out of our minds, but this simple touch is a foreign country for us. One I very much want to take up dual residency in.

I pause at the end of the second chapter, unsure how long I've been reading, but willing to keep going until my voice is hoarse if it keeps her here on my couch.

"She really can't stand that cowboy," Wren says.

"And yet, he's obviously smitten with her."

"That doesn't happen in real life." She flips my hand so hers is beneath it and uses her other to trace slow patterns over my skin. If I died and this is heaven, nobody zap my heart back to life. "Is this what you thought would happen when you joined a romance book group?"

"Yes, but I had my eye on Fran."

She whistles a low note. "High hopes."

I already told her about Rosetta's repeated invitations, but making a friend happy wasn't the only reason. "I joined because I thought it might help with my anxiety. Get some exposure therapy in a contained situation."

"Is it helping?"

"They do put me on the spot a lot." I squeeze her hand beneath mine.

She shifts to face me better. She's exquisite like this, relaxed on my couch. "What else do you need more exposure to?"

Don't even ask, kitten.

"Reading aloud to a beautiful woman would help."

She rolls her eyes, but she's still got a grin going. "Look at me, doing my part. I could help you prepare for that town hall presentation if you want."

Dread creeps in behind the comfort of the evening, playing peekaboo from the shadows. I was trying not to think about that, despite Lila's chipper texts for us to coordinate for the slideshow. A date's been set for next month, a glaring red square on my calendar. My quick escape the other day seems to have barely registered with her. Or she's pointedly ignoring it.

"I don't think it would be the same one-on-one. My triggers have more to do with crowds and being the center of attention among strangers."

I was prepared to be uneasy during book group, but the ladies quickly revealed themselves to be over-eager grandmas and dispelled my nerves. A room full of a hundred Sunshine residents there to decide whether the town can afford to spend money on my trail plans won't give off nearly the same harmless vibes.

Wren dips her head, scrunching her eyebrows together to stare me down. "You underestimate how intimidating I can be."

"I don't underestimate anything about you."

Her mouth takes on an unimpressed slant. Not sure why she wouldn't believe it. She's a capable and impressive woman, no matter how much she likes to deflect attention from it.

"Is that why you stopped working at your family's lodge?" she asks. "Because of the crowds?"

"That's part of it. I was more comfortable when it was smaller, but I never really fit in there as an employee. We all knew Charlie's plans to turn it luxury weren't for me. My grandpa encouraged me to open my own shop."

"The grandpa from the picture?"

I nod, gliding my thumb over the smooth skin on her hand. "He wanted me to follow my passion."

More to the point, he never wanted me to feel trapped into following his. He was adamant I find what I love and stick with it—and I don't think he just meant work.

"And that's bikes?"

I exhale a soft laugh. "You sound so shocked."

She straightens, smoothing out her expression. She has no idea how much I love it when she doesn't hide what she's feeling —even confusion about why I like my job.

"I'm not trying to. I really want to know."

"My passion was doing my own thing, and bikes were a means to that end. I enjoy bikes, both riding and repairing them. Like you said: I like to get my hands dirty."

"Let's pretend I didn't say that."

"Impossible." I'll never forget it, or the fire that danced in her eyes when she stood right there in front of my bookshelves.

"Working with customers in your shop doesn't bother you?" she asks, redirecting.

"We don't usually have more than a few people in the shop

at a time. It's low stress. And it doesn't hurt that I'm an expert in the field."

She tilts her head, scrutinizing my face. "You know, I never noticed how humble you are."

A chuckle rumbles through me. "If it helps, I never felt that way at the lodge. I was always off balance and out of place. But with Get in Gear, I don't question myself. And there's pride in helping other people enjoy something I love, whether that's a single ride along the river or starting a lifetime with the sport."

"Which brings us back to your presentation."

She's good. But I already knew that.

"You're adorably tenacious."

"I've been told. I'll help you, though. I'll be your practice audience. You can give your speech, and I'll boo and throw tomatoes at your head."

"I wasn't planning on an angry mob."

"See? You need me."

"I never thought I didn't."

Wren's gaze drifts over my face to my mouth. Seconds tick by. "Maybe you should read another chapter."

She sounds so breathy, I don't want to go back to the book. But I'm not above doing anything she asks.

By the time the fictional couple walk away angry from their argument in chapter three, Wren's trying to hide a yawn. It's late, and I know she was in the bakery early this morning. Her car was already in the alley when I rolled in after nine.

"Sorry," she says from behind her hand. "It was a pie prep day for me again. Six o'clock is a stupid time to get to work."

"That's why I don't open until ten."

She collapses against the back of the couch, her shoulder not quite touching mine. "Don't rub it in. You don't have to build the bikes."

"Yes, I do. The bikes come partially disassembled."

"They do?" She stares up at me, her head resting on the cushion. "With instructions like an Ikea dresser?"

"Pretty much."

"Hmm. Only partially disassembled, though."

"Sometimes I get requests for custom builds that I make entirely from scratch."

She sags another inch closer to me. "That's more like it."

"Maybe we could get a bike for you sometime."

"Oh, no." She slides her hand from mine and escapes off the couch. "Don't start trying to get me to *do things*."

I stand and follow her across the room. "Wanting to 'do things.' How horrible."

"I already have a bike, for your information. It's an unrideable rust pile in my garage, and that's the way I like it."

"You know best."

"I do. And—" She points at me like I've got a target on my chest. "That's why I'm going to help you with your presentation."

"Okay." Might as well start giving in now. I plan to do a lot of it with her. "As soon as I have everything prepared, I will let you pelt me with rotten tomatoes."

She nods, pleased with herself. "Thanks for catching me up on the book. I wouldn't have known how annoying cowboys are otherwise."

"Thanks for ignoring my stumbles." Why the word "verisimilitude" is in that book, I can't guess.

"You barely made any. You have a really nice voice. I listen to a lot of audiobooks, and your narration is way up there."

I'll remember that.

"And to think, a few weeks ago you said the sound of my voice made you wish you could weld your ears shut."

Her cringe makes me regret the poorly timed joke. "I do have a way with words."

I take a step closer, keeping her focus on me. "If it helps, I've always been more concerned with the way you look at me."

She backs up until she's against my door, her hands behind her. "How do I look at you?"

As if she doesn't have a volcano of heat in her eyes right now.

I close the last scrap of distance between us until we're nearly touching. "Like you can't decide if you'd rather fight me or kiss me."

Her laugh comes out breathy, her gaze stuck on my mouth. "It's a really tough decision."

"Not for me." I rest one hand just over her head, and the other sifts into her hair. I've been itching to run my fingers through those wild blond strands all night.

"Fighting is less ambiguous," she whispers. "I need super clear romantic signals."

Running my fingertips along her scalp, I cup the back of her head. "I was awfully clear with my signals when we kissed the other day."

Her hands find my chest, her fingers dancing over the fabric. "It's a big leap to make, though. Enemies to lovers."

I hover over her mouth. "I was never your enemy."

She tilts her face up, straining to get to me without actually moving closer. "You're a big fan of torture, aren't you?"

"I'm a big fan of taking my time."

I trail my fingers from her hair, down behind her ear until they graze along the slope of her neck. Her skin is so unbearably soft, I'm afraid my calloused hands will leave marks. I'll just have to be sure I'm extra gentle.

She shivers beneath me, so warm she's practically burning up. One of her hands drifts from my chest down to my waist, lightly flexing to tug me closer.

"Please kiss me." The barest whisper.

I lean in until my mouth is almost on hers, my fingertips skimming over her skin. "What kind of bird do I have tattooed on my arm?"

Her blue eyes flash, her gaze darting between each of mine. Her mouth parts, and I feel her intake of breath as much as hear it. For three long seconds, I expect her to argue with me again and run off into the night.

But she relaxes in my arms. "A wren."

I nod slowly, that sweet, soft word exactly what I needed to hear. "That's right. Wren."

Everything I've longed for is voiced in that single syllable. Her eyes widen as if she heard it, too, but then my mouth is on hers. Claiming as surely as I'm surrendering.

If our first kiss was a frenzied dare, this is an unhurried promise. There's no rush. No fear of getting caught or coming to our senses. Our kisses soothe the ragged uncertainty I've been drowning in, bringing me back to the surface for air. We're both in this together.

She makes soft little sounds, and I swallow each one down. Her hands slowly trek over my shoulder and waist, mapping my body in tentative touches. With each kiss, her exploration grows bolder, more relaxed. Her fingers slip over the nape of my neck and into my hair, lightly tugging at the strands.

I want this kiss to be controlled and gentle, but she's making me forget why. The sounds that groan out of me are anything but soft, and she smiles against my mouth. Triumph all you want, kitten. I have no problem falling to my knees for you.

Eventually, we draw apart with tandem sighs. I press my forehead to hers, my hands smoothing over her back and down her arms. I know she needs to leave soon, but I won't be the one to suggest it.

"Are you sure the cold tub doesn't work?" she says.

I rumble a low laugh. "Very sure."

"I guess I should go before…"

She doesn't fill in that blank, but my imagination is more than up for the task. "Probably a good idea."

I slowly move out of her space, reluctantly releasing every point of contact. She's gorgeous like this, a little dazed and kiss-drunk in my house. She's breathtaking when she's wild and angry, too, so it's likely I'm a poor judge. I have Wren-blindness and find her achingly pretty no matter the context.

"Text me when you get home," I tell her.

She nods like my worry bordering on overprotectiveness is a given now. "Goodnight, Shepherd."

That deserves another kiss. I dart in close to press my mouth to hers in thanks. Praise. Adoration. Everything. I want to hear her say my name at all times, in all ways.

"Goodnight, Wren."

TWENTY-TWO
WREN

HOW SOON IS TOO SOON to show up at someone's house? Let's pretend you have a vague but blanket invitation that you've thoroughly abused already. Do you go every night the way you want to and reveal just how ridiculously obsessed you are? Or do you play it cool like a normal person and give it a day or two?

I opted to behave like a normal person. I'm really not suited for it.

I've spent the last couple of nights at home, fighting the urge to drive into the canyon like I'm going through withdrawals. In theory, I have a solid distraction. Rosetta's prediction came true —my e-book hold for the romance group came up yesterday. I've read a little, but I don't have much enthusiasm for it.

The book is fine, don't get me wrong. I love a female character who knows what she wants and goes after it, and this one delivers. But apparently, I'm easily spoiled. I want Shepherd to read it to me.

My stomach tilts. I'm such a pathetic little ball of longing, I get all gooey inside just thinking about him. What happened to strong, independent Wren who never got mushy over a man?

She melted like chocolate after a couple of smoldering kisses, that's what.

It wasn't just the kisses that turned me to goo, though. He's genuinely a good guy behind his too-cool-for-school façade. One who's steady but driven, serious but easily lightens heavy moods. He's kind of dreamy in all the ways.

Ugh. I'm so gross.

If I'm being weird, nobody's noticed yet. Mom was too busy talking about how our new hires are doing while we baked this morning to question the hazy look on my face. And Tess has a full schedule of custom orders this afternoon to keep her attention. She's at one of the front tables, meeting with a couple to come up with their perfect wedding cake. Everyone's distracted from what's going on in my life, and that's just the way I like it.

A shadow darkens Blackbird's door and pushes through. Shepherd doesn't look any different from normal. Longish dark hair he runs his fingers through as he crosses the room. Neatly trimmed beard that highlights his jaw and mouth. A dark green flannel layered over a gray t-shirt and jeans.

And yet, my body zings like a roman candle's gone off inside me, sparking and fizzing all over the place. When his gaze hits mine, a dopey smile pops onto my face. Unbidden, but undeniable. His is more of a smirk but just as immediate.

He slips his hands into his jeans pocket when he reaches the counter in front of me. "Krause."

For months, that word has dropped over me like an unspecified insult, an indistinct dig that never failed to get me to retaliate. So why does it feel like flirtation today?

Oh. Oh, wait. Has it *always* been flirtation? I might need to sit down for a minute.

"Callahan." That came out way breathier than normal, but okay.

"What's fresh today?"

I roll my eyes. He's asked me that question approximately one hundred times. I give the response I've doled out just as often. "It's all fresh every day."

He nods, his mouth twisting as he glances over the case before fixing his attention back on me. "How do you know which ones are fresh?"

It's a ridiculous game. Made even more ridiculous by how long it took me to realize what prize he was after every time he asked.

"Mom and I did the baking this morning." Which he must know, since my car was in our spot when he arrived. "She made the cranberry silk, pumpkin, chocolate-peanut butter, and French silk pies. I made the peach, pear, lemon meringue, and Dutch apple pies."

He seems to ponder his options. I hold my breath the barest second.

"I'll take a Dutch apple."

My pride does a shameless victory dance in my chest. "Whole or a slice?"

"How about a hand pie?"

"Got it." I slip one into a paper bag and pass it over the counter.

He peers into the bag and frowns as if that flaky, golden-brown goodness did him wrong. "It's pretty small."

I cross my arms and jut out a hip, ready to trust fall back into my usual snarky attitude. "That's the same size our hand pies always are."

He's never complained before, but maybe now he's finally comfortable enough to admit the truth.

"Then I should probably come in again later this week to get another one."

I try to keep my stupid grin under control, but it's reckless. It wants to spill across my face and make it obvious how this little change in our routine zips through me like a lightning bolt.

Behind him, Tess glances over at us, narrowing her eyes as if she's making calculations. Normally, I'm a whole lot louder when Shepherd shows up. I probably look more annoyed, too. Smiles are out of the question. But thankfully, she returns her focus to the couple at the table and goes back to talking about cake flavors and decorations. The snoop.

I shift my gaze to Shepherd.

"Are you sure you'll be that hungry?" I aimed for skeptical but hit 'bated breath' instead.

"I'm always hungry, Krause."

Just like that, I am a fireball soaring into the sky. He's always been able to set me off, but now he's achieving much more enjoyable results.

Before I can come back down to earth and offer up a sassy response, his sister walks through the door with Leo Dalesandro right behind her.

"Oh, hey." Charlie doesn't sound thrilled to see Shepherd here, but Leo slaps him on the shoulder in bro-greeting on his other side.

"Getting a sweet treat to help you through your day?" Leo asks him.

Shepherd's gaze locks on mine. "It's the only thing that keeps me going."

Unfair of him to do that when I'm still smoldering.

"What are you two doing here?" he asks.

"*I* came to place a special order." Charlie jabs her thumb Leo's way. "*He* insisted on tagging along."

"Hey, we're a team. It's important for us to work together." He winks at her as if they're the only two people in the room.

Meanwhile, she fixes her attention on me as if he *isn't* in the room. "You know all about our new wedding venue. We're having a grand opening celebration in a few weeks. It's a mix of showing off the space and a fundraiser for the children's hospital."

"That's sweet to add that part." I don't follow Leo's career closely, but I know he's always doing fundraisers for kids. He's got the right persona for it—loud and full of enthusiasm.

"We got the idea to have a dessert bar—"

"My idea," Leo says. "FYI. I'm the ideas man."

Charlie takes a deep breath. "Leo got the idea to have a dessert bar—"

"Thank you." He gives a little bow.

Charlie looks like it's taking all her patience not to dropkick the man. Considering he's as tall as Shepherd and almost twice as wide, it'd be a Herculean feat. But the way steam's practically rising off of her, I'd say she's up to the task.

"So we need to order pies," she continues. "The event's the first weekend after Thanksgiving, and I know you guys get busy around the holidays so I wanted to get our order in early."

"Friday or Saturday?" Shepherd asks.

"Friday." Leo slings an arm around his shoulders. "Want to be my date? I've tried to find somebody to go with me, but I keep getting shot down."

I've always marveled at just how different Charlie and Shepherd are in looks and personality. She's petite, with red hair and a spirited attitude. He's tall, dark, and broody. But right now, they're wearing the exact same smirk.

"It's hard to imagine somebody turning you down," I say. Leo would probably have a line of women out the door if we just gave it a few minutes. There was brief talk about him starring in a reality dating show after retirement, and his fangirls lost their minds.

"Maybe you could be his date," Charlie says.

"No," both Shepherd and Leo answer simultaneously.

I don't even care that the handsome, famous, and flirty Leo Dalesandro just rejected me so blatantly. Shepherd's deep "no" turns my body up to a simmer.

"Then I guess you're out of luck," Charlie says. "Can we focus on the pies, please?"

Leo whacks Shepherd on the chest, one arm still around him. "Charlie told me the wedding venue was your idea. I didn't know you had marriage on the brain."

Shepherd watches me as if he's completely unaffected by his friend's teasing.

"It was her idea to turn the barn into a wedding space," he says. "I just encouraged her to make it happen."

"You reminded me of when I used to have weddings for my Barbies in the barn loft." Charlie nudges Shepherd with her shoulder. "That sparked the whole thing."

"I have good ideas, too." Leo feigns a pout that doesn't mesh well with his good-natured demeanor.

"A fifty-foot waterslide really isn't wedding-appropriate, no matter how much lawn space we have."

"I meant you being my date to the gala."

Charlie stares at him for a minute. I guess Shepherd's not the only one who blurts out his inside thoughts. I'm pretty sure she's wishing Leo had stayed in Texas when he retired. She turns to Shepherd as if Leo isn't there.

"You also deserve credit for helping me convince Mom and Dad." She looks up at him with a dash of big brother-adoration in her eyes. "That was the hardest part of the entire process, and I owe a lot of it to you."

"Your parents are not easy to win over," Leo says. "Like a certain someone."

Charlie sighs and moves closer as if she wants to climb over the counter and join me back here. "I would love to place that order, please."

"Sure." I grab the store's tablet from behind the counter and pass it to her. "You know how our special-order system works. How many pies are you thinking for that weekend?"

"Thirty."

Leo raises his hand like he's bidding on a cow at the county fair. "Fifty."

She maintains intense eye contact with me. "I'm placing the order for a variety of thirty pies."

"Always go bigger, Chuck."

Her gaze darts sideways, her mouth pressed into a thin line. I don't think she likes her nickname.

"You're expecting a pretty large turnout then?" I ask to refocus her on me. They sometimes place special orders for guest events at the lodge, but those usually max out at ten pies.

"Several hundred at least. Between wedding vendors and couples, and Leo auctioning off a bunch of sports memorabilia, it should be a huge event."

"A gala," Leo says. "That's what we call it in the biz."

Charlie focuses on the tablet, scrolling through to mark down her pie selections. Leo releases Shepherd and sidles up next to her. He doesn't throw his arm around her, but he flexes his fingers like he's itching to.

"Maybe I should help you with that, teammate."

"I should have just phoned it in," Charlie mutters.

"Never phone it in." Leo shakes his head at her. "Always give it one hundred and ten percent."

"Have you ever been stabbed with a stylus?"

He grins at her, but I doubt she sees it. "Once."

"Are you glad you don't work at the lodge anymore?" I ask Shepherd.

"Very."

"Are you going to the gala?" I'm not fishing for a date invitation. I'm not.

But...I would certainly consider going. If I happened to be invited.

"I doubt it."

I'm cramming down unnecessary disappointment when my phone starts buzzing like mad in my pocket. I pull it out to check.

Shepherd's does the same thing. We make eye contact over our phones.

"Menaces," we both say at the same time.

TEXT THREAD

Isabel: Movie night was such a hit, what do you say to a dinner out?

Isabel: Maybe this weekend?

Nora: I haven't finished the book yet

Nora: Can we promise we won't reveal spoilers?

Rosetta: Nobody ever promises that

Ada: I think we'll find enough distractions from fictional romance

Barb: I can't eat anything spicy

Fran: Hoping for spice is the whole reason we're going out

Ada: Great idea, Isabel

Ada: Magnifico, maybe? Or Lemongrass?

Barb: Lemongrass is Thai. That's spicy

Nora: You can order it mild

Barb: I vote Magnifico. Delicious Italian food and no loud music

Rosetta: Agreed

Isabel: Lemongrass doesn't have loud music

Barb: I never said it did

Fran: We can show up a little dressy, too

Fran: Really make a date of it

Ada: Is everyone in? Maybe some of us have other plans for the weekend?

Ada: If anyone has plans, let us know and we can reschedule

Ada: We only want to do it if everyone can attend

Wren: Magnifico sounds good

Shepherd: Does anyone need a ride?

Fran: If you're offering

Nora: He's not

TWENTY-THREE

SHEPHERD

AT SOME POINT, I'm going to dump my phone and only communicate with people via fax. Send me antiquated messages during work hours or nothing at all.

Every new message I get from Lila about the town hall presentation kicks my anxiety higher.

Lila: Let's set aside some time to go over your slideshow ideas

Lila: Do you have your presentation to run by me yet?

Lila: No rush. Still plenty of time

Lila: And I don't have final approval or anything

Lila: Just offering to look it over!

Lila: I'm drumming up a lot of interest for you!

Lila: You're going to do great!

I thought I'd be nervous about having dinner with Wren tonight, but it's Sunshine's tourism coordinator who's got my palms sweating.

I arrived at Magnifico early, but nobody in the book group thought to make a reservation for a Friday night. While the wait staff works to get a table for eight together, I'm on a leather seat in the waiting area, doom scrolling my text messages.

I've been working on the presentation in my off hours, but I'm not ready to share it with Lila yet. I'm not sure I'll ever be ready to actually get on stage and make my impassioned plea for community support.

Shepherd: I'm getting there

Feels like a lie, but I hit *Send* anyway.

Wren walks through the restaurant's doors looking like the embodiment of a warm hug. She's wearing a long, brown, thick-knit cardigan over a graphic tee. It's printed with *The Female Gaze* over an illustration of Medusa, hair-snakes going wild.

Marry me already, Krause.

Her eyes light up when she sees me, and my heart leaps. I've stopped by the bakery twice this week, and it hasn't been nearly enough.

"Am I actually early?" She glances around the small waiting area, probably looking for the rest of our friends. A few other larger parties fill the space, but no meddling women from the romance book group.

"You're right on time." I've been here for a good ten minutes with no sign of them. My anxiety goes into overdrive if I'm late to anything.

She looks me over, her gaze warming as she takes in my rust-colored sweater.

Yes, I took Fran's advice. Probably a bad idea on most counts, but tonight, something other than flannel felt like the right choice.

"I feel underdressed," she says.

"You're perfect."

Her skeptical smile draws me closer, but my phone starts buzzing in my pocket. I would ignore it, but Wren's phone apparently does the same thing. She looks at hers, too.

> Ada: Is anyone at the restaurant yet?

I type a quick message.

> Shepherd: Wren and I are here

> Ada: Oh, good. I'm having such a terrible case of allergies tonight

> Ada: I can't make it, I'm so sorry

"That doesn't explain the others—" I start to say, but more messages pop up.

> Isabel: I so wanted to have dinner with everyone tonight, but I have a headache

> Barb: I also have a headache

> Nora: I started making caramels and can't leave them or they'll burn

> Rosetta: I have an emergency meeting at the library

> Fran: I had pasta for lunch. I can't eat it again for dinner

> Isabel: You two enjoy your night!

> Isabel: Talk books! Have fun!

They lured us in with Italian food, and we stumbled straight into their trap.

"The caramel one is pretty serious," Wren says, trying not to laugh.

"They're as subtle as a sledgehammer."

She forces a frown. "Two headaches, though? Is this amateur hour?"

"They have no faith in me asking you out on my own."

"They're right to be worried. That 'you have plans' line was not your best work." Her mouth tips into my favorite smirk.

We're in a crowded vestibule or I would show her my best work. Since we have no privacy, I lean down to whisper in her ear, grazing my mouth over her soft skin, my hand on the small of her back, pulling her in. The warm scent of cinnamon envelops her. "Do you want to stay and have dinner with me?"

Her shiver elicits a low hum of satisfaction from my chest.

"Might as well," she says, eyes bright. "Otherwise, you got all dressed up for nothing."

I tell the hostess about our change in plans. Luckily, the long wait is only for larger parties, and she leads us through the busy restaurant to a two-top in the back. Wren and I sit down, the lively Italian music drowning out the conversations around us.

"I wish I could be as bold as they are," Wren says over her open menu.

"You think you're not bold?" She's the boldest, brightest woman I've ever known.

"Oh, I am. I just think I could be worse. Those ladies are really inspiring me to up my menace game."

"I won't stand a chance." I never did.

We place our orders, and the waitress walks away, leaving us to our relative privacy.

"How does August like his bell?" I ask.

Wren lights up as if he's at the table with us. "He loves it. Rings it whether anyone's around or not."

"Told you."

"But at least I don't have to worry about him running into people now." She lifts a shoulder. "Not as much, anyway."

"How is your apartment hunting?"

Her joy fades out. "I'm mostly avoiding it. I want a place of my own. I should have one by now, right? But I'm either finding sketchy places that will let me live there, or really nice places that don't want me."

"What are the grounds for that?" I have no basis for comparison since I've always lived somewhere on my family's property. But it doesn't seem right that a place would ban someone like Wren.

"I've been rejected by a few of the nicer apartment complexes because I don't have any rental history. Sort of the 'Entry level job, five years' experience required' dilemma. Without that, they want an extra fee which I'm too bitter to pay, and I can't bear to ask my mom to cosign on an apartment. I'm almost thirty, for goodness sake."

"And the sketchy places?"

"So gross. Smells, security issues, weird landlord vibes."

I refuse to let my imagination run free with that one. Definitely don't want her in a place that makes her uncomfortable.

"I wish I didn't tell Leo he could stay in my old cabin, or I'd let you live in it." I'm already considering kicking him out. He would find a place just fine.

"How do you have two houses? Seems like millionaire stuff."

"It's buying extensive property sixty years ago stuff. My grandparents built a house for themselves and two small cabins for employees when they ran the lodge. My parents took over the house and let Charlie and I live in the smaller ones when we were old enough. So that cabin's not legally mine, but if Leo weren't in it, it would be yours for the taking."

"You wouldn't mind me going through your old stuff?"

"No. I like the idea of you in my bedroom."

Her cheeks go pink, but she flashes me a haughty look. "A man with big dreams."

"No doubt."

She sips from her water glass, her eyes scanning the restaurant. When they land back on me, she pins me with a silent challenge. The slight eyebrow raise she gives me when we banter that says *I dare you.*

"How is your trails presentation going? Should I start looking for soft tomatoes?"

I chuckle softly. I guess my assumptions about what she was thinking got away with me there. "Not yet."

She waits, apparently leaving her taunting behind. She and Lila must be on the same page tonight. This wasn't my preferred topic of conversation.

"I'm getting close. I think. But it's hard to judge when my imposter syndrome makes me think every idea I have is going to get booed."

It's a mostly technical presentation filled with verifiable facts and figures, but I'm still dragging my feet over it as though it's my magnum opus. Mostly because every word is going to have to come out of my mouth. If someone else were giving it, I wouldn't think twice.

Her gaze softens. "I would never guess that about you. You're always so confident."

"I've perfected my act." Not something I would admit to anybody else.

She hitches a shoulder. "So have I."

I shift one hand to the center of the table, palm up. She eyes it, and I almost think she's going to resist. But she slides hers against mine, locking her fingers around me. Perfect.

"I'm sorry I keep joking about tomatoes," she says.

"Nobody's going to boo you. I'm sure your presentation will convince everybody at that town hall."

"You haven't heard it yet."

"No. But I know you care about biking and the trails. You can be really convincing about the things that spark your passion."

I bask in that praise, determined not to ruin it with the sexy retort I want to make. What else can I convince you of, kitten?

"Stop with the smirking." Her scolding doesn't have much weight when she's doing the same thing.

"I'm hearing that I've convinced you to let me rehab your bike." It's a weird thing to want, but it combines my two favorite things. Restoring an old bike for the woman I'm crazy about? Don't make me beg.

"Maybe. But only because August keeps asking me to ride with him."

"This is happening." Even more so for August than me.

Our meals arrive, cheesy pastas with a hearty loaf of bread to share. Wren slathers a piece with butter and takes a generous bite. Her nose scrunches as she chews.

"Not good?" I ask.

"Not as good as yours," she says after she swallows. "What's your secret?"

"I'll show you sometime." Despite the teasing from the book club ladies, I like the sound of spending an afternoon making bread together. There's a lot of downtime in the process. I'm sure we could find things to do.

We eat for a while in comfortable silence, punctuated by festive music and a dozen voices talking around us.

"So the wedding venue at the lodge was your idea, huh?" she says.

"No, Leo's just the king of exaggeration."

"I'm starting to see that. And you're fine with whatever's going on between him and Charlie?"

"I'm staying out of it." Hard to do when he's not shy about his interest in her. He regularly texts me, fishing for advice I don't give. "But I would be okay with it if she wanted to be with him. He's a good guy."

"Charlie doesn't seem like she's going to make it easy on him."

"I endorse this."

She stabs at a noodle on her plate. "I wish I could retire at thirty-two."

"I hear that." We can't all be NFL heroes. Then again, all the broken bones and surgeries that finally made him give up the sport weren't a breeze. "What would you do if you could?"

"Easy. I'd go to New Zealand."

"Really?" I don't know what I pictured her answer being, but I can see that for her.

"I've always wanted to go. They have so many gorgeous beaches, and they're all so different. One where the sand is littered with tiny little seashells you can dig your toes into. Another one that's all this thick, volcanic residue that's so soft and spongy, it's like you're on another planet. Classic beaches with palm trees and gentle surf. And there are a bunch that have natural hot springs so you can dig your own hot tub right on the beach."

Her eyes are bright, her voice a little higher than usual as she describes it. I love her enthusiasm. I want to wrap this moment up like a gift to open again and again.

"Sounds kind of outdoorsy," I point out.

"I maintain that sitting on a beach on a beautiful island country isn't the same thing as riding a bike a hundred miles over a mountain or sleeping in a tent with bears."

"If you say so. I've heard they have a few non-beachy things to do, too."

She makes a sour face at me. "I've made it clear how I feel about doing things."

I chuckle. "You're right. It was wrong of me to suggest. It sounds like you've thought about this a lot."

"It's at the top of my bucket list."

"Why haven't you taken a trip yet?" Not that it would be easy for everyone, but she's obviously eager to go.

Her excitement deflates like a sad party balloon. "I planned to. It just didn't work out."

I wait, unsure if she's going to tell me more. I want her to open up to me, but it's not the kind of thing I can get by pushing. She would push right back.

"Hope and I were going to go after college," she says. "We saved up, had ideas for where we would stay and everything. But then Tess got pregnant with August, and I couldn't justify a big vacation from the bakery when we were all adjusting to life with a newborn. I was going to go when he got a little older, but then the diabetes stuff happened, and it felt selfish to take that much time for myself."

I want to tell her it's not selfish to need time for herself, but for now, I listen.

She sighs, drawing invisible circles on the wooden tabletop. "Now everything's settled with August, and we finally have more help at the bakery. I could get the time off. But everybody's paired up. A girls' night is one thing, but a girls' vacation across the ocean? Not happening. I could go alone, but I'd rather be with a friend."

Offering to take her to New Zealand sits on the tip of my tongue. I wouldn't even care if the only thing I saw there was Wren in a swimsuit on endless beaches.

Actually, that's starting to sound like the ideal itinerary for any trip.

It's probably too soon to start planning international vacations together. Even if I'm ready to grab my passport and board a plane with her at my side. But I might have an acceptable compromise.

"Have you been to any of the hot springs around here?" I ask.

She wrinkles her nose again. "You mean the one at the commune farther up the canyon? Isn't that a nudist colony?"

"You can visit the hot spring at the commune without being a nudist."

"So you've been."

"Yes."

"Were you naked?"

"You're fixated on my naked body, Krause." Never change.

"I'm worried about everyone else's retinas getting seared away by the image." The way she's watching me, I don't think she's too concerned about her own eyesight.

"Forget the commune. I want to take you to one of the other hot springs a short drive away from here." I heave out a sigh. "But for the record, all of the hot springs are clothing-optional."

She shoots me a deeply unimpressed stare. "Trying to get me undressed on our first date is not a good look."

"*We* would wear swimsuits. Most people do." I don't want to drill down to percentages, but "most" seems pretty accurate from my visits.

"But some just let it all hang out?" She cringes, no doubt imagining the worst. "Are they our age? Older? Is it a deeply wrinkly time out there? Or are they muscular and overly tanned and really *proud* of everything?"

Honestly, I've seen some things. But a few awkward experiences aren't enough to make me give up on all the good ones.

"You're missing the point. The hot spring I want to take you to is a series of small rock pools in the middle of the forest. They range from hot tub temps down to bathwater. It's not the same as digging one on a beach, but it's a close second."

"People just put their naked butts on the rocks, though? Is that sanitary?"

"Wren." It's a warning as much as a plea. "I'm trying not to think about anybody's naked butts right now."

Her mouth tips up into a wicked smirk. "Not anybody's?"

This woman will be the death of me. At least I'll go out doing what I love.

"A team of volunteers cleans the hot springs regularly."

She cringes. "It's outside, though."

"Like most hot springs are."

"What are the beneficial properties of this hot spring?"

"What?"

"You know. Does it have special vitamins and minerals in it? Does it cure wounds and heal bug bites? Does it have any mystical legends surrounding it?"

"No. Well." I lean forward a touch. "There is one."

She mirrors me. "What is it?"

"There's a legend that says anybody who enters the hot spring with pure intentions will fall irrevocably in love with their companion."

She blows a raspberry. "Pass."

I lean back against the booth. "I tried."

She stares me down, her mouth twitching. I just wait. "Okay, fine. It sounds like fun."

Inside, I'm celebrating with bottle rockets and firecrackers. I try to keep it to a serene smile on the outside, but I'm well aware what a victory this is.

Even before factoring in Wren in a swimsuit.

She tilts her face closer, looking stern. "But if we get there and it's a bunch of naked old men, I'm out."

"Agreed."

TWENTY-FOUR

WREN

I REALLY SHOULD NOT HAVE ORDERED dessert. The pasta's going to do a number on my stomach as it is. But the zabaglione sounded so good, I couldn't resist. Plus, it's still early. And fine. If I'm being totally honest, I'm not ready for the night to end. Even if Shepherd is trying to widen my activities bubble to include outdoorsy things.

And possibly naked people.

But I'm enjoying myself. Despite this night happening entirely due to scheming ladies and subterfuge.

Okay. Maybe I'm enjoying making Shepherd squirm, too. I might have unnecessarily licked my spoon as I ate my creamy custard dotted with strawberries. The way his gaze is stuck on my mouth like nothing in the world could be more important than whatever my lips do next? Kind of intoxicating.

He clears his throat, his eyes tracking the movement as I lick a spot of custard from my lips. "What, uh...what kind of state is your bike in?"

He's so cute, searching for a solid distraction. I'll have mercy on him.

"The tires are flat and crunchy. I wouldn't trust the brakes.

The handle grips are brittle and falling apart. There's rusty bits everywhere. I don't know what else." I picture it, forgotten in a corner in the garage. "The license plate that says 'Girl Power' is in good shape."

That seems to focus his attention away from my mouth. "That's all doable. I can come pick it up sometime. I doubt you'll want to ride it before spring, but I can have it ready for you in a couple of weeks."

"How much will fixing all that stuff cost?" If it's going to come close to the price of a basic bike, I won't bother. I'm not even sure I want to ride in the first place. I sure don't want to spend a lot of money on the experience.

But oh, it would make August so happy if we could ride together when he visits.

Shepherd looks at me like I'm speaking Dutch. "There's no cost."

I see what he's doing, and I'm not sure how I feel about it. "There must be some cost. Replacing those parts isn't free. Your labor isn't free."

He just pins me with a dead-eye stare. "I'm not going to charge you, Wren."

Ugh, saying my name like that is so rude. Now I probably look as dazed as he did a minute ago with the spoon incident.

"Is there a friends and family discount at Get in Gear?"

"Something like that."

"Does that mean we're friends now?" No! I was supposed to ask all cynically with a tough edge to my voice. Not soft and uncertain, like something vital hangs on his answer.

He must hear it, too. The man smirks—my new most-slash-least favorite sight in the world. "Something like that."

My phone buzzes in my purse. Shepherd turns to where he left his on the booth beside him, and it's buzzing just as insistently. Our friends are back in the chat. I'm starting to regret finagling my way into that invitation to romance book club.

Well. Not really.

> Isabel: I hope Shepherd and Wren were able to salvage the evening
>
> Isabel: Did you have a nice night without us?
>
> Fran: And is another night without us on the horizon?
>
> Barb: They might not want to do a tell-all in the group chat
>
> Nora: But we all want to know
>
> Rosetta: This might not be the best approach

Shepherd scrubs a hand over his beard. "I didn't think ahead to this part."

I start typing. "We can be menaces, too."

> Wren: We decided to wait until everyone could join in the fun
>
> Wren: I had ramen at home
>
> Wren: Made good progress on our next book
>
> Wren: No idea what Callahan's doing

Shepherd grins over his phone. "You just broke six hearts."

"They deserve it. You can't pretend you're not meddling and then pry for details on the results."

Anyway, if they know their nefarious plans are working, they'll just get more daring. Really, it's not about us. It's for the good of all of Sunshine.

I tap on my phone. "Those ladies are lemon pies with ginger

cookie crusts. Sharp flavor with aftertastes that never let you forget it."

> Ada: You were supposed to stay and have dinner together
>
> Fran: It's such a romantic restaurant
>
> Nora: Poor Shepherd, all alone
>
> Isabel: He won't be alone for long, mark my words
>
> Fran: That tall drink of water will snag somebody, I have no doubt
>
> Shepherd: I'm still in the chat
>
> Fran: I know you are [winking face emoji]

"They're so confident in you." I ignore the weird jealousy creeping through me over the idea they might have some other woman on the back burner for him. Give me a minute here, people!

He laughs. "To an unsettling degree."

> Isabel: I can't believe after all that planning, they actually left without having dinner together!
>
> Isabel: Could we have made it any more obvious for them?
>
> Isabel: What are we going to do, girls?
>
> Rosetta: You're still posting in the main chat
>
> Isabel: ...
>
> Isabel: It's the allergy medication
>
> Isabel: It's making me type nonsense

Wren: You said you had a headache

Isabel: I do

Isabel: Caused by allergies

I snort. "They're not very good at butting into people's lives."

"Their plan was a success."

He's right. We had dinner together at a small table in low lighting and held hands through half of it. They would be screaming and jumping up and down if they knew.

"When are you going to let them know the truth?"

Why does his question feel like he's asking about more than just our scheming friends? And why do I not have an answer? I can't just blurt out what's going on in my private life to people. Mostly because I'm not entirely sure myself.

"I'm going to let them simmer for a while," I say.

A description that applies equally to me.

The check arrives, and Shepherd lays down his credit card.

I grab my wristlet wallet next to me. "We can split it."

"I've got it."

"But I still owe you for that drink." I think about the way he stepped in with the guy at the bar. All protective and territorial and handsome. I just blur out the rest of the evening when I reminisce.

His smirk makes my heart flutter. "You can still buy me a drink sometime, Wren."

Well. Okay, then.

When we get up to leave the table, our hands lock between us like this kind of PDA is something we do all the time. Natural. Not at all making a strange tingling sensation rush through my body like I just took a leap off a bridge with a bungee cord attached to my ankles.

Or so I'd imagine.

In the parking lot, I guide us to my car while we work out days for him to get my bike and for the hot springs excursion he's so excited about. That one's tougher, since we both need the day off, but we manage to find times that line up.

And it's not nearly enough. I'll see him in a few days at my house for the bike. A handful of days after that, we'll go to the hot springs. But all I can think about are the stretch of days in between.

I used to hate this man's face. Kind of. And now, the thought of not seeing it for more than a few hours makes me curiously sad.

We reach my car but don't let go of each other.

"Thanks for letting Isabel and the others coerce you into taking me to dinner." I gaze up at him, telegraphing my hope for a goodnight kiss loud and clear.

"No coercion necessary, Wren." He gazes back, no doubt calculating just how slowly he can make his move.

I hate waiting.

So why am I? I've let him take control before, but that doesn't mean he gets to keep it forever. It's my turn again.

I reach up to take his face in both my hands. Ugh, this man is the cutest. With his messy hair and dark, broody eyes. His beard I want to run my fingers over until he purrs like a cat. His mouth with the bottom lip a little fuller than the top. He is exceptionally kissable.

So I indulge.

I pull him down to meet me, our mouths pressing together as his hands find my waist. He lets me take charge, following along where I lead. Gentle kisses here. A little more passion there. I lick the edge of his lower lip, and he groans open for me.

I thought I wanted to move to the alley. Then, I wanted to live in the doorway of his cabin. Now, this parking lot is pretty excellent. I just want to be wherever Shepherd Callahan is kissing me.

This is right. This is good. We should kiss like this every night.

But probably not in front of a busy restaurant downtown. A car honks as it drives by, breaking the spell we were under. We pull apart just enough to see each other clearly.

"Goodnight, Wren."

His low voice is like a gentle wave, rocking my boat as I drift out to sea. I'm...maybe a little dazed from that kiss.

He smirks down at me, sparking my dignity back to life. I straighten but don't quite manage to leave his arms.

"Goodnight, Callahan. I come in late tomorrow. Don't park in my space."

The man just smirks harder. My pulse races to a frenetic beat.

"You hate it when I don't park in your space."

I really do.

TWENTY-FIVE

SHEPHERD

THIS IS WORSE than I expected. Neglect is one thing, but mistreatment is something else entirely.

Several cardboard boxes are stacked on Wren's bike. Not just tilting precariously between the handlebars and the wall, but resting on the seat, too. Her bicycle was hidden away among other forgotten items and became one with the garden variety garage junk.

Not to judge. The boxes could be filled with priceless artifacts. But the scrawl on the side of one that says *August's baby toys* makes me doubt it.

"I should have pulled it out of here before you showed up." Wren grabs the uppermost box off the stack to start a new pile next to the bike. The hem of her shirt lifts as she stretches, revealing a stripe of pale skin I want to explore. Her long-sleeve T-shirt today has a raccoon on it. This one says, *Raise hell and eat trash.*

I help her move the boxes out of the way. "This is a fascinating window into your world."

The garage at her house is filled with the usual: boxes, garden tools, bins of Christmas lights. Some of it's neat and tidy, but other sections are cluttered. Like the parts they use the most get their attention, and the rest fades into obscurity. Seems pretty normal.

"It's not my world." She leans over to tug the box on the handlebars out of position. "Tess is the sentimental one. This is all August's baby crap."

She's trying to pretend she doesn't care, but it's impossible for her to say the word "August" without revealing her heart. Her soft spot for him is wider than an ocean. It's endearing and simultaneously hits something unpleasant inside me that wants her to have a soft spot for me, too.

Because I'm apparently jealous of children now.

"You still have your old bike," I point out. Surely, some of the other boxes in here belong to her, but I'm not low enough to go on a hunt for them. Yet.

"That's because it's too crummy to donate." She steps back, hands on her hips, to stare at the fully revealed bicycle. "It's pretty bad, isn't it?"

"It's not the best."

It's a black Electra seven-speed. Grease and a few spots of rust mar the frame. The black fenders have been scraped up. The flat tires are brittle and the tubes inside are probably shot. The rubber handlebar grips are cracked and coming off, and the saddle is misshapen from being used as a storage shelf.

I can't wait to get started.

"If we should just chuck it in the garbage can, you can tell me that. It won't hurt my feelings. In fact, I might prefer it. Let's do that now." She grabs the seat as if she's going to roll it off the nearest cliff.

I put one hand over hers to stop her. "It's not garbage, Wren. I can do this."

More to the point, I want to. Not just because of my impulse to restore it, but because it's a small thing I can do for her. Her independence calls to me, but I want to take care of her, too.

She gazes up at me, dust motes dancing in the air between us. "It's going to be so much work."

"I like a challenge." More than she realizes.

"And it's all for free, apparently." Her tiny frown indicates how she feels about that.

"I'm a generous man." Currently trying not to think about all the things I'd like to give her.

She blows a loose strand of hair out of her face. "You're kind of insufferable sometimes."

"Same to you, kitten."

Her eyes spark. "I told you that's a terrible nickname."

"I know. But I'm saving 'goddess' for the right time."

"Oh my gosh." She turns away to free the bike's handlebars from the crowd of boxes around it, failing to hide her smile.

I help her get the bike out of the graveyard of long forgotten things and heft the middle of the frame onto my hip. Crossing the garage, I take it to where I backed my truck into the driveway and lay it in the cargo bed. When I turn, she's at my side, hands in her back jeans pockets.

She shivers, but I don't have the satisfaction of being the cause of it. The brisk fall air is already too much to be out in for long this evening.

"Do you want to come in for a minute?" she asks. "Mom and Daniel aren't here right now. Not that that's incentive or something. That would be so wildly inappropriate. 'Nobody's home, come over.' I'm just saying—you know what? Never mind."

"I'd love to come in." I wouldn't pass up an opportunity to see the home where she grew up even if her entire family was inside.

"Great." She spins, peeking at me over her shoulder as she crooks a finger. "Follow me."

Anywhere.

She leads me through a side door into the kitchen. It's been lightly remodeled, but the bones of the old Craftsman house are still intact, from the L-shaped galley kitchen to the curved archways that lead from room to room. The living room has two big sofas facing each other, framing the fireplace. Light floods in from the dual front windows. A collection of children's books sits next to the coffee table. It's comfortable, if surprisingly beige.

She tosses a hand toward the room. "Pretty basic, I guess. Do you want to see my room?"

She scrunches her nose as if she regrets the question. I sure don't.

"I can't wait to see the dartboard with my face on it."

"It's actually a punching bag with a flannel shirt over it."

She heads up the stairs, and I trail behind, struggling to keep my eyes anywhere but on the glorious view in front of me.

At the top of the landing, family photos and little kid art line the walls. She moves to a door at the far end before I can get a good look at any of the pictures. Walking in, she spreads her hands wide. "Ta da."

Now *this* is Wren's room. Bold fuchsia and yellow accent the quilt on the bed topped with half a dozen throw pillows. Frames in a variety of colors decorate one wall. A vision board hangs over the desk, crammed with photographs, fabric, and mementos. The desk itself is covered in strange yarn creations.

"Are these your weirdos?" I move closer to inspect the small stuffed animals. There's at least ten oddly shaped creatures here, each bearing an eclectic variety of appendages, eyes, and accessories.

She joins me in admiring the colorful assortment. "Those are my guys."

I pick one up. It's dark green, with spikes down its back like a dinosaur, but big webbed feet like a duck. The head has seven eyes that goggle up at me. It's also got a curving red topknot like a quail that bobbles when I move.

"You can see they're absolute nonsense." She flicks a finger over the topknot. "But that's the whole point. They're impossible to mess up."

"I don't know what it is, but it's cute."

"Then that one's yours." Her smile falls. "I mean, if you want it. Not that you would. It's a scientific abnormality with uneven stitches and—"

I hug it to my chest as she tries to grab it from me. "I want it."

She relaxes again, her mouth tipping back up. "Okay."

"So this is your refuge." I can't decide what I want to look at most. Her collage of photographs. The vision board. Her low bookshelf stuffed with paperbacks. The collection of enamel pins stuck in a long lanyard.

One says, *Ask me about my existential crisis.*

She sits down on the edge of the bed. "It's my woman cave." She scrunches her nose. "No. That's awful. It's my lair. That sounds way more mysterious and evil."

"It's a good lair. But I hate to think of you shrinking yourself down in here to make other people more comfortable."

She should shine as bright as she can. Let someone else cower if they can't handle it.

"It's not like that. Mom and Daniel aren't dimming my sparkle or anything. This is a self-imposed exile."

"I'm not understanding."

She flops onto her back. Her shirt rides up again, revealing her belly button. I want to trace a fingertip over that cute divot in the worst way.

"I've never had to watch my mom make out with someone

before." She stares at the pale blue ceiling like she's trying to block the scene from her mind.

"Aww, Krause. Are you telling me PDA makes you squeamish?"

"Hers does. She's basically been a nun for the last twenty years, and boy, is she making up for lost time. I can't walk into a room now without clearing my throat or banging around so they know I'm on my way. I have seen things, Shepherd. I'm traumatized."

Traumatized. Because her mom's been kissing her new boyfriend.

She huffs a breath, propping herself up on her elbows so she can glare at me properly. "Stop laughing."

"The way you talked, I thought they were icing you out or trying to get you to move away. Not just being affectionate in front of you."

"It's not just affection. There are *sounds* involved."

This doesn't stop my laughter.

"You'd be the same if it was your parents," she says.

"It is my parents. They still make out every time they get the smallest scrap of privacy. My mom can't resist smacking my dad's butt when he walks in front of her."

They try to tone it down in front of guests, but now and then, Charlie sends me a text letting me know they've been caught: PCRH. For *Parents Caught Red-Handed.*

Not my favorite texts.

Now Wren's the one laughing. "Butt-smacking, huh? Your dad must still have it."

"Let's not talk about my dad's butt right now. The point is, I hated their constant kissing and cuddling when I was younger. But as an adult, that's the only kind of relationship I want. A best friend I can't keep my hands off of."

Her eyes light like she's quickly coming around to the idea, too. It would be so easy to prowl my way over to her and pin her body down with mine. Show her just how difficult it is to keep my hands to myself when I'm with her. Her lips part as if she knows exactly what I'm thinking.

A door slams somewhere in the house, and we both startle.

"Holy Cheez-its." She launches off the bed and heads for the door.

"Wren?" her mom calls through the house. "What is Shepherd Callahan's truck doing in the driveway? You didn't steal it, did you?"

Wren freezes. "Why didn't I think of that? I could have been joyriding in your truck ages ago."

"'Holy Cheez-its?'" I repeat.

She darts a hand out to smack my chest but only manages a light caress with her knuckles. "Habit. I guess it's too late to shove you out my window and make you jump off the roof."

"Sounds like it."

She exhales a long-suffering sigh. "Fine."

I follow her back down the stairs. Maureen Krause and Sheriff Daniel O'Grady stand by the front door, tracking our progress like we're aliens beaming down to earth.

Maureen looks remarkably like Wren and Tess—long blond hair, blue eyes, similar heart-shaped face. She's bundled up in a warm sweater and scarf. Sheriff O'Grady is more imposing, with his gray hair cut into a severe buzz and the stern gaze of a man who's been in law enforcement all his life.

"What exactly—?" Maureen lifts a hand to point at us but drops it again.

Her reaction is understandable. She's only ever seen Wren and me bicker. Suddenly, we're caught leaving Wren's bedroom? I'd have questions, too.

"Callahan has trouble sleeping at night all alone in his cabin in the woods," Wren tells her. "I offered him one of my little stuffies to comfort him."

I lift the green mutant still clutched in my hand and shake it as evidence. Mostly to get Sheriff O'Grady's steely gaze off of me. It doesn't work.

Wren's sass seems to break her mother out of her confusion. "You'll have to forgive her, Shepherd. Snark is her love language."

"I'm used to it." I'm also used to the pert frown on her mouth. Probably disliking a very specific word in that sentence.

"Shepherd." The sheriff holds out his hand, and we shake. "Mo says that's Wren's old bike in the back of your truck."

I admire the way he's asking me a question without actually asking. Not that I'd want to endure much direct questioning from him about Wren.

She hasn't been straightforward with them, but I opt for honesty. About this much, anyway. "I'm going to fix it up for her so she can ride with August."

Maureen reacts as if I told her I rescue children from burning buildings in my spare time. "Oh, Shepherd, how sweet. August will love that."

"But don't say anything to him until I'm ready," Wren adds. "Just in case it turns out I can't actually ride anymore."

"You can always learn again," I tell her.

"Very close to doing things," she sing-songs.

Her ridiculousness brings out a rumble of laughter. "I forgot we would hate that."

"Are you staying for dinner?" the sheriff asks me. I can't quite bring myself to think of him as Daniel. Especially not when he's sizing me up like he's searching for evidence. "Mo and I are going to make butternut squash mac and cheese."

"He would, but Callahan is a busy man." Wren nudges my arm, apparently trying to herd me through the house.

"I promised my sister I'd go see her progress at the lodge," I tell him honestly. "If I don't follow through, there will be blowback."

"I'm looking forward to seeing the renovated barn at the gala," Maureen says. "It's going to be a special evening from all I hear."

"That's the rumor." Not that I know enough to confirm or deny. Acquaintances and even a few customers have asked me about it. I have to refer them to the lodge's website.

"We can take a rain check on dinner." The sheriff snakes an arm around Maureen's waist. "Another night, maybe with the whole family."

"I—"

Wren practically body slams me, one arm around my back, the other on my chest, urging me sideways. I appreciate the lack of personal space, but her desperation to get rid of me doesn't give me warm fuzzies.

"We don't want to make Callahan late for Charlie. She'll tear him a new one."

"Wren." Maureen looks ready to deliver a reprimand, but Wren's already pushing me through the living room toward the back door.

"It was good to see you." I lift a hand as Wren manhandles me outside. Once she gets the door slammed shut behind us and we're in the safety of the driveway, I look down at her. "That was subtle."

"It's kind of soon for family dinners, isn't it?"

Her reluctance makes sense. Squeezes something tender in my chest, but makes sense. This thing between us is new. I wouldn't want to be on display at a family dinner, either.

Except...with Wren, I wouldn't mind. But she's not there yet.

"I mean, yes, he's sometimes here when Tess and August

and Ian come over for dinner, but now he's issuing invitations for the whole family?" She wraps her arms around herself. "A little presumptuous if you ask me."

The tightness in my chest eases like somebody lifted a bowling ball off of it. Which is insensitive, since Wren is clearly uncomfortable about the changes with her mom's relationship. But for a minute there, I thought she was taking two major steps back in *ours*.

I can't make demands, but I want all the forward momentum.

She exhales a soft groan. "I just realized. He's going to have Thanksgiving dinner with us, isn't he?"

I tuck her hair behind her ear, trailing my fingers along the delicate skin there. "Why are you upset about the sheriff?"

She stares at my truck instead of me. "I know I sound like a thirteen-year-old girl who hates her new stepdad. I'm happy for Mom. I really am. I just don't know how we're supposed to navigate all this stuff."

"Which stuff?"

"I don't know. The 'this man is now part of our lives' stuff, I guess. It's been just the three of us forever, August notwithstanding."

"You don't have to do anything major. Just get to know him a little at a time."

"Is that smart, though? Do we really want to get attached to this guy?" She drops her voice but doesn't lose her bite. "He could change his mind. He could decide to leave tomorrow, and even if we asked him to stay—"

She snaps her mouth shut. Her shoulders slump, and she drags both hands down her face. Her eyes grow so sad, my arms ache to reach out and pull her to me. A ragged groan slips out of her, but she finally meets my gaze.

"I don't ask for things like this often, so please understand the gravity of what I'm about to request." She takes a deep breath. "But could you hug me, please?"

I step in and wrap her up in my arms, one hand cradling the back of her head, the other tight across her back even as I grip the stuffy she gave me. "Always, Wren."

We stay like that in the driveway for a long time, her arms tucked up between our chests. I hold her, blocking out the cold as we breathe through it. I don't know what she's processing, but it's significant that she's willing to process it with me.

After a while, she shifts, moving to embrace me in return. "I'm not the first person to suggest it, but I should probably go to therapy."

I squeeze her tighter, lightly caressing as though I can fuse her broken pieces back together, whatever they are. "I can refer you to the practice I go to if you need a suggestion."

"That would be good." She rests her forehead against my chest. "This is so bad. Mental breakdowns are not attractive."

I run my hands over her back. "You don't have anything to worry about, Wren. Would it comfort you to know just how attractive I find you?"

She laughs, but releases me, dragging her hands across my sides as she takes a step back. "I don't know if comfort is the right word."

I tilt my head down. "Do you want to talk about it?"

"I'm fine. That crisis was nothing."

She's aiming for her usual indifference but doesn't hit her mark.

"I'm here for you. Anything you need."

Her little smile works its way straight through my ribcage and into my heart. "You know that thing where you're upset about something but you're frustrated because obviously, it's not a big deal, that can't be what's making you upset? And then you realize what's actually making you upset and now you're even more frustrated with yourself because *that*? That is the cause of the trouble?" She throws her arms out wide. "That's pretty much me right now."

"Surprisingly relatable."

"Thank you for...you know."

She's painfully bad at the emotional side of things. That's okay. I'm not always the best, either. Maybe together, we can work it out. But for now, I can offer her a distraction.

"You mean the other night when I kissed you until you forgot your name?"

Her mouth drops open into an indignant O. "Sir. I kissed *you* that time."

I flash her my smuggest smirk. "You sure did, kitten."

"You'd better go meet up with your sister or *I'm* going to tear you a new one."

I take a couple of steps backward but hold up the stuffy. "Thank you for this guy. Does he have a name?"

"Cheeseball. Like his father before him."

"Aww. Touching." I round the back of the truck. "See you, Krause."

"Bye, Callahan."

In my rearview, I watch her wait in the driveway until I turn onto the street, my ribs aching like I left my heart back there with her.

TEXT THREAD

Wren: Out of curiosity, can you add handlebar streamers to my bike?

Wren: August admired some at the park today

Wren: I want to get a pair for his bike, too

Shepherd: I can set you up with a little razzle dazzle

Wren: I heard they make the bike go faster

Shepherd: Verified. They create a slipstream effect

Wren: Are you home?

Shepherd: It's almost ten at night

Shepherd: Yes, I'm home. Where are you?

Wren: Home

Wren: Just thinking about how quiet it must be out there

Wren: Like spooky quiet

Shepherd: I don't mind the quiet

Shepherd: But I like that you're thinking about me late at night

Wren: I'm thinking about your cabin

Wren: You aren't part of it

Shepherd: Whatever you need to tell yourself

Wren: Daniel's trying to arrange for Tess and me to meet his kids

Wren: Adult kids, to be clear. His son's older than Tess

Wren: Easton and Evie

Wren: Bit of a theme

Shepherd: Are you okay with that?

Wren: I guess. It seems like he's pretty serious about making a life with Mom

Shepherd: He wants to be part of your life, too

Shepherd: He was protective of you the other day at your house

Wren: He was not

Wren: All he did was ask you to dinner

Shepherd: Where he would have interrogated me about my intentions

Wren: What are your intentions?

Shepherd: Be specific. I have many

Wren: Do you ever play yacht rock on your guitar and stare broodily into the fire?

Shepherd: Come by some night and find out

Wren: Goodnight, Shepherd

Shepherd: Sweet dreams, Wren

TWENTY-SIX

WREN

"YOU DIDN'T MENTION the hike we'd have to take to get to the hot springs." Panting would be unladylike and an embarrassment, but I am breathing *hard*.

"I most certainly did."

Shepherd walks in front of me carrying our tote bags full of towels and snacks. The trail through the forest is practically overgrown with ferns and shrubs, and we have to stay single file. When the path isn't riddled with tree roots and rocks, it's muddy. My sneakers are already inches deep in it. The smell of pine trees and dirt overwhelms my senses.

It's also shockingly cold. There's no snow, thank goodness, but our breath fogs in front of us and I'm already debating the wisdom of stripping down to my swimsuit once we get to the hot spring. I'm about to break out in a full-body goosebump.

I grumble at myself for agreeing to do this in the first place.

Days off are meant for sleeping in until you start to feel gross and wearing pajamas all day long. Burrowing in and reading, only getting up for snacks and emergencies. They were never intended to be used for rolling out of bed at a decent hour and walking through the woods like a lumberjack in search of his next victim.

Shepherd, naturally, is dressed for the job. He's got a thick flannel jacket on over jeans and boots, his long hair and beard making him look like he yearns for a good clearcut. He's only missing the axe and ear-flap hat to complete the picture.

I'm dressed less iconically. I opted for baggy sweatpants, a gray sweatshirt with *Please go away* printed on it, and a messy bun that wobbles atop my head. No makeup because why bother when I'm going to steam it all off. If Shepherd wants an all-natural date, he gets an all-natural Wren to go with it.

An all-natural Wren who has zero trekking-in-the-woods skills.

"I think I'm experiencing some mild cardiac arrest." All this pounding blood can't be good for me.

"We can still see my truck from here."

I spin around. Shepherd's black truck is just visible through the mass of trees. A little sound of dismay croaks out of my mouth.

"We're not even going uphill," he says, amusement coloring his voice.

"So I'm not an outdoorsman."

His low chuckle drifts back to me. "Would you like me to carry you the rest of the way?"

I purse my lips as he easily maneuvers on the trail. Something comes over me, I can't explain what. I watch myself as if I've been hypnotized, skipping forward a few steps until I'm just behind him. And then, before I can stop it—I smack him on the butt.

He freezes. The utter silence in the woods alarms me as much as my behavior. He turns around in slow motion. I've always known giving in to the intrusive thoughts was a bad idea, but the absolute blaze in his eyes proves just how dangerous it can be.

"Oh," he says low. "Is that how it is?"

He moves a fraction of a step closer to me, and I lunge backward. "No. Butt-smacking is a one-way street."

"I don't think so." He takes another step forward.

He is *prowling*, and some hidden part of me is here for it. The rest of me really doesn't want to take that smack.

"Stop." It's almost a shriek. "You don't want me to run into the woods and break my ankle all because you needed to make things even, do you?"

"Then don't run."

But running's all I know how to do.

He moves closer, the heat in his gaze almost crackling between us. I don't take off tearing into the wilderness, but only because I don't know what threats lurk in the forest. At least with *this* dangerous creature, I have some idea of what he has in mind.

He leans in and presses a soft kiss to my mouth. Just before he pulls away, he says, "I'll let you anticipate it."

Then, he smirks and resumes his trek through the trees like an absolute beast. He knows I won't be able to think about anything but the oncoming butt-smack now.

Dread and hope have never coiled so tightly together.

Eventually, we reach a rustic wooden shelter. The sloped roof is overgrown with moss, and the picnic table beneath it is covered in graffiti and carvings. Shepherd moves past it to a railing overlooking something.

"I guess we're here." I can't see anything from where I'm standing, but there are other signs. I fan the air in front of my nose.

I've learned from my research on hot water beaches in New Zealand that the smell of sulfur is a given, but I've never experienced it before. The smell hangs in the air like a skunk just carelessly paraded through. It's not overpowering, but it's not one of the qualities I'm looking for in a pleasant afternoon, either.

"That's being outdoorsy for you," I say. "It stinks."

Shepherd laughs and gestures for me to join him. I pick my way closer and have to take in a big breath of sulfur when I get there.

We're at the top of a series of pools spread out in front of us like a giant step ladder. They're formed by boulders, with waterfalls tumbling from one pool down to the next. The first few are pretty big, funneling into smaller and smaller pools before it reverts into a natural stream at the very bottom.

The water is surprisingly blue. Surprisingly tempting, too, in spite of the smell and the cold.

"It's so pretty."

Shepherd grins at me. "Then you're still in?"

I can't believe it, but yes. "I'm still in."

We climb down wooden steps to a landing by the first pool. A trio of people float there, ignoring us as they talk together. I guess pretending nobody else exists comes in handy when naked people enter the mix. From here, the stone steps become less uniform as they carry from ledge to ledge. They're also wet from all the steam in the air, and there's no railing.

Shepherd takes my hand. "It can get slippery."

He leads us down to one of the smaller pools, passing a few more people as we go. So far, everybody's wearing swimsuits. Not that I'm trying to snoop on people's soaks, but it seems like the alternative would be pretty obvious.

"I'm starting to think you were joking about the nudity thing," I say.

"Count yourself lucky." He pauses to look at me over his shoulder, his dark eyes alight with a challenge. "Unless you were hoping to see something."

"You're in prime butt-smacking position, sir."

His smirk is the thing of legend. "Can't keep your hands off me."

Ugh. He's not wrong.

He finally stops and lays out a picnic blanket with a waterproof side before arranging our bags on top. Then he starts unbuttoning his shirt.

I swallow hard, tracking his progress. "We just go for it now?"

He told me there's no changing rooms out here, so I've got my swimsuit on underneath my sweats. Back in his truck, I brought a full set of clothes for when we get back to his cabin. But right now, that's not doing me any good.

Especially when he's peeling off his flannel jacket to reveal the gray T-shirt beneath that's got a death grip on his shoulders.

"Just go for it." He leans against a nearby rock so he can pull off his shoes and socks.

His bare feet touch the rough stones, and he hisses, flexing his toes. Not a ringing endorsement. But he pulls off his T-shirt and quickly sheds his jeans. He's wearing his blue swim trunks, FYI. The hot spring might be clothing optional for the general public, but this is a clothes-on kind of date.

He glances over at me. "Feeling shy?"

"No." The warm pool with the steam rising off of it looks inviting. But to get there, I have to expose most of my body to borderline frigid temperatures. It's not as bad as a polar plunge, but it's got to be somewhere close. "I'm trying to psych myself up."

"I'm committed now. I have to get in." He sits at the pool's edge and lowers himself into the steaming water. The groan he makes as he sinks deeper is obscene.

Tantalizing, but completely inappropriate.

He dips down until the water laps his chin, but he doesn't

dunk all the way under. Because, oh yeah, actual brain-eating amoebas might lurk in these waters.

I could be reading in bed right now.

He sits against the rock ledge and watches me from the pool, one eyebrow darting up in challenge. This infuriating man. He might as well cluck like a chicken. Can't he just let me sit on the sideline in peace? I was perfectly happy not *doing things* before he came along.

But...I can't let him win.

My groan has more bite to it than his did, but I pull my sweatshirt over my head, shuck my shoes and socks, and peel off my sweatpants. The cold makes any self-consciousness about what he thinks of my two-piece suit impossible. I'm not modeling, I'm narrowly avoiding frostbite. I creep over the frozen rocks and crouch so I can swing my legs into the pool.

The hot water caresses me, soothing my chilly toes. I sink lower until my butt hits rock, the toasty water warming me up. I might make the same satisfied sound Shepherd did.

"Not bad, right?" He's got his requisite smirk on.

"It's okay." I glance up toward the higher pools, but from this low angle, only the series of waterfalls are visible. "Not a lot of people here."

I like that he chose a small pool. The water's warm but not so hot my skin's turning bright red, and the size is just right for two. If I stretched out my arms, I wouldn't be able to touch him. In fact, this pool might be slightly too big. I scoot to the next rock over, narrowing the distance between us.

"It's early, and coming on a weekday helps. There are a few places like this in the area, so it spreads out the potential crowds. But more people will show up later in the day. You should see the crowds in the summer."

"I wonder if Lila knows about the hot springs. Maybe she's

got another festival in the works. She'll encourage people to visit them all and do a hot springs crawl."

"She might. She's awfully enthusiastic about her job." His frown says he's been on the receiving end of Lila's enthusiasm lately.

"Has she been calling you about the presentation?"

"She texts. A lot."

Hmm. I'm not sure how I feel about Lila texting my boyfriend more than I do. I need to step up my game.

Wait—boyfriend? No. We're just hanging out. Just two bros chilling in a hot spring. Two bros who kiss occasionally. We don't need to define what's going on between us.

Do I want to define it, though? I've never cared to before. But that's just it—I've never *cared*. And with Shepherd...I think I really do.

Stupid hot springs with their mystical properties, making me poke around in my emotions after a five-minute soak. A fiberglass hot tub full of chlorine would mind its own business. It wouldn't get my heart fluttering around in my chest, making me question exactly what I want.

I can't think about any of that while I'm staring at Shepherd's naked body. Not that I'm *staring*. And it's not his whole body that's naked. But the water only comes up to his armpits, exposing his shoulders and the tops of his tattoos. The little wren on his arm dances just below the surface.

That's not really helping things, either.

"Are you ready to practice with me?" I ask.

He swallows, his gaze dipping to the hollow of my throat. "What?"

"For your presentation."

Nobody look too closely, but I might be smirking, too. I guess I'm not the only one staring.

"Oh. I'm almost there."

He doesn't sound too sure, but this probably isn't the time to grill him.

"If cold plunges help with anxiety, do hot springs make it worse?"

His gaze locks on my mouth. "I might have an elevated heart rate right now."

"You cheeseball." I stretch out to poke his leg with my toe. "I might, too."

"Come here." He grabs my foot and pulls me closer, sliding me across the pool and into his lap. I wrap one arm around his shoulders, the other floating in the water in front of us.

"Careful," I say softly. "There's no PDA at the hot springs."

"That's not a rule." He glides one hand over my back, finding my free hand with the other. He runs his thumb over my knuckles, and I shiver. How can a person shiver in a hot spring? "What's your verdict?"

The crazy part of me thinks he's asking what I think about *him*. As if he read my mind and wants to know if I've sifted through my tangled feelings and come to a conclusion or not. If I'm ready to slap labels on both of us and dive into something more.

The logical part of me knows it was an innocent question about the hot spring. And is frankly alarmed at how loudly the crazy part of me wants to scream *yes*.

"I thought I would hate it, but I kind of don't. It's peaceful. Really beautiful." Our fingers intertwine in the water. "Smelly, but...I don't mind it here."

His hazy, soft smile makes the fluttering in my chest go wild. His dark brown eyes shimmer with light reflected off the pool as he gazes at me. One tiny push is all it would take to send me tumbling over the edge of a cliff into the unknown.

"I have some good ideas now and then."

I can't bring myself to ask about the rest of his good ideas. Even if I really want to know.

"Do you come here a lot?" He's such a nature nerd, he made it sound like he's a regular.

"A few times a year."

"I bet you bring all your dates here." Not sure why that came out of my mouth. I don't want to imagine him here with anybody else. Definitely not with Rose, cuddling up exactly like this. Soft, sweet, gentle Rose. A bit of a buzzkill, that Rose.

He kisses me, pulling me out of my thoughts.

"I only wanted to bring you here."

And there I go. Right over the edge.

TWENTY-SEVEN
SHEPHERD

I SHOULD HAVE KNOWN it would be a mistake to bring Wren to the hot springs. I sometimes come here to relax and clear my head. It's peaceful, if I time it right, and the waters soothe me. Now, the vision of her in this pool will be so ingrained in my memory, any visits without her will be a poor imitation.

And, honestly, not especially relaxing.

I run one hand along the smooth lines of her back as she sits on my thigh, my other hand holding hers beneath the surface. The sound of the water bubbling from one pool to the next muffles any conversations from above.

"So you usually just come here by yourself?" she asks.

One of her hands splays across the nape of my neck, caressing my hairline so lightly, it's driving me crazy. Her finger-nails scratch over my scalp as she massages, setting my nerve endings on fire.

Now that I'm in the middle of it, I'm realizing this entire scenario was probably a bad idea.

"I'm usually on my own. Charlie used to come out with me, but she's been bad at taking time off lately. Leo's joined me a couple of times. *That* one gets naked."

Wren giggles against me. The sensation is both a delight and a torture.

"Seriously? Wait, wait." She closes her eyes. "Let me picture it."

I pull her against me, dancing my fingers along her sides until her squeals pierce my ears. "Don't picture it."

She squirms in my arms, shifting so her back is to my front in an effort to avoid my tickles. "But he was in the running for Sexiest Man of the Year!"

"Sadly, he didn't get the votes." I won't tell her he was actually discouraged about that for months. But I guess when you're used to winning the popularity contests, it's hard to adjust when you lose.

She settles, relaxing against my chest. Leaning back, she rests her head on my shoulder, letting her legs float while I hold her to me across her upper arms. Her toenails are painted bright yellow, and her feet bob at the surface. She pulls them back under, no doubt protecting them from the breeze moving through the trees.

"I didn't vote for him, FYI."

"Who did you vote for?" Not that I actually want to know. The other contenders that year were three world-famous actors and a beloved pop star. All of them with clean-cut images, toothpaste commercial smiles, and throngs of adoring fans. Highly punchable types. I have no need to find out which is Wren's favorite among the bunch.

She shrugs, wrapping her hands around my forearms. "I forget. Some lumberjack-looking dude probably."

It's a good thing she can't see my smug face right now.

We relax for a while, listening to the waterfalls above us. She traces my tattoos, sliding her fingers along the trees, river, and mountains. Each touch is a gentle test of my control.

"Is this one for your grandpa?" she asks, running her fingertip over a mountain peak on my biceps.

"All the mountains are for him. He loved them. He would have disappeared into the mountains and built a cabin out there if it weren't for my grandma."

"Sounds familiar." The affection in her voice wraps around my ribcage, holding tight.

"He was better with people, though. He loved having guests in the lodge and showing them all his favorite places in the canyon. Nothing made him happier than meeting strangers and turning them into friends." He was the epitome of hospitality, something I could never achieve no matter how much I tried.

Most of the time, I don't try very hard.

She slips her hand around my forearm to grip it. "You're not bad with people. You're just selective. You're good with a few people at a time."

"Maybe at my best with only one."

She hums a happy little sound. "Wasn't it hard for you to leave the lodge, though? The family responsibility must have weighed pretty heavily."

"It did. Even after my parents encouraged it, I put it off. But Grandpa knew what I was feeling and convinced me to go my own way."

"Find what you love and pour your whole heart into it."

My only regret is that I didn't act fast enough for him to see my shop open. He passed away while I was in the planning stages, but he loved hearing what I had in mind.

"That's really special. Tess had to threaten to start her own business before Mom would let her even expand ours. I think Mom has a hard time seeing happiness for us outside of the family limits."

That's an interesting way of phrasing it. "Are you happy at the bakery?"

She stretches her legs, pushing closer against me. "I actually really love it. I like coming up with new recipes. Mom made that concession over the summer, too. So I get to experiment with flavors. And I like our customers. Some people are big fans of my work. I should tell you, I have a stalker. He comes in every week, desperate to see me and taste anything I've made."

"Sounds like a man obsessed. What would his pie flavor be? Mud?"

She hesitates a moment, dipping those yellow-painted toes in and out of the water. "I think...something rich like chocolate silk. But with an unexpected crust, like crushed pretzel. And a bourbon cream topping to give it some kick."

I've never been so flattered by a description of pie before.

"What's your pie flavor?"

"A grapefruit custard. Almost too bitter to eat."

I clutch her closer, instinct driving me to protect her from herself. "Is that really how you see yourself?"

"I don't know. Maybe a lemon curd with a blueberry meringue. Tart, but with a hint of bright freshness."

"I like the sound of that."

"I'm happy at the bakery," she says after a minute. "But I don't like feeling as if I don't have choices in my own life."

I wasn't all that good at my family's business, but I understand feeling like your choices have already been made for you. Where I lived, where I worked—they were foregone conclusions I had to break away from. We were in similar spots, once.

"You always have choices, Wren. When you figure out what you want, I have no doubt you will make it happen. Whether that's finding a different job or a different place to live. Even taking a long vacation you've been thinking about for years."

"Not everybody agrees."

"I know. I've been there, too. But you deserve every happiness you want."

Her soft smile makes my heart melt. "I do deserve happiness, don't I?"

"Absolutely, you do."

"What if my happiness involves a little smacky-smacky?" She raises one hand to tap an imaginary rump.

Laughter rumbles through me, along with a shot of adrenaline. "I never said you couldn't. I only said it goes both ways."

We sink lower in the water. It's so cold out, any wet skin exposed to air is immediately an iceberg. At this point, it's going to be impossible to get out again.

With Wren in my arms, I can't even care. I will live as a half-frozen prune if that's what it takes.

"What else do you want to do when you go to New Zealand?" I ask. "Other than lie on beach after beach."

A plan I wholeheartedly endorse.

"I had it all figured out. I'd stay in tiny houses close to the beaches and go into town for ice cream every day. There are these caves that they take you through in canoes and the ceilings are full of glowworms, so the caverns twinkle like stars. There's whale watching on the South Island, and it'd be cool to experience some Māori culture."

"A lot of those things sound suspiciously outdoorsy."

"It doesn't count as outdoorsy if it's in another country."

"Is that how it works?"

She slowly bicycles her legs in the water, and I memorize the sight. "It's not really that I hate all outdoorsy things. I just... never wanted to feel like I had to change myself to make a guy like me. I've done it in the past. It didn't work."

Protectiveness barrels to life in my chest. I want to hunt down whoever made her feel like she had to be anything other than exactly who she is. This goddess doesn't need to change herself for anyone.

"You're holding me kind of tight. Are you hulking out again?"

"Sorry." I relax my arms and press a kiss to her temple. "I don't want you to be different, Wren. If I ask you to do things with me, it's not because I want you to like exactly what I like. It's because I want to experience things with you. And if you don't want to do them, that's okay, too."

She nods, but I'm not sure she believes me.

"I think you're perfect just the way you are."

Her laughter rocks through my chest. "Perfect? You must have me confused with someone else. I'm snarky and rude, and I—"

A man and woman slowly descend the stairs next to our pool. At a guess, they're in the age range of the women in our book group, with graying hair and faces etched with lines. They wear sandals as they traverse the wet rocks, but they've got absolutely nothing else on.

Wren freezes, staring straight ahead. The couple continue on to a lower pool as if we aren't here. They gradually disappear from view, probably dipping into one of the coolest levels.

Wren dislodges herself from my arms, spinning stiffly to face me with wide eyes.

"Too much for you?" I ask.

"Maybe. Wow. They really just let it all..." She shimmies her hands in the air.

"Yup."

"And there was not a stitch of..."

"Nope."

"See, I thought I was bold, but...I'm not that bold."

"Something to work up to."

Her sassy smirk hits me square in the chest. "In your dreams, Callahan."

She very much is.

TWENTY-EIGHT
WREN

THERE'S something especially intimate about seeing Shepherd's bedroom. We've kissed a dozen times, but being in the room where he sleeps is like he's wrapped all his innermost secrets up with a bow and handed them over. When we got back from the hot springs, he let me shower and change in his room while he rinsed off using the cabin's outdoor shower. Because he's a self-sacrificing gentleman and all that.

I'm not much of a self-sacrificing lady. I resisted the urge to snoop through his cabinets, but I shamelessly used his body wash and shampoo in the shower. I smell like a bike-repairing lumberjack who lives in the forest, and I have no regrets.

I change into leggings and a long-sleeve shirt, putting my hair into two braids. The hot springs were more relaxing than I expected—minus the nudity—but it doesn't compare to being freshly washed in a temperature-controlled environment safe from brain-eating amoebas.

Creep that I am, I stand in Shepherd's bedroom for a minute and just look. I touch nothing, but I'm pawing through his stuff with my eyes. The walls are sloped like I thought, with a big window in the middle revealing an expanse of forest. His bed cover is a soft-looking gray that I have the worst urge to cozy up underneath. He has a couple of books on his nightstand, but I can't tell from here what they are. The green stuffy I made sits on one of his pillows, judging me for enjoying this moment so much.

I never perfected cartwheels when I was a kid, but my heart is sure doing them now. It's not that big of a deal. Just a stuffy on his bed. It doesn't mean anything. But I snap a picture of it and make it my phone's lock screen like a lunatic anyway.

Pretending to be a model of self-control, I grab my tote bag and leave Shepherd's room. Immediately, I almost run into him in the short hallway between the two bedrooms up here.

He's changed into a hunter green short-sleeve T-shirt and black sweatpants. Weirdly, the sweatpants aren't even what gets my heart rate kicking up. It's his socks. They're a marled gray and are somehow more private than seeing his bare feet.

All I can think about is him padding around the cabin in his cute little socks. Cozying up on the couch while his feet stay toasty. Cooking dinner in the kitchen in his sock feet. I want to witness every single scenario. On repeat.

Do I have a thing for feet? Or am I just really, really weird about Shepherd?

"Everything okay?" he asks.

Because, oh yes, I'm staring at his feet. I am normal some-times, I swear.

I snap my gaze up to his. "All good. Your shower's really nice."

The whole cabin is. Nothing fancy, the way Lila described the guest cabins at the lodge, but not so rustic I expected the water to come out brown. It's cozy and warm, and I think I'd like to stay forever.

I am a master of restraint and do not say that part out loud.

"Good." His mouth tips up, and my stomach tumbles right down the stairs. "Are you ready to learn how to make bread?"

I frown at him. "I know how to make bread, Callahan."

"Sorry, let me rephrase. Are you ready to learn how to make good bread?"

I gasp like a dowager in a historical romance. "Rude."

I slip past him and down the stairs, telling my heart to knock it off. It's not normal to get *excited* when someone's intentionally being a pain. And yet, here I am. Loving it.

I drop my tote bag by the front door and go to his kitchen, spreading my arms wide. "I'm here. Enlighten me."

He glances around. "Do you have something for taking down notes? You don't want to forget anything."

"Are you going to make this as difficult as possible?"

"Most likely." He moves closer until we're toe to toe. Maintaining eye contact, he slowly leans down and presses a quick kiss to my mouth. "But there will be perks."

I slip on a mask of indifference. "You mean the bread?"

"Oh, Krause. You're going to learn so much today."

I snort, but I really do want to know his secrets. Mostly, so I can exploit them for myself. And...okay, I'm looking forward to spending the day baking with him. I have issues, what can I say?

He gets out his mixer, and my veneer of indifference goes to crap. I never would have guessed that a man owning a KitchenAid appliance would get me hot, but apparently my issues run deeper than I thought.

"I'm going to need a minute before we start."

He plugs it in, glancing at me over his shoulder. "Okay there, Krause?"

"No. Why is everything I learn about you some kind of shock to my system?"

"How am I blowing your mind now?"

I frown at his phrasing. Also his smirk. "You must be more serious about baking than I thought."

"Is that a problem?" He's still teasing, but a hint of sincerity lurks beneath his question.

"No. I just never knew."

He pulls ingredients from his pantry and sets them on the counter. Bread basics I already know: flour, salt, yeast. This recipe isn't revolutionary.

But *Shepherd* is.

"I told you I worked at the lodge for years, but I struggled to find my place. Front desk was a misery, and anything dealing with special events was right out the window. Housekeeping was fine, and I helped with maintenance when I could." He pulls measuring cups and spoons from a drawer and lays them out next to the ingredients. "More often than not, I wound up in the kitchen with my grandma. Whatever she baked for our guests, I baked, too."

The more I learn, the more my tiny, ice-cold heart melts for this man. Maybe it's melted already. Nothing but a puddle of goo and admiration. Possibly even more contents I can't centrifuge out right now.

"I'm not skilled enough to come up with new recipes like some people." He takes one of my braids between his fingers and smooths over the twists, lightly tugging at the end. "But I learned enough from her to feed myself well."

"That's really sweet."

He runs his hand back up the braid. "Always so surprised."

Enamored is probably the better word. But actually saying that? Impossible.

"As a woman who's not sweet myself, maybe it's always a surprise to experience it in someone else."

His eyebrows tug together, his gaze intense. "You're sweet, Wren."

Of all the things he's said to me, this one feels like the biggest lie. At the hot spring when he told me I was perfect, the down-deep part of my soul wanted to believe it, but I'm not that delusional. I don't want him to tell me things just to make me feel better. And maybe that involves both of us accepting the truth.

"I'm really not, though. You know better than anyone. I was a jerk to you for actual years. As opposed to, say, your ex-girl-friend, who is the literal embodiment of sweetness to everyone."

Oh, wow. I'm just laying it all out there, huh? Blurting things out is way more fun when it's snarky commentary and not my deepest insecurities.

It's impossible to get that toothpaste back in the tube, so why not smear it around a little?

I slip away from him, moving down the counter toward the array of ingredients. "I'm not anything like Rose." A name I already wish I didn't actually say out loud. "And I'm not jealous."

A comment that doesn't help my case at all.

"But I'm not sweet and kind and good like her. I don't think I can be. Just so that's out in the open."

The pause that comes after that emotional vomit feels like the longest of my life. Seconds click audibly in my head like there's nothing in there but a giant grandfather clock. I stare at his bag of flour as if my life depends on whatever's written on it. Is this the part where Shepherd remembers he's dating a jaded, bitter woman and decides to cut his losses?

"Do you want to know why I ended things with Rose?" he asks.

Not really, no. But I basically asked for this by throwing his ex in his face. "If you were looking for someone with a sweeter disposition or softer-looking hair, I don't know what to tell you."

"I ended things with her for two reasons. First, no matter

what I asked her, she never had a preference for anything. 'Do you want pizza or pasta?' She'd say, 'You choose.' 'Do you want to watch a romcom or an action movie?' She'd say, 'Oh, I don't care.' 'Do you want to go on a bike ride with me?' She'd say, 'Anything you want.'"

I go on staring at the flour. I can imagine very limited scenarios where I would tell Shepherd, "Anything you want."

"I don't know if she was doing it because she thought I wanted her to or if she really didn't have opinions on anything. More than just being generally annoying, I knew I could never truly be with her long-term. She had no strong opinions, no deep interests, no preferences. No challenge."

He says the last word as if he's talking about a whole lot more than just choosing what to eat for dinner. I finally look up, and his gaze is locked on mine. Blazing hot. Demanding I hear him.

"There was no spark between us." He takes a slow step closer. "But you...you would never tell me you had no preference or opinion. You would never let me decide everything."

I can't help my eye roll because no, I would not. I would probably fight him even on things I wanted to do just for the principle of it.

A low rumble works through his chest as he reaches me. He lifts a hand to trace his fingertips along my jaw, making me shiver. He rests his thumb on my lower lip, and I might be internally combusting right now.

"I heard you, though." Apparently, I'm not done with the big, embarrassing revelations. "You were talking about me in the shop, and you said I'm loud and obnoxious. Too much."

I hate how repeating it even all this time later makes me want to run. Fight. Anything but face it.

He slides his thumb over my lip. "I don't remember saying that, but I'm sure I did. After Rose, who felt like she was intentionally trying to be too little, I *wanted* your 'too much.' I like that you take up space when you walk into a room. That you voice your opinions even when people disagree. That you're unapologetically yourself. I'm sorry you heard what I said and thought I was insulting you. It was never a slight, Wren. It was admiration."

My understanding of us tilts on its axis, sharpening this new perspective like I'm sitting in an optometrist's chair. *"Wren Krause is too much in every category that matters."* And he *likes* that?

His thumb keeps making its slow arc over my lower lip, making it difficult to fully process this confession.

"What—" I have to swallow because the words are stuck in my throat. "What's the other reason you ended things with her?"

He tilts his head closer to mine, and I lift my chin automatically. "The feelings I was having for the firecracker blonde who worked next door."

When his mouth meets mine, every touch is a soft reassurance. A silent promise backing up the words he spoke out loud. As unlikely as it sounds, Shepherd sees me, even at my worst, and still wants me. Still values me and likes me and cares for me. His tender kiss is a reminder that I don't have to be somebody else. I just have to be me.

In the most mortifying betrayal by my own body, a tear leaks out of one eye. Then the other. I hold him tighter, begging him not to notice my ridiculous tear duct malfunction. But my tears must reach his hand where he still holds my face because he pulls back.

He swipes his thumbs over my cheekbones.

"Wren." So soft, it's like a heartfelt vow.

Ugh. What a mess am I? I run my hands over his arms, searching the images tattooed there.

He must see right through me because he chuckles. "You won't find it."

"You don't know what I'm looking for."

"There's no rose there. Only Wren."

How did we get here? I used to think this man was my nemesis, whose only goal in life was to make me miserable. Now, I'm crying in his arms, and he's telling me I'm the only one for him. It should have been impossible.

I run my thumb over the cute, fat little bird on the inside of his arm. "Why did you get this? I wasn't very nice to you by then."

The idea of someone getting a tattoo in my honor is crazy enough when I'm at my best. But at my worst? I don't get it.

"You know why."

I shake my head. He can't make me say everything.

This man has the audacity to smile. "I got it because verbally sparring with you made me feel more alive than anything else ever has. Because the window you gave me into your heart was enough to make me crave more. Because every time you walked into my shop to argue, my soul said, 'That's her. She's ours.'"

I should tell him I feel the same. That even when I thought I hated him, I needed to see him. That the days he didn't come into the bakery left me hollow, like I'd missed out on something important. That I looked forward to our banter with an almost religious devotion.

I should tell him that these last several weeks have been the best of my life. I want to talk to him every day and see him every night. I want to share myself with him, even when it's terrifying to give someone that much of me. And I love how much he shares back as if he's not afraid of anything. I want to tell him there will never be enough Shepherd Callahan in my life.

Staring into his deep brown eyes I used to think I couldn't

stand the sight of, my heart swells up with love for this man. It presses on my ribcage and shifts my organs, demanding more space. It strains and grows until it should burst, but it just adapts and takes over. My heart is filled with Shepherd, and all I want is more.

But. It's terrifying enough to experience—I can't add saying the words out loud, too. Not yet. Instead, I fake a scowl, pretending my eyes aren't still streaming silent tears.

"Ugh. I'll never be able to go back to men who don't read romance novels."

He levels me a serious look that sends fireflies dancing around in my chest.

"No. You won't."

TWENTY-NINE
SHEPHERD

OF ALL THE ways Wren and I could spend the hours while our bread dough rises, she wants to hear my bike trails presentation. I might have chosen an activity with a lot less talking, but it's exactly like I said—she does her own thing unapologetically.

I get out my laptop so I can show her the slideshow Lila and I worked up while I talk. It's mostly pictures of the fire roads and graphs and stats about other similar projects, but it will give her an idea of the result I'm going for. Wren sits next to me at the dining table, her bright eyes betraying nothing of the big emotions she processed earlier.

I had no idea she'd given Rose a second thought, let alone that she'd felt inferior to her in some way. Rose and I were never serious—she asked me out one day at Perk Me Up, and in an effort at being open to trying something new, I'd agreed. We had just enough time together to discover we were incompatible before I realized my feisty new business neighbor had already worked her way deep beneath my skin.

I wish Rose nothing but the best, but I don't regret my decisions for a second.

Except maybe the one where I agreed to let Wren help me prepare for the town hall meeting.

Putting the final touches on the presentation hasn't eased my anxiety. If anything, it's cranked it up another notch. Having the speech ready just adds to the looming dread hanging over my mental calendar, like two storm clouds colliding to create a tornado. The date creeps closer, destruction imminent.

I've got my notes on a tablet I can refer to during the presentation, and I call those up. My fingers shake on the touch screen, my heart already beating against my ribs like it wants to escape. In a frustrating twist of fate, Wren is perfectly calm while I have a mild crisis right before her eyes.

If my palms are sweating from the prospect of giving this talk in front of her, how am I going to handle standing in front of a hundred people? Or more—Lila's drummed up enough interest in the meeting that there's talk of needing overflow space. I'd hoped scheduling it the same night as Moonlight Lodge's gala would cut down on the audience, but apparently the two interest groups don't overlap. I told her I don't want to hear any more details from her end. It's going to take all my imagination to pretend the people in the room with me are somewhere else. I don't need to know about anyone listening in from a second location.

Wren runs a hand over my knee, bringing my spiraling thoughts into focus. I exhale, debating chickening out, but her soothing method works. I launch into my speech, clicking through the slides where appropriate. I try to use the same voice of authority Lila coached me on for when I do this for real. I need to be convincing. Affable. Someone Sunshine can trust. Logically, I'm the best person to give the presentation.

But anxiety doesn't like to listen to logic. Anxiety tells me I'm going to say the wrong words. Lose my train of thought. Throw up. And that's before anxiety really gets cooking.

Twenty-five minutes about bike paths and community impact is a lot to put Wren through. But she listens attentively, examining each new picture that comes up as if the details matter to her. She keeps her hand on my knee, squeezing lightly when I *do* lose my place and fumble over words. Not a good sign when I can't get all the way through it in my own kitchen.

But she's comforting to have here with me, even if I wish I didn't need the extra help.

When I finish, she applauds. "That was great, Shepherd."

I try for a smile, but this trial run didn't reassure me.

"Expanding those trails could really make a difference for Sunshine, huh?" she asks.

"It's hard to quantify community quality of life indicators about something so specific, but tourism numbers in other areas are pretty straightforward. So yes, it should benefit Sunshine on several fronts." I sound like a short-circuiting robot. I don't want her to see how I'm flexing my hands beneath the table like one, too.

She catches it anyway. The softness in her eyes when she recognizes my discomfort is like a tiny little knife to my heart.

She takes my hand and stands. "Come here."

I seem to have no self-control when she touches me, and I follow her without a second thought. She leads me to the couch and indicates I should sit. When I do, she tucks up against my side, tugging my arm around her shoulder.

Thankfully, I can take it from here. I wrap both arms around her, holding her close. The tension coiling through me fades away on each slow breath. Snuggling Wren is a completely impractical method for dealing with my anxiety, but it's now my all-time favorite.

Somewhere by the door, her phone buzzes. She sighs against me, kicking both her feet over my legs.

Our book group friends haven't let up with their eager hints about Wren and me. They'll probably want to take full credit when they find out we're actually together.

"Did you finish the book?" she asks.

"Yes." Everybody dropped their walls and declared their love. It took almost four hundred pages, but they got there.

"I haven't yet. I've been too busy." She lightly presses her fingers against my chest.

"You don't regret a minute of it."

She just laughs. "I heard once that some people with anxiety like reading romances because you always know things are going to turn out okay in the end. Is that true for you?"

"I don't know. Some of those third act breakups can be pretty brutal."

"Is that a hint for the book?"

"No. It's a comment on love stories having heart-wrenching moments right before they end happily."

"A tale as old as time." She draws small circles over my chest. "Would your presentation be any easier for you if people you know are in the front row?"

I snake my arms tighter around her. "Probably depends on which people I know."

She releases a little growl of frustration. Ah, yes. One of my favorite sounds.

"I mean me, obviously. If I was there, would that help? Or just make you stress more?"

I love that she's trying to accommodate my anxiety even as she's looking for ways to soothe it.

"It would mean a lot to have you there." It won't magically cure my anxiety over being on stage, but having a comforting face to focus on could help.

"What if you had a big support group with you? Like Leo and Charlie and your parents?"

"That might help, but it doesn't matter. They're busy that night."

She tips her head back to look up at me. "What do you mean?"

"The town hall meeting is the same night as the gala at Moonlight Lodge."

She stares. "What?"

Then, she shifts so she's sitting up and straddles me, gazing hard into my eyes. "They scheduled their event for the same night as your big presentation?"

"To be fair, my presentation wasn't on the town hall calendar yet when they set up the gala."

"Can they reschedule?"

I smile over how hard she's trying to find a solution for me. "It's pretty late for that."

"Do they at least feel bad about missing out?" A little line forms between her eyebrows as if she needs to convince my family of their transgressions.

"I didn't tell them."

She takes me by the shoulders. "Why not?"

"What's the point? They can't reschedule, and neither can I. It's not their fault it sometimes feels like..."

I search for the right words but don't like any of the options.

"It sometimes feels like...?" she says.

"They encouraged me to venture out on my own, and I appreciate that. I know they're here for me if I need them. But sometimes it feels like I'm not what they want me to be."

My parents would never say that, of course. They love and support me to an absurd degree. That doesn't change the fact that I haven't lived up to their hopes for me. I left the family business behind and forged my own path. There's got to be some amount of disappointment tied up in that.

She runs her hands from my shoulders down to my elbows. "Because you don't work at the lodge anymore?"

"It was the same when I worked there. Maybe worse." I slide my hands over her hips and up to her waist. "It was like being the last piece of a puzzle, but I didn't fit where I was supposed to go. Leo meshes better with them than I do."

"That's not true."

She's so worked up in my defense, it's adorable. And somehow both soothes and presses on an old bruise. "Leo's been working at the lodge for a couple of months and has not only helped plan the biggest event they've ever seen out there, but he's going to emcee the whole thing. Stuff like that is second nature to him. I could never."

I'm envious of my famous friend—what a cliché. I don't want what he has or wish my life was different. But I'm well aware I was never much of a benefit to my family's business. He's become central without even trying.

"Who cares about Leo? Snore." She runs her hands up the sides of my neck to cup my jaw. "The guy who built his bike shop from the ground up? Who's going to give a big speech and sell this town on a cool new project even though it's *not* second nature to him? That's the good stuff."

She leans in close, running her fingers through my hair. "Plus, black sheep are kinda hot."

The warmth of her lips makes all thoughts of Leo and the lodge fade into the background. Her soft kiss grounds me in the here and now. The feel of her in my lap. Her nails on my scalp. Her mouth, nipping at mine.

After a minute, she pulls back, still petting and soothing me with her hands. "I know what it's like to feel like you can't be what your parents wanted."

I run my hands to the small of her back, pulling her closer. "Your mom?"

She shakes her head. "My dad. Things were bad before he left. They fought a lot. He threatened to leave a bunch of times before he finally did. As an adult, I can see that he was just testing whether Mom would beg him to stay. As a little girl..."

She smooths the front of my shirt, not meeting my gaze. "I thought I could get my daddy to stay. If I did the right things, if I was sweet and good and kind all the time. If I was the best girl, he wouldn't follow through on his threats. But he did, and...ugh, it's so stupid. It's been so long, but I think there's a part of me that feels it's safer to be the worst girl instead of trying to be the best girl and have people leave anyway."

"Wren." I pull her in close, locking her to me. My heart breaks, imagining her as a little girl thinking she could save her parents' marriage if she only stayed on her best behavior. And then despairing that it wasn't enough.

She pushes back, finally looking me in the eyes. "To be clear, I *am* the worst girl. This isn't an act or anything. I really am full of snark and rage and bitterness."

I glide my hands up her back. "I know. I like that about you."

She rolls her eyes, and her mouth takes on that skeptical slant I know so well.

I'm reminded of something Rosetta texted us weeks ago. That people read enemies to lovers because they like the idea of someone seeing us at our worst and loving us anyway. Just because Wren doesn't believe it doesn't mean she doesn't want it.

"You're also full of love and loyalty and a fierce protectiveness. I like all your parts, Wren. I like *you*."

I want to say so much more. I love you. I inked you on my skin so I'd always have a piece of you with me. There is nothing you could do that would make me give you up now.

But this day has already witnessed a host of emotional revelations. I don't need to add to the weight of that. So I do what I do best. I needle her. Just a little.

"For the record, I like you when you're bad."

She snorts, falling against me to nuzzle her nose along my neck. "You are such a cheeseball."

When it comes to her, I one hundred percent am.

Ada: As a reminder, book group is this weekend

Ada: Show up ready to eat lunch and talk romance!

Fran: Would be a whole lot better if we could see some romance, too

Fran: But alas

Fran: We are thwarted at every turn

Isabel: Perhaps we should come up with more activities for us in between meetings

Barb: If dinner at a nice restaurant didn't work, I don't know what will

Fran: Dancing could help

Nora: The couple in the book went two-stepping

Nora: It seemed pretty romantic when they did it

Nora: Does anyone know where we can go country dancing?

Barb: I will not be dancing

Ada: It's not a bad suggestion, though

Rosetta: I vote for a paint night

Isabel: That's not very romantic

Fran: Anything can be romantic if you're with the right person

Fran: [crying emoji]

Nora: I don't think that's what you meant

Rosetta: Does it have to be a romantic activity?

Nora: It does if we're trying to get you know who together

Ada: Ladies!

Ada: Let's focus on book group, please

Wren: Who are we trying to get together?

Ada: The couple in the book, of course

Shepherd: Are we taking credit for that?

Isabel: It's like we're part of the story, isn't it?

Barb: My knees are too stiff for dancing

THIRTY

WREN

NATURALLY, I'm the last to show up to book club. I've got two pies with me because I'm feeling generous today—a pear and a cranberry silk. And, truth be told, I'm feeling more than a little mushy. It's a weird sensation. I'm not used to all the softness. Possibly still fighting it. The problem with turning to mush is that it spreads. Everything brings a dopey smile to my face. When a yacht rock song comes on the easy-listening channel in the bakery. When someone rides past on a bicycle. When I see any kind of bird, no matter the context.

When I see my nemesis-turned-hot-springs-guide standing in Ada's kitchen, and I want to run over to him, jump into his arms, and smooch him so hard the ladies all faint.

Shepherd looks really, really good today. Not all that unusual, let's be real. I might have once been deluded about him being a jerk, but I was never confused about how attractive he is. His green flannel shirt is pre-rolled to the elbows, forearm tattoos on display. His hair is especially messy, and I'm here for it. But it's his eyes that make me need to double check that my feet are still on the floor.

He looks into my soul and just *knows* I'm thinking about whether he will catch me if I come running.

But absolutely every last woman is watching me like they expect some kind of over-the-top reaction. Swooning. Spite. They have a preference, but they'd probably accept either. The weight of their eyeballs on me presses me down, squashing my outward enthusiasm for Shepherd until it's a much more manageable size. Practically nonexistent. I rein in the giant smile that almost overtook me and tack on a smirk.

"I see we're all here already," I say.

"We're just about to eat. Come on in." Ada waves me inside, shutting the door before any more cold air can sweep inside. The ladies will surely have a lot to discuss over brunch with the possibility of snow this week.

I cross the room and set my pies on the table next to an assortment of food. I spot a golden-brown loaf of Shepherd's bread but don't pay attention to the rest of the dishes. I'm too busy staring at my man.

"Callahan."

I'm trying to keep things low-key, but the tiny quirk of his mouth throws a glitter bomb in my chest. Nothing but sparkly joy. We probably should have secretly met around the corner before book group to kiss for a while to take the edge off.

Why do I get all my good ideas when it's too late to do anything about them?

"Krause."

And now I'm imagining all the places we could meet up for clandestine kisses. It's a long list.

But, no. Everyone's still eyeing us. All except for Barb, who's opening the pie boxes to see what varieties I brought. Thank goodness someone has a little decorum. Kind of.

"It's so sweet of you to bring these, Wren." She examines both and promptly serves a thin slice of each onto her plate.

"I aim to please." I shoot Shepherd a look. "Sometimes."

"For what it's worth, I'm very pleased, Krause." His deep voice twists something in my belly. If we're trying to be chill about not hating each other anymore, I'm not going to make it very long when he talks to me like that.

Rosetta comes between us, empty plate in hand. "Thank goodness you're both here today. I need to know if modern dating is as bleak as this book made it out to be."

"No spoilers," Nora calls as she fills her plate behind us.

Rosetta shoots her a quelling look. "It's not a spoiler. It's a reference question."

"It is pretty grim out there." Luckily, I haven't had the same level of hilarious but horrible experiences the book's heroine did, but I've had some real loser dates. Thanks to the magical love-bestowing hot spring, I think I'm on the right track now.

Which, sadly, I can't say out loud. And probably wouldn't even if I could. My private win isn't for these ladies to pick apart and glory over.

"Finding only duds, Krause?" Shepherd doesn't try very hard to sell the image we're still at odds. His smirk is too close to a genuine smile. Like he's gloating that those other guys didn't work out.

I tip up my chin. "I've added to my Greek god requirements list since last book group. It's a lot for any mortal man to live up to."

"Any qualities you want to share?"

Um, no, actually. My list would be too specific for anyone to miss.

"I don't want to crush your dreams all at once," I tell him. "I'd rather do it slowly and really savor the experience."

His eyes light like he's imagining me *savoring* an entirely different experience. Oof. I can't say anything to this man without him reading nonexistent spicy undertones in it.

Practically nonexistent spicy undertones.

"My dreams are ready to be slowly destroyed by you anytime." His invitation drops between us like a gauntlet, the challenge in his eyes sparking the fuse that sets me on fire.

Look, I know there's something wrong with me. Everyone I love has told me dozens of times for a variety of reasons. But saucy play-fighting with Shepherd gives me that burst of adrenaline you get on a really good rollercoaster. Exhilaration with a twinge of fear from not knowing what's coming next, a potent combination that's instantly addictive. I need another ride.

Wait—no. I took it too far for book group.

Isabel slides over on our other side, boxing us in. "I agree with Rosetta. You two can tell us all about what it's like to be single and dating. Maybe share some personal experiences. Most of us haven't been in that scenario for fifty years."

"Speak for yourself," Fran says. "I am single from time to time."

"I'm not sure I'll have much to add." I really don't want to be in the hot seat while they grill me about dating apps and eligible men. I have very little experience with either. "I try to avoid that whole scene."

"Krause, at a loss for words?" Shepherd's teasing puts me right back at the top of the rollercoaster. "I'd love to see it."

"I'll just sit back and let you tell us about your impressive dating career. I've got thirty seconds to spare."

His smirk is a thing of beauty. "Is that what you want? For me to go into detail about my dating life?"

I might gulp. I don't want him to tell them about us. Talking about a guy I don't have feelings for is easy enough, but the idea of sharing about someone I do care about—more than any guy I've ever cared about—sends me reeling down that rollercoaster. Only this time, my safety strap is loose, and I'm holding onto the grab-bar with all my might so I don't go flying.

"Please, Callahan. Some of us are trying to eat."

Isabel keeps glancing at him and then me, mentally wringing her hands over us. Guilt twists through my stomach that I'm intentionally causing her worry, but I can't just blurt out the truth, even if Shepherd seems willing.

"What did you two think of that dancing idea?" Isabel's romantic schemes for us are sinking before her eyes, but she's bailing for all she's worth. "Maybe we could all try two-stepping someday."

"Not all of us." Barb points a fork her direction. "I will gladly sit that one out. Besides, we're only doing it to try to force those two—"

"We're agreed, then." Ada slips in front of Barb before she can finish outing the group's true intentions where we're concerned. None of it's subtle, but I'll play stupid for their sakes. "We'll go two-stepping in a week or two. In honor of the couple in our book, of course."

"Two-stepping isn't easy," Nora says. "Everything I've researched says it takes skill to master."

"I'm always up for showing off my skills. How about you, Krause?"

Shepherd sure is making it hard to be good. Or bad. Whichever version of myself has to snark and pretend I'm completely unaffected by him.

"I don't dance." I really don't. Coordination is not one of my gifts.

"I'll teach you everything I know."

My belly dips as I imagine it. This man is the worst menace of them all.

———

For the record, sitting next to Shepherd and discussing romance book themes while I'm tied up in knots over him was a bad idea on all counts. Naturally, the ladies tried to pair us up on a couch, but with limited seating inside, he refused to take one of the cozy chairs. We're on straight-back dining chairs while the older ladies enjoy the comfortable seats in the living room. My back aches, but my heart is swooning over how much of a gentleman he can be.

A broody, saucy, flirty gentleman.

"I thought the big grovel was so romantic." Rosetta gets a dreamy look on her face. "Standing up for her *and* learning how to sew to help her with her small business? That cowboy is an inspiration."

Barb sniffs. "I thought it was overdone. Sewing ruins the masculine image of his rodeo riding past."

I scoff. Traditional gender roles just don't want to die out. "If anything, sewing made him more attractive. He did something totally outside of his comfort zone to support her. She didn't ask him to, but he did it anyway because he needed to do it. For her. It's extremely thoughtful and romantic."

Nora coughs. "Do you happen to sew, Shepherd?"

"No, ma'am, but I've been thinking about learning how to crochet."

That earns a round of *oohs* and *aahs*. The man knows how to work a crowd. And, apparently, me.

Why am I sitting here picturing teaching Shepherd how to crochet? Side by side, our shoulders pressed together while I demonstrate stitches. Maybe at his cabin while the fire's going. It's not even a romantic activity. And yet, my mushy heart loves the idea.

"Last time, you said you agreed with the hero that love is a lie, Wren. Do you still think that way now?" Ada watches me as calmly as an entomologist sticking me into place with a pin. Or more accurately, a heartless kid who rips the wings off of flies.

Have I really changed my mind about something so huge after six short weeks? Maybe the bigger question: has Shepherd changed my mind? Do I really feel different down in my bones, or am I trying to be the sunshine girl who believes in love to get him to stay?

My heart races, my body going tingly as if I finally flew right out of the rollercoaster. Like those nightmares where I lose gravity and jump way up high into the sky, only to start plummeting back down again.

At least in my dreams, I wake up before I hit the ground.

"I think it's real." I tread carefully across conversational ground littered with traps and pitfalls. "But fake versions are so common, it's hard to tell the difference. And nobody wants to get stuck with a cheap imitation."

That lands about as well as a rude gesture in the middle of a church service. The ladies stare at me like I just offered to pop off my head. I don't look Shepherd's direction. I'm not sure I want to know what he's thinking.

"You must have related well to our heroine," Rosetta finally says. "After so many bad relationships, she didn't recognize the real thing when it came calling."

"I didn't like her." Barb picks at the last of the pie on her plate. "She was rude and indifferent to the hero for too long. He should have cut her loose when he had the chance."

Rosetta laughs. "Thankfully, that's not how it played out in the book."

"It's how it played out in my head. He found someone sweeter, who won't take his love for granted."

That tingly, flying-out-of-the-rollercoaster sensation coalesces deep in my stomach like the first indications I'm about to lose my lunch.

"Isn't it interesting how we'll accept any number of rude or indifferent behaviors from the male love interest, but when it's the woman, she has to be sweet and likable all the time?" Rosetta glances around at each of us, spearing us with one raised eyebrow. "I don't know about you all, but I am not as saccharine as we expect a romance book heroine to be."

The group erupts over this, half in agreement, half defending the concept of a "likable heroine." I barely listen. I stare at the book of national parks on Ada's coffee table, having a wee little crisis.

"*He found someone sweeter.*" Thank you for so succinctly describing my new nightmare, Barb.

Shepherd doesn't add to the noise. I side-eye him, but he's just staring back at me. Possibly contemplating how much he really wants an unlikable heroine of his own.

"Now, ladies." Ada raises her hands, bringing the commotion to a halt. "Maybe we should call it a day. I like my furniture, and I'm afraid some of you might start throwing things."

Embarrassed chuckles move around the room. Ada gives us our options for next month's book group: a romcom pitting coworkers against each other for the same promotion, and a contemporary romance set in a small town that's infused with a touch of magic. We settle on the magical romance and pick up our things to head out.

I help Ada divide and box up the leftovers. It's no accident she doles out the largest share to Shepherd. These ladies are determined to take care of him like one of their own. It's sweet.

Ugh. I can't escape the word.

Rosetta pulls Shepherd off to the side, talking quietly in the living room. I edge around the kitchen island, getting closer without being too conspicuous about it. Because yes, I am a terrible snoop. I want to hear more about how wonderful he is with the kids in the volunteer program. It sounds freaking adorable.

"Lucy's a gem," Rosetta's saying. "She's thoughtful and friendly, and just the sweetest thing. I think it'd be the right fit for what you're looking for."

My stomach revolts against everything I ate at brunch—is she trying to set Shepherd up with someone? Did she already give up on smashing us together through book group and found another woman for him? I might have played my indifference this morning too well.

"Thank you, Rosetta," Shepherd says. "That sounds perfect."

I might have played my indifference too well for longer than just today.

Perfect. He told me *I* was perfect. My mushy heart that's been steadily growing to fill my whole body deflates down to the sad, sorry cherry pit it was before. Nobody wants to find a pit in their *sweet* cherry pie.

When he said all those soft, romantic things to me the other day, I didn't say them back. I barely said anything at all. My throat closed up, and I couldn't scrape the words out. How long will he be content with sharing his heart if I don't share mine back?

Not very long, I guess.

"What kind of magic do you think this new book has in it?" Nora asks me. "I don't want to read anything with devils in it."

"It's got flowers all over the cover," I point out. "I doubt anything that cute and whimsical has dark magic in it."

"You can't judge a book by its cover," Barb says like she invented the adage.

Nope. Like if you were to look at me right now, you'd never know my insides are torn up like a hurricane ripped through my ribcage, smashing my teeny, tiny heart.

Shepherd moves forward to grab his stash of leftovers, his shoulder brushing along my back as he does. I suck in a breath as if the gentle touch seared my skin. He focuses on me, that stern little line dipping between his eyebrows.

"Okay there, Krause?"

I flash the biggest smile. "Yup!"

His eyebrows tug tighter together as he frowns at me. Okay, that might have been more enthusiasm than his question warranted. Also, there's probably no more obvious sign of distress from me than an actual smile. It's like a giant SOS.

I let it fall right off my face. "Just getting ready to go."

"I'll walk out with you."

A couple of the women *ooh*, but Rosetta shushes them. Right. Because we're done with that now. She's already got somebody lined up to replace me. I thought we were friends, Rosetta.

Out on Ada's front porch, I gulp in cold air, letting the shock pinch my lungs. Shepherd side-eyes me as we walk down the steps. His focused attention is worse than the room full of staring women. Probably because he's seen me at my weakest and most vulnerable and knows the signs.

Once we walk far enough away from Ada's house that nobody could see us if they were watching, he stops on the side-walk. "I need to talk to you."

My stomach sinks like the messy center of an under-baked cake. That's never good, is it?

He holds his brunch leftovers in one hand and rakes the other through his hair. "I did something you might not like. We never really talked about exactly where we stand, and I might have crossed a line—"

I do not want to have this conversation. I would rather watch Mom and Daniel make out for an hour than endure whatever Shepherd's about to tell me. About *Lucy*. Whoever she is, I hate her. I hope she gets rocks in her shoes, and her bra strap twists.

"Can we put a pin in that for another time?" I stare at a space just to the side of Shepherd's head. It's like eye contact but without the emotional wreckage. "I got a bad headache in there. I just want to go home and lie down."

Now I'm using the fake headache excuse. I'm as bad as our book group ladies.

He moves closer. "Do you want me to come over and help out? I could—"

"No!" I lurch backward. "No, you don't need to. I just want to sleep for a while."

Like maybe the rest of my life.

He stills, his gaze roving over me like he's searching for evidence of my symptoms. I look away just in case he finds some. Not of the headache, but of my crazy. Hoo boy, is there a lot of that in here.

"Okay. Text me if you need anything."

I hate how sad he sounds. But I hate the sadness raging through me more. Somehow, those meddling women at book group were both the rise and downfall of the best moments of my life.

"Will do." I get in my car, but he just stands there, waiting. Watching.

Maybe this is all for the best. I'm obviously not fit for human interaction. I am a grade F person. And isn't this what I deserve? I was such a jerk to him for so long, it's fitting that as soon as I realize just how wrong I was, he has the same revelation about me.

He waves as I pull away from the curb. I wave back, fake smile stuck in place. My little cherry pit heart writhes in my chest like its tethered to him, and any distance between us makes it cry out in agony.

That's another reason to hate *Jane Eyre*. The perfect imagery I can't get out of my head no matter how disgusted I am by the book's hero.

I drive through Sunshine, punching buttons on my car stereo, looking for a good angry song to sing along with. Of course, I get only ballads and peppy, hopeful music. *Everything's fine* music. *Lies* music. Switching it off again, I slump against the steering wheel as I come to a four-way stop.

I wanted to *care* for once, and this is what happens. But what am I supposed to do? Drive back to Ada's and beg Shepherd not to go out with Lucy? Confess all my messy feelings? Show him my soft and tender underbelly I keep protected like a wounded armadillo?

That's not me. I'm not the girl with the big, blubbery emotions.

Am I?

THIRTY-ONE

SHEPHERD

WREN'S A HORRIBLE LIAR. I knew something was up from the second she flashed me her big, fake smile at Ada's. It was like a teller in a bank trying to look like everything's fine while a robber has a gun pointed at her.

I can't figure out what got her so rattled. I've sifted through the conversations at book group and can't come up with what affected her so much. Her comment about cheap imitations of love sure got to me, though.

That's exactly how I feel, too. Anyone I was interested in before Wren was just a flimsy knock-off version of love. Those were pale, washed-out imitations, but what I feel for her is bright Technicolor. She and I are the real thing. But I haven't told her in as many words yet. And maybe it's time.

I drove by her house, but her car wasn't parked in the drive-way. Not knowing where else to go to find her, I head to my cabin. I'll text her once I get there, and hopefully we can talk soon so I can tell her how I feel and confess what I've done.

I overstepped, but just how far remains to be seen.

My truck bumps over a pothole when I turn onto my gravel drive. Normally, driving through these trees brings me back to center. My cabin is a refuge I can't wait to return to. But today, I only want her.

I'm in luck—her car's parked out front when I pull up. She was sitting in the Adirondack chair on the porch but pops up when I park. She strides across the porch and crosses back to the chair. Pacing.

That's not ominous or anything.

I get out of my truck and come around to the bottom of the stairs. "Okay there, Krause?"

It's obvious she's not. She flexes her hands more rapidly than I do when I'm trying to stave off a panic attack, and her eyes are wide like she's processing more than she can handle.

"Don't go out with Lucy." The words tumble out in a rush, forming one word. *Don'tgooutwithLucy.*

"Lucy?"

"I don't want to lose you to some sweet, kind, blah-blah-blah, perfect woman." She frowns, but when it disappears, she looks like somebody unraveled one of her precious crocheted weirdos. "I want to keep you for my own sad, shriveled heart."

I have to bite my cheek to keep from laughing. She's too upset for me to ruin this by interrupting. But hasn't she realized yet that the only thing I want is to be in her *glorious, overflowing* heart?

She takes a step closer but doesn't leave the safety of the porch. I'm six steps and five feet too far away from her. Any amount of distance is too much.

"I should have told you how I feel about you when we made bread and you said all those romantic things to me." She cringes, and her body language crumbles as if she's shrinking in on herself. But she rallies, standing straighter. "I was scared. And if I'm saying all of this too late, then I only have myself to blame."

She considers and juts out a hip. "Really, I also blame you because you can't take a girl to a magical hot spring where people fall in love and think she won't fall totally in love with you, too."

My heart goes supernova, wiping out everything in its vicinity with blinding exhilaration. "You love me?"

She nods. "Probably an unhealthy amount. Like, unhinged levels. So you can't go out with Lucy and fall for her instead."

I stalk up the stairs, my gaze locked on hers. "I don't know who Lucy is."

She has just enough time to look confused before I kiss her, lifting her up into my arms. She swings her legs around my waist, locking us together. I kiss her exactly like the obsessed man I am, striding forward until her back hits the front door. I use the leverage to keep her there, pressing my body against her, and I do not stop until she gasps for air.

She loves me.

I finally draw back enough to speak. "You absolutely beautiful madwoman. I am so in love with you."

Her face lights up, her wide blue saucer-eyes brimming with tears. I press soft kisses to each of her cheeks. "You are my first thought in the morning and my last thought at night." I kiss her temple, nuzzling into her hair, reveling in the warm scent of apples. "You are everything I crave in the exact right amounts." I kiss along the slope of her neck down to her collarbone. "Spark. Tenacity. Humor. Passion. Your gorgeous heart."

Wren gasps, holding me around the shoulders, kissing me back everywhere she can reach.

"Being with you, it's like...you take my breath away, but for the first time, I can breathe deeply, too." She cringes again, trying to burrow into my neck, but our positions don't allow it. "I'm a cheeseball sometimes, too, okay?"

Then, she looks up at me and bites her lower lip, sending a shot of lightning through my veins. "But only for you."

"Agreed."

I kiss her again, and I'm well aware we're making out against my door. It's cold out, and I should take her inside to warm up. But this moment means too much to break, and I refuse to stop for anything.

Except maybe one question.

I pull back and catch my breath. "Who is Lucy?"

She rolls her eyes, poking her fingers into my upper back. "You know. The woman Rosetta wants to set you up with."

The name clicks back into place. I was too excited by what Rosetta was saying to remember little details like the woman's name. A common factor of my social anxiety. Names are blips of sound that don't register, even when I'm trying to hold onto them.

"You heard that?"

She hitches a shoulder, glancing away. "I was right there. I didn't know she would try to set you up in front of me."

"Lucy's what I wanted to talk to you about earlier."

She takes in a big breath. "I know."

She so obviously doesn't.

"Lucy's not for me. She's for you."

"That's flattering, but I'm not interested in dating Lucy."

I drop a kiss onto her mouth. "Cheeky. I told Rosetta about your apartment hunt this week at the library. I didn't explicitly tell her about us, but she's a smart woman. She didn't need it spelled out. But she asked around, and she found someone who has a place that could be good for you. Lucy."

"Really?"

"Lucy has a small house with an apartment over the detached garage. She's got a roommate in the house, but the woman who was living over the garage moved out. It doesn't sound like she has any unusual rental history stipulations or sketchy vibes. But I got her number so you can call her and find out for yourself."

Wren's soft expression hits a tender spot in my chest. "You're helping me find an apartment?"

"I'd do anything for you."

Her mouth twists as she battles a smile.

I tilt my face closer to hers. "But you have got to stop eavesdropping on partial conversations and drawing conclusions."

She blows out a breath. "I know. I'm sorry. I'm not good at confronting people."

I lift an eyebrow. This woman is *excellent* at confronting people.

"Okay, I am," she concedes. "But not when I'm feeling small."

I hold her tighter. I don't ever want her to feel too small to let her usual confidence shine through. "Promise you'll talk to me when you're worried about things."

"I will. I promise." She squirms against me so I have to adjust my hold on her. "Will you take me inside now?"

A chuckle rumbles out of me. "Yes. It's pretty cold out here."

"I don't feel cold." Something sparks in her eyes as she gazes at me, and her grip tightens on my shoulders. "Will you take me all the way inside? Upstairs?"

I press closer, running my nose against hers. "If I take you upstairs, I'm never letting you go again."

Her grin is all smug triumph. "I'm good with that."

"As you wish, goddess."

THIRTY-TWO

WREN

"THIS PLACE IS SO STINKING CUTE!" I've walked through the one-bedroom apartment over Lucy's garage three times already, and I can't stop staring at everything. The huge front windows that overlook the tree-lined neighborhood. The shiny checkerboard tile in the kitchen. The sloped ceilings just like in Shepherd's bedroom.

Oof. I'd better not think about that last one too much right now if I want to behave like a somewhat normal person.

But the addition is comfortable and snug. It's probably ten minutes from the bakery and fifteen from Mom's house. Even longer to Shepherd's, but there was never much hope of cutting down that commute. Best of all, it's one block from a park with a big play structure perfect for Wren Wednesdays with August.

"The house and everything is really my aunt's, but she passed it over to me while she goes out living that RV life. She's in Arizona right now. I think." Lucy, for the record is also super cute. She's roughly my age, petite and curvy, with golden-brown hair and dimples in her cheeks when she smiles. Which she does a lot.

Daniel has mentioned RVing to Mom a few times. I'm not

even going to think about what it would be like if those two ran off to travel Route 66 one day. Hmm...but then, I would be in charge of the pie side of the bakery. Might not be so bad, after all. Retire, you lovesick fools.

"What are utilities usually like?" I had to pull up a website with questions to ask potential landlords. I've already asked her about trash, parking, and pets, and I'm running out of ideas.

She gives me a few numbers, and I nod along like it's neck day at the gym and I have to get in every rep. The rent is super reasonable for such a nice place. Not as cheap as Tess's family discount on her duplex, but nowhere close to what it could go for. I keep wandering through the rooms, trying to find a catch, but I haven't spotted a flaw yet.

Shepherd stands off to the side, watching me flit from room to room, a happy smirk in place on his mouth.

It's probably stuck there permanently after last night. Mine probably is, too.

"Olive and I have barbecues out back in the summer," Lucy says. "Sometimes we do s'mores around the fire pit in the winter, but not as much. Olive's my roommate, I probably should have said that. You don't have to join in, but it's nice to feel like we can be friends. No pressure."

She looks hopeful, though, like maybe she needs this as much as I do. I wasn't looking for a new place to live to expand my social circle, but...I like the sound of that. Lucy seems like she'd be fun to know. And I could use more friends in my life.

Am I...growing? How disgusting.

"I'd like that," I say anyway.

She grins, making her dimples pop. Attempts at socializing would be a bad sign from any other landlord, but it's different when it's a woman my age with just one apartment to rent. I assume. If it turns out it's just a way for her to sell me essential oils, I'll bail.

"You should know my brothers come around a lot, but they're completely harmless. And of course, they won't bother you up here. I'll warn Nathan that you have a boyfriend, and all will be well." She shoots Shepherd a reassuring look that has the opposite effect.

"Do I need to be worried about Nathan?" He seems to be regretting helping me find this apartment in the first place. And also might hunt the guy down to have a little conversation of his own.

A jealous Shepherd is a hot Shepherd. Really, all versions of him are.

"Flirting is his default communication style, but I'll tell him to knock it off." Lucy gives me a stout nod. "She'll be fine."

"I prefer broody guys anyway, so it would never work out." He seems pacified by my addition. Lucy just giggles.

"What else would be helpful to know?" she asks. "One of our neighbors runs a plow service so the streets always get cleared even though we're not covered by the town. We have a pretty competitive holiday lights competition every winter. Last year the Cohens won with their spectacular Hanukkah display. They had a giant inflatable dreidel and everything. So, if you have ideas for what we can do to try to top that this year, I'll be open to them."

"It sounds like a great neighborhood." Which is a comfort, since I'm weirdly missing my old one and I haven't even left yet.

"Everybody's really nice. What else? I teach high school English. I keep pretty normal hours during the school year, but in summer, anything goes. If you text me and I don't answer, I'm probably at a good spot in my romance book and can't be distracted from my writing."

"You write romances?"

Lucy pales, her eyes widening comically. "I meant to say

reading. Obviously, I don't write them. That would be so weird, right?"

"I think it'd be super cool. I love romances."

She relaxes, and her smile reappears. "Then we'll have plenty to talk about. If you decide to move in, I mean. Obviously, it's all up to you. I'll give you guys some time to talk about it, and you can come knock on the back door at the main house when you're ready."

"Thank you." I watch her slowly disappear down the open stairwell on one side of the living room until I hear the door to the rental open and close.

"Is it strange that the stairs are inside the apartment?" I ask Shepherd. It's the only oddity I've found.

"It's probably so they can't ice up in the winter."

"Oh. That's smart." I make my way over to him, peeking around the room again as if I'll spot a family of mice I missed earlier, having a tea party on the vinyl wood-look floor. "Do you see any red flags?"

"Just Nathan."

Aww. My man's gone so surly.

My mouth twists as I fight my smile. I sneak closer and run my hands up his chest, delighting in the soft flannel fabric over his perfectly touchable pecs. "Are you jealous now?"

He loops his arms around me, reeling me in. "I've always been jealous over you."

"That is disturbingly adorable."

"Can you see yourself living here?"

I turn to glance around at the living space and kitchen, leading to the bathroom and bedroom in the back. It's only about six hundred square feet, but it would all be mine. I could watch whatever movies I wanted to. Go to bed when I choose without being asked why I was up so late the next morning. Decorate, cook, and live however I want.

Beautiful, chaotic anarchy. I want it.

"I can see it. The only trouble is telling my mom."

She hasn't forbidden me from getting my own place, but from all her dire warnings when Tess moved out over the summer, her disappointment was obvious. She liked us all together, as close as possible for as long as possible. I don't want to hurt her feelings, but I can't go on living in my childhood home forever.

"Do you want me to be with you when you tell her?"

"That's sweet." Of course he would offer. He might be the most supportive person I know. "I can do it. But thank you."

I snuggle in closer, not quite kissing, but making my intentions extremely obvious. "I might ask for some help when I move, though. I'll need to find a man with a big truck and rippling muscles."

I tilt my chin up until our mouths are a breath apart. "Do you know anyone?"

He hugs me closer, one hand drifting into my hair to hold me in place. "Don't tease." He kisses me once, softly. "I'm here for you, whatever you need."

"Are you sure? That's a lot of stairs to climb."

His eyes darken as he gazes down at me. "I can always be persuaded."

I melt against him. "I've got that covered. You see, that's a magical stairwell. There's a legend that says anybody who carries boxes upstairs with pure intentions will fall in love—"

He dances his fingers along my ribs before I can finish, nuzzling against me as I laugh.

I'll consider him successfully persuaded.

HOLIDAYS AT BLACKBIRD'S are always criminally busy, but Thanksgiving is the worst offender. Someone's in the back making pies during all business hours so we can keep up with the demand. Our normally moderate crowds turn into an unending flow of customers, most of them frazzled and making last-minute purchases for their special dinners. My pores ooze pumpkin.

But the income boost helps tide us over during slower seasons, so I can't complain.

Ha. Not true. I go into great detail in my complaints.

The day is winding to a close and Jamie and I are cleaning out front. Tess is in the back finishing up with prep work for tomorrow, and Mom is probably somewhere at home making out with Daniel.

It's fine.

My favorite customer walks through Blackbird's door, decked out in multiple forms of flannel and worn gray jeans. The smile that pops onto my face when I see Shepherd is automatic. Like a reflex or buying up every sarcastic shirt I see.

He approaches the counter, gaze stuck on me. We haven't

been able to see each other nearly enough since the other night. Our *big* night. Where we showed how we feel about each other with mouths, hands, and a whole lot of skin. I went to his house the next night, but it was a pie-baking day, and I fell asleep while we cuddled on his couch. I drooled on him, which was mortifying enough, but he somehow saw it as endearing.

The bar seems low for his affection if drooling on the man makes the cut. Probably a good thing for me.

"What can I get you, Shepherd?" Jamie is an eager beaver.

I wave him off. "I've got him, thank you."

I consider trying to temper my grin, but it's too late in the day to put on an act. I let my smile hang out like that couple at the hot spring. *All* the way out.

"What's your favorite pie in the case today?" How can a perfectly simple question get this weird bubbling sensation going in my stomach? Am I *giddy*? Over Shepherd?

Gross.

I hope it never stops.

I squint at the pie case as if I don't know. "We've got a new flavor this week." My hands go stupidly sweaty. "It's a chocolate silk pie with a pretzel crust, topped with bourbon cream."

Realization tips his mouth up ever so slowly. "That sounds amazing, Wren."

He could tone down how flattered he looks. It's not like I got a tattoo for him.

"It's our most popular pie today." I lift a shoulder. "After pumpkin, but that doesn't count this close to Thanksgiving."

The number of pumpkins that have given their lives to the cause this week is appalling.

"I don't mind being second. I'll take a whole pie, please."

"We don't have any whole pies left in the case." I hate how his little smile drops. He thinks I didn't plan ahead for this? "But I might have saved you one in the back."

I slip through the swinging door, passing Tess wrapping a cake to decorate tomorrow. I open one of the industrial refrigerators and grab the pie I set aside from my first batch this afternoon. I'd thought about bringing him the tester pie I made earlier in the week to try it with him but couldn't do it. If it'd turned out awful, we'd be eating bites of crappy pie together. Nobody wants that.

"We reserve pies back here all the time, you know." Tess watches me pull several cautionary sticky notes off the pie box. "You didn't have to word those threats in such detail."

"It got my point across."

She shakes her head at me, but goes back to finishing up at her workstation. Good. I don't want her snooping around in my private life the way I do in hers.

Out front, Jamie's helping a customer who walked in just before we close for the night. I round the counter and hand the boxed pie to Shepherd. "On the house."

The pie-lust in his eyes fades into something stern, but I hold up a hand before he can argue. He can fix up my whole bike, but I can't give him a pie? No way. "We'll figure something out. But you get that one for being the inspiration behind it."

Oh, no. Is my smile *shy*? Why am I like this? Just because I'm bursting with hope he likes the pie flavor pairings I came up with while thinking about him? Silly goose.

But his return smile is wildly reassuring.

"Also, it's kind of an apology. I don't think I'll have the energy to come over until after Thanksgiving. I'm so exhausted in the evenings, and tomorrow I'm on August duty." I don't want to admit it might be even longer—with all those pies Charlie ordered for Moonlight Lodge's gala, we'll be swamped more than usual next week, too.

I'd try harder to carve out an hour or two for him, but he really didn't like me driving home in the dark when I was so tired the other night. Ramping up his anxiety like that isn't worth it.

My house isn't really an option, for obvious reasons.

His mouth quirks. "What about Thanksgiving? My family eats dinner at mid-day."

"I like the way you think." And am way too excited to have that on my calendar to look forward to.

He watches me for another minute, silently challenging. I can guess what he wants me to do. I just don't have it in me. I've always hated losing to him in our face-offs, but I can't kiss Shepherd Callahan in my bakery.

"See you tomorrow, Wren," he finally says.

I nod, wishing I had the courage to just lay one on him. Just smooch the heck out of him and not worry about the consequences.

Except, why don't I? Jamie's the only one out here to bear witness, and who cares what strangers on Maple Street think? I've never let their opinions bother me before.

I jog through the store to catch up with him just outside on the sidewalk. It's dark already, but he's fully illuminated by the glow of the bakery. "Shepherd."

He turns, and I grab the lapels of his flannel shirt, tugging him down to meet me. He's more than willing, wrapping his free hand around my waist as his mouth meets mine. We're like those old-timey couples kissing one last time before one of them ships off to war. Only, in this case, the war is the lunacy of the Thanksgiving holiday.

When I finally pull back, he's smirking up a storm. "Can that come extra with all my pies?"

"Cheeky." I press another quick kiss to his mouth. "But good idea."

We part, and he backs toward his shop. "Goodnight, goddess."

Unfair of him to use that nickname when I'm trying to be a force of self-control and restraint.

"Goodnight, cheeseball."

Jamie's customer leaves the bakery, and I hold the door open for him before walking back through. I'm contemplating the wisdom of going over to Shepherd's tonight even though I have to wake up at five in the morning, but I stop short in the middle of the store. Hope is leaning against the pass-through wall between our shops, a giant grin eating up her face.

I try to erase mine, but my post-Shepherd glow probably gives away even more than the floaty expression.

"Things have progressed, I see." She might as well be twisting her handlebar mustache like a cartoon villain.

I smooth out my apron and tip my chin up. "You didn't see anything."

"No, we saw it." Jamie's not exactly gunning for employee of the month.

I roll my eyes at him, but head over to Hope, who's grinning her pretty little head off. "Please tone it down. Your gloating is interfering with people's WiFi connections."

"I would just like to say, 'I told you so.'"

I can't even hold onto my mad face. That's how mushy I am over Shepherd. "Congratulations. You're smarter than I am, blah, blah, blah. You win."

"Are you happy?"

My heart flutters its answer, which luckily, she can't hear. "Why do you have to go and ask a question like that? That's ridiculous."

"I'm going to take that outburst as a 'yes.' I'm happy for you, too."

"Stop it. Gross. We're not doing this." I've never been on the receiving end of Hope's romantic enthusiasm. It's pretty soon to judge, but I'd call it a love-hate thing. Like a grandma hug that's comforting at first but goes on way too long.

"Will Shepherd join us for our next night out?"

"I don't know. I haven't asked him." I smooth out my apron, running my fingers over the pocket. "But probably, yes."

Hopefully, our next night out isn't for a while. I need time to get past my urge to poke people in the eye just for seeing us together.

Hope squeals silently, shimmying her shoulders. Best friends who love you too much are the worst.

"Do your mom and Tess know?"

I glance at the door that leads into the back. It's lucky for me Tess is too obsessed with her cakes to hang out in the front lately. She might even have a wedding cake she's working on for this weekend. "I haven't told anybody."

And really, do I have to? I don't need to go into detail about my dating life to satisfy their curiosity. So what if I'm happier than I've ever been? That's not their business, is it? That info is on a need-to-know basis.

Hope tries to get a severe face going. "How long do you think you can keep it a secret? You obviously can't keep your hands off him."

My dopey smile returns, sending Hope into fresh paroxysms of secondhand joy. *A best friend you can't keep your hands off of.* I never knew it until he said it, but that's exactly what I want, too.

"Oh. I have some non-Shepherd news to tell you."

She starts beaming again. "You call him Shepherd now."

"Quit it." But I'm shining brightly, too. "I got an apartment."

"Really? When did this happen?"

"Just a few days ago." I can't think about what else happened that weekend or we'll both turn into sappy loons. "It's really cute. Nobody knows about that, either."

The smile falls off her face. "Wren. You need to tell people things."

I blow out a breath. "I know. I will. In my own way."

Maybe I'll write a group email. Send them a voice note. Glue together words from the newspaper in a ransom-style letter.

She tries to smother a yawn with her hand. Things are busy over at The Painted Daisy this week, too. She's always semi-comatose by the time Black Friday and Small Business Saturday are over.

"After this week, we need to sit down at Delish and talk, okay? You have to tell me everything."

"Not everything," I grumble. Some things are just for me. Like the way Shepherd whispers *goddess* in my ear, and all my nerve endings whip out their pom-poms and cheer.

"Most things then. I really am happy for you." Her earnestness threatens to get me choked up. My best friend who's been baffled by my resistance to all things romantic must be doing a full-on dance party in her head.

"I'm happy for me, too."

"I'm happy for you, too," a male voice echoes.

I sigh. Jamie's on thin ice.

The thing about dropping a chaos bomb is that you have to time it just right. If I had revealed my secrets at the beginning of Thanksgiving dinner, I would have left myself open to hours of interminable questions. Saving it until we've finished eating and are putting plates in the dishwasher was the only way.

Choosing which bomb to drop first was the hardest part of my plan.

"I found an apartment."

The kitchen hushes at my blunt announcement. Ian and Daniel both have their hands in soapy dishwater, while Mom, Tess, and I are putting leftovers into glass containers. All four of them stare at me.

"It's a really cute one-bedroom addition over a garage. Two women my age live in the main house. I only met one of them, but she's really sweet." I apparently can't stop using that word. It fits Lucy, though. Who may or may not secretly write romance books. "I'm going to move in next Sunday."

I pop a maraschino cherry out of the fruit salad and into my mouth. Its candy sweetness is a nice contrast to the sharp confusion on everyone's faces.

"I didn't know you were looking for a place." Mom's neutral voice reveals nothing. Typical.

Daniel dries his hands and steps closer. "I never meant to run you off."

"You're not." I share a look with Tess. "I've been looking for a place since before you came along."

Half-heartedly, but I have been looking a good long while now.

"Is it in a good neighborhood?" Ian asks. Aww. Protective big brother-in-law-to-be. When he gets his butt in gear and asks her.

"Yeah. It's really nice." I'm already making plans for how I can decorate my little garage apartment for the big holiday lights battle.

August steps out from behind Ian. "You're not going to live with Nana anymore?"

Ugh. This little guy has had a lot of changes in living arrangements over the last few months. His sadness is understandable, but I work to reassure him.

I drop to one knee, and he rushes into my arms. "No, I'm

going to have my own apartment. But there's a park we can walk to with a big slide and swings and a merry-go-round."

His grin eases most of my worries. "I like parks!"

I stand up again. "I know you do, buddy."

"I still feel like we're part of the problem," Mom says.

"You are." She sucks in a breath, but I laugh to soften the blow. "Mom. I'm twenty-nine. How long did you think this arrangement could last?"

She stands straighter, her mouth pert. "Well into your forties."

I know she's only mostly joking. She's loved having us all under one roof, but even she must see it can't go on forever. "Thankfully, we're not testing that theory."

I have another theory: that Mom's desire to keep her chicks in the nest has only been part of my reluctance to get my own apartment. The rest is all me.

Big changes are scary, okay?

Tess comes over to give me a hug, the sap. "I'm proud of you."

The way she's looking at me, Tess came to the "all me" conclusion a lot sooner than I did.

"Yeah, yeah. You should be offering your man to help me move my things."

"How did I get involved?" Ian asks. He might be a grump, but the tiny lift at the corners of his mouth says he's secretly pleased to be included.

"I was talking about August," I tease.

"I can help!" August shouts. "I can carry your weirdos!"

And maybe snag another one, too. He can pick anything he wants.

"It won't be much of a moving day. Everything I own is in my bedroom." It's going to be mighty empty in that cute apartment while I work up the nerve to spend money on furniture.

Lucy didn't have extra fees, but it's still a big chunk of dough to hand over.

"I've got a small dining set and a couch in storage that you might like," Daniel says. "If you're interested, you're welcome to them."

This intimidating man who puts bad guys away for a living sounds remarkably hesitant. Almost as if there's some kind of longstanding precedent where I run out of the room whenever he offers me anything. I've really been the worst.

"Thanks, Daniel. That would be a big help." My smile is small for an olive branch, but it's a start. "And we can still do movie nights sometimes, right?"

He stares for half a second, then looks at Mom for confirmation he heard me right. Then back at me. "Of course. I'd like that."

"Great. Maybe invite Easton and Evie, too." If we're going to do the family thing, we might as well do it right.

His subtle smile—and Mom's more radiant one—make me happier than I thought it would. "I will."

"Cool. Oh, just as an FYI, I'm going to take a two-week vacation this spring. I'm going to New Zealand." Hopefully with Shepherd, but I'm taking that trip even if he can't come with me. I've waited too long. I'm finally going to cross the ocean.

Tess looks like she wants to eat me up with a spoon. Mom is a little more stunned but doesn't argue.

"I have to go. I have plans tonight." I take a step backward and pull the pin on my final chaos grenade. "Oh, and Shepherd Callahan is my boyfriend. Don't be weird about it."

The kitchen erupts into a tumult of questions as I walk away.

THIRTY-FOUR
SHEPHERD

"THIS IS the only way to spend Thanksgiving." Wren's voice is already a little sleepy. I love how relaxed she is, even if I selfishly hope we're not going to nap the afternoon away.

We're lying on my couch, her head on my chest, our legs tangled together. I've got a wood fire going in the stove, the occasional snaps and crackles the only background noise. I was going to show her that I finished her bike, but she threw herself into my arms as soon as I opened the door, and I got distracted. The bike can wait.

I subtly pinch myself to be sure this really is my life.

"I have plenty of leftovers if you get hungry." My mom sends me home with even more food than Ada does.

Wren groans. "I ate enough mashed potatoes to cover a small planet."

"What about a slice of chocolate-bourbon-pretzel pie?"

She snuggles closer against me. "Maybe just one small-to-medium piece. In a little while."

I still can't believe she made a pie flavor for me. It's added to that molten spot in the center of my heart where she lives, melting everything she touches.

She moves her fingers in tiny circles over my stomach. "Are you ready for next week?"

She doesn't have to specify. The town hall meeting hangs over my head like a guillotine glinting in the sun.

"As ready as I can be." I know the presentation backward and forward. I've repeated every line until my voice went hoarse. I know what Lila's going to say to introduce me, and where to click through for each slide.

But it's still a dark smudge in my mind, like a grease spot I can't clear away.

"Just look at me when you need to focus."

I run my hands over her fleece-covered arm. Her Thanksgiving attire is a pink hoodie that says, *Exhausted by Existence.*

"Looking at you will ruin my focus in entirely different ways."

"Did you at least tell your family?"

I make a negative sound in the back of my throat, which earns an angry little growl from her.

"Shepherd."

I should not enjoy her scolding me so much.

"This is so important for you," she adds, driving her point home with a gentle poke to my stomach.

"It's just a technicality in the approval process. It's not an awards ceremony or something." And honestly, Lila *could* give the entire presentation if she wasn't so determined it should be me.

"But it's a big deal for you to overcome your anxiety to do it."

I suppose. Doesn't make it more of a win in my book.

"Would you want them to be there if they didn't have that dumb gala?"

I try to imagine my parents and Charlie showing up for me at the meeting. Cheering me on the way Grandpa always did.

Showing me in tangible ways that what's important to me is important to them. "Yes. I would want them there."

She lifts up onto her elbow so she can glare at me. "See?"

"But I'm not going to ask them to choose between me and their event at the lodge. That's just putting unnecessary pressure on everybody."

She lies back down, grumbling. "I guess. I still disagree with you."

I crane my neck to kiss the crown of her head. "I like that you're so upset in my defense, but I promise you, it's fine."

"Then I'll just have to be your rock. You're going to be awesome and convince everybody how great your trails idea is, and Sunshine will become a big tourist trap for bike nerds."

"Aww. You know what I like to hear."

She pinches my side. "And if some of your customers wander next door for a slice of pie, I won't complain."

"I always tell new customers to visit your bakery."

She pops up again. "You do?"

I push a lock of hair behind her ear. "Of course."

"So all this time, you've been advertising my business and defending me and pining for me, and I never knew?"

"Pretty much."

She leans forward to kiss me. "That's the saddest thing I've ever heard."

I can't help my laugh. "Thank you."

She snuggles back in again. "Just so you know, my mom and sister are going to the gala. Everybody's *so excited* to see a fancy barn. Ooh la la. 'We're getting married where animals used to live.' What's the big deal?"

She's trying to sound bitter, but I've learned a few things about Wren's deflection methods.

"Do you want to see it?"

"Yes." She laughs against me. "There's so much hype around it. I have to know what it looks like."

"Want to go over there and check it out right now?"

She rolls on top of me, her face almost pressed against mine. "Really?"

"Sure. Charlie and Leo headed back after dinner to get some last-minute preparations ready. They're probably still there."

Wren scrunches her nose. I love how her face paints a vivid picture of what's going on in her head. "On Thanksgiving?"

"Charlie's a workaholic. I'm sure Leo would rather watch the game, but that's probably why she thought she could escape to the barn."

"Let's do it." Wren slides off me and holds a hand out to help me up. I stand but don't let her go.

"What do you say to riding our bikes there? It's only three-quarters of a mile to the lodge."

She groans. "You keep getting me to do things."

I lean down to kiss her. "I want to do all the things with you."

She smiles against my mouth, proving she doesn't hate *doing things* as much as she lets on.

She pulls back as if she's been stung. "Wait. Do you mean *my* bike? Are you finished already?"

"It's out in the garage."

"I thought it was going to take you weeks."

"I've had time to kill." Thinking about her, but that's obvious.

We bundle up in coats, and I find a pair of gloves for her to wear. The dusting of snow we had this morning is gone now, but the bite in the air isn't. Just to be safe, I tug one of my knit beanies over her head.

"Happy now?" she asks, smirking up at me.

"I'd be happier if you were dressed head to toe in my clothes. Or better yet—"

She puts her hand over my mouth. "Please stop being sexy when I'm five minutes away from crashing my bike."

I take her hand. "You're not going to crash."

I lead her outside to my detached garage. It's more of a workshop, since my old truck can't fit in there. It's bitter cold out, but that hasn't been much of a problem while I've worked on her bike. Being in the cold plunge twenty-four-seven wouldn't kill the fire she's lit inside me.

"You will eat your words when I'm in the back of an ambulance with life-threatening injuries after ten minutes of cycling."

My anxiety can't get very worked up about that ominous imagery when I cleared and smoothed the path to the lodge myself.

Her reminder about the presentation, on the other hand...

It doesn't matter that I'm committed and there's no backing out. Running away from my responsibilities sounds like a great idea. Except, of course, I can't let down everyone who's counting on me to get this project approved.

And Lila would murder me in my sleep.

I let Wren into the garage. Instead of the delighted gasp I was anticipating, she laughs.

"How many bikes do you own?" She stares at the vertical bike rack on one wall.

"Four." Plus some junkers I tinker with, but those don't count.

She tries to cover up a snort but can't manage it. "Why?"

"Different purposes for different bikes." I gently take her by the shoulders and direct her to the main attraction. *Now* I'm rewarded with her delighted gasp.

"I can't believe you did this." She moves to where I left her bike in the center of the workshop and lightly runs her hands over the frame and seat. She pulls her fingers through the black-and-pink streamers I added and tests the new handlebar grips. "It's like brand-new."

"With a few extras." I point at the black device I attached to the handlebar.

"Is this..." She hovers a finger over the button next to one of the grips. "Is this the loudest bike horn in the world?"

"Seemed appropriate."

Her devious grin makes my stomach flip. "Can I?"

"Knock yourself out."

She presses the button, and a sound like a high-pitched car horn fills the workshop. Wren cackles and pushes it again. "You're going to regret your generosity."

"Never."

Before I can blink, she's got her arms around me, rising up on tiptoes to kiss me. "Thank you. This is the coolest thing. But don't expect me to ride it all the time."

"I have very low expectations." She's always enough, whatever she does.

I grab my mountain bike off the rack, and we walk them outside. She sits on her bike, bouncing a couple of times on the new seat as if she's gearing up for our short ride.

"You're going to do fine," I tell her.

"It's been ten years." She looks at the dirt path ahead of us like there's a root canal waiting for her at the end of it.

"I'll make you a deal. If this doesn't work out, I'll get one of those baby trailers to pull you around in."

Her mouth drops open, and an indignant sound croaks out of her. "Eat my dust, Callahan."

I am madly, deeply in love with this woman.

She starts pedaling, and her worries must evaporate with every turn of the wheels. Not a wobble in sight. I trail behind, enjoying the view of Wren on a bike, streamers flowing in the breeze. When I pull up alongside her, the grin on her face makes my heart kick.

"Shut up," she says, rolling her eyes. "It's not a big deal."

"It is to me, goddess."

We pass my parents' house and the smaller cabins where Charlie and Leo live.

"Okay, those cabins are really cute," she says. "You guys all lived so close together."

"You can see why I needed more space."

"Relatable. I told my family about the apartment today. Among other things."

"What other things?"

"Wouldn't you like to know?"

I very much would. Wren's not big on PDA or revealing her feelings, so I know getting her to claim our relationship publicly will take time. Doesn't mean I'm not secretly hoping.

She slows when the path merges onto lodge property. The guest cabins are spread out and surrounded by trees for maximum privacy, but the main lodge and outbuildings are impossible to miss. I take the lead, coasting down to the old barn.

Charlie had its white paint refreshed, but otherwise, it looks the same from the outside. I dismount and lean my bike carefully against the building. If I damage the paint, Charlie will send me a bill.

"Did you play Barbies out here with Charlie when you are little?" Wren asks.

"Her Barbies never wanted to play with Darth Vader, so no."

"But that would make the perfect morally gray love interest situation."

I pull open the side door, and Wren and I both stare inside. I am only marginally aware of the changes—the refinished hardwood floor, the new paneling that makes the interior look rustic yet sleek, the miles of bright string lights overhead. A different change is center stage.

In the middle of the room, Charlie's kissing Leo.

I don't usually pay attention to other people kissing, but they are *really* into it. So much that they don't even notice us in the doorway. A meteor could probably rip through the barn's ceiling, and they still wouldn't come up for air.

Wren takes my hand off the door, letting it silently swing shut again.

"I'm glad you brought me out here," she says. "This was really illuminating."

I groan out a laugh. I can't tell if I want to punch my best friend or bleach my eyeballs. Both work.

"The parts I saw of the venue look really nice," she goes on. "And it's obviously a romantic spot."

"Too soon."

Wren's still holding my hand and shakes it. "Okay there, Callahan?"

"Yeah. I guess this is happening." I'm fine with it. I am. I just didn't expect to find out quite like that.

"Looks like it. You know what will cheer you up?"

I finally focus on her. "Finding our own romantic spot?"

"You wish." She drops my hand and hops on her bike, popping up the kickstand. "Trying to catch me!"

She pedals back up the path, blasting the loudest bike horn in the world as she goes.

That will do plenty to cheer me up. I'll catch her—right after I send my sister a text.

Shepherd: CLCRH (Charlie & Leo Caught Red-Handed)

THIRTY-FIVE
WREN

I AM A GOOD GIRLFRIEND, I tell myself like I'm my own self-help audiobook. This is not overstepping. This is just the right amount of stepping.

Acting on my impulses isn't always the best move. Every time they backfire on me, I swear I've learned my lesson. And yet, here I am, back at Moonlight Lodge with just a few days left to go before the gala/big bike trails presentation. If the women in book group have taught me anything, it's that sometimes meddling makes life better for everyone.

I should probably let them know that at some point. Far in the future.

Usually when I walk through Moonlight Lodge's swanky lobby, I'm carrying pies. Today, it's just me and my adrenaline, urging me to rush in swinging my sword of righteous indignation.

Some of that urge to go in guns blazing fizzles when Charlie's mom spots me from behind the front desk. Because that's also *Shepherd's* mom. I've never been nervous around Emily Callahan before, but I might have a lil' sweat going on this time. Her mom radar could clue her in about Shepherd and me.

She beams, though, in perfect customer service mode. "Wren. It's good to see you."

"Same to you, Em—I mean, Mrs. Callahan." Smooth.

She smiles over my little flub, even though I usually just call her by her first name. "What can I do for you?"

"Is Charlie available?" My first instinct was to head straight for the barn, but I don't want to get in trouble for nosing around the lodge without a guide. And my favorite guide happens to have no idea I'm out here.

"She's in the barn getting everything finalized for our big event on Friday. Do you want me to call her down?"

"I can meet her there, if that's okay." I'd rather do this in the relative privacy of the barn. It might get messy if I have too much of an audience.

She gestures at the hallway that leads outside. "You know the way."

"I do. Don't worry, I'll be back on Friday with your pies."

Emily just laughs. "I've never had a doubt about Blackbird's delivering when they say they will."

Aww. She is the nicest. I hope she stays that nice after she finds out I'm dating her son.

I walk the short path from the main lodge out to the barn. Déjà vu hits me when I move to open the door. Leo's probably with Charlie. That's what I hoped when I came out here, but if I catch those two kissing again, I'm going to seriously question their work ethic.

Thankfully, when I pull the door open, they're on opposite sides of the room. Charlie catches sight of me, and her face does this weird grimace. Like she wanted to smile but then panicked.

"Hi, Wren." She moves closer, weaving between the fancy white tables set up throughout the space like a pro. "Is everything okay with our order for Friday?"

"All good. I'm not here about that."

A more natural expression overtakes her face. "Thank goodness. What's up?"

"I know you're busy, but I need to talk to you. It's about Shepherd."

Her smile crumples again. "Oh, gosh. He said it was no big deal, and now he's not even talking to me about it? I'm going to call him right now and get this out in the open."

She pulls her phone from her pocket, but I rush to stop her.

"It's not about that, either. And obviously, I don't even know what *that* is. I'm just saying...it's not about whatever you're thinking."

Charlie freezes, phone in hand. "He told you."

"No, he didn't say anything." I glance away, hoping to get this over with ASAP. "I might have been here, too."

Charlie's shoulders slump, but Leo grins like a cat who just cornered a mouse. He has zero concerns that I saw him kissing his best friend's sister. "What were you doing out here with Shepherd on Thanksgiving?"

Just racing him on the bike he fixed up and falling asleep cuddled against him on his couch. Don't make a big thing out of it.

I won't give satisfaction to his gloating question. "Unless you want to explain what you two were doing *in here* on Thanksgiving, I don't have to answer that."

"Oh, I'll tell you."

Charlie smacks his chest. "You won't."

He takes her hand and holds it to him. "I'll tell everybody."

"That's not as reassuring as you think it is." And yet, the woman's smiling.

This is getting way out of hand. "Please, let's focus on Shepherd."

"Yes, Wren. Let's focus on Shepherd." Leo couldn't sound any more like a hypnotist implanting a trigger word if he tried.

I'm pretty sure the next time I say that name, I'll wind up clucking like a chicken.

"Take it down a notch," Charlie tells him. "I want to know what's going on."

Leo sobers infinitesimally, but they both turn their focus on me.

Right. What I came here for.

The thing is, this isn't easy for me. I would go to bat for my family in a heartbeat. Same with Hope, my oldest and truest friend. But outside of that tiny circle, I don't have any other ride-or-dies. I'll have to lay a lot of personal cards on the table to get through this big request. That's not the type of risk I usually take.

But for Shepherd, I'll do anything.

"You know about the trails expansion he's working on, right?"

They both nod. At least they know some things. I don't have to start from scratch.

"He has to give a big presentation at a town hall meeting to try to get the project approved." I don't want to say anything about his panic attacks yet. I have no idea if that's common knowledge and won't be the one to reveal it. "It's a thirty-minute speech in front of at least a hundred people."

From the surprise on Charlie's face and Leo's low whistle, they already know about Shepherd's anxiety.

"Why hasn't he told us about it?" Charlie asks.

"Because it's this Friday." Their stunned expressions are morbidly satisfying. This isn't their fault, but I'm still inclined to blame them that he felt he couldn't speak up. He needs to know his family supports him, even when their goals don't perfectly align.

"He knows you guys are committed to your gala." I stop for a second to really admire everything I didn't pay attention to last week. It's a gorgeous space. I can almost see all the wedding cakes Tess will deliver here. "But this presentation is really important to him. The trails could do a lot for Sunshine's tourism and businesses, not just his. It's a multi-million-dollar project that's resting on his shoulders."

I played it cool when he went over the money side of it in the presentation the other night, but I had no idea bike trails were that expensive. "It's going to be a massive undertaking, all because *Shepherd* had the vision to make it happen. I think you know it's hard for him to be in the spotlight like this, but he's going to anyway because it's that important to him."

But it's not a selfish endeavor. I'm pretty sure he'd do something similar even if he wouldn't stand to gain anything from it, simply because he wanted to help out.

"Shepherd thinks he has to be some kind of lone wolf, but that's not who he really is. He stands up for other people and defends them and supports them. He's there for everybody else. He's a pack animal." I pause to take a breath. "And it would mean a lot to have the people who love him be there for him, too. If his sister and best friend—"

"And parents."

I spin around to see Emily and Nick Callahan in the open doorway. Somebody went a little crazy with the WD-40 because that thing is silent.

My heart races into my throat, but I can't stop now. "And parents. If all of you could be there, it would let him know how much he means to you, too. And maybe it would steady him when it's hard for him to speak in front of a crowd."

"I can't believe he offered to do that," Leo says.

"I don't think offered is the right word. But he's following through because people are counting on him. I know you've got an important event here Friday. But I want to make sure you remember how important Shepherd is, too."

Emily and Nick join us in the middle of the barn.

"And Shepherd is important to you, too?" Emily's got too knowing a look in her eye to accept anything close to a denial.

And why would I want to deny it? Shepherd Callahan is steady and loyal, funny and smart. He can be a pain in my butt, too, but I wouldn't want him any other way. So what if I'm not used to sharing my love life with people? I never had anyone worth sharing before.

I nod. "He's the most important."

TEXT THREAD

Isabel: Roxy's has two-step dancing on Thursday and Friday nights

Isabel: Let's pick a night in December we can all go

Barb: Not all of us

Nora: You won't at least come to watch?

Nora: You can point out everything we're doing wrong

Barb: Who has time for that?

Fran: It's bound to be a hoot

Ada: I've heard it's quite romantic

Nora: If you like country music

Rosetta: It's easy enough to pick up

Rosetta: If you have the right partner

Barb: If we're planning to back out again at the last minute, I'll just do that now

Isabel: I don't know what you're talking about

Isabel: I didn't plan my headache

Wren: Allergies

Fran: I call dibs on Shepherd

Fran: I bet he's a good dancer

Nora: I thought Shepherd would dance with all of us

Wren: Now, ladies

Wren: I don't share my man

Ada: ...

Isabel: ...

Rosetta: ...

Nora: Is this true?

Shepherd: Yes. I am a good dancer

Shepherd: But it's also true that I'm Wren's man

Ada: Hallelujah!

Isabel: Finally!

Barb: So we can cancel dancing?

Rosetta: I hope everyone's happy with the outcome

Wren: Extremely

Shepherd: Never been more satisfied with a book club

THIRTY-SIX

SHEPHERD

TRYING to look casual and unaffected when my vital organs feel like they've been chopped to bits on a butcher block is tough work. It's way too late to ask Lila to cover the entire presentation, but the thought has crossed my mind.

Approximately seven hundred times.

"The turnout's even better than I hoped." Lila's twisted in the seat next to me, eagerly watching the crowd behind us.

I haven't turned to look, but the ambient noise is loud enough I'd guess the auditorium is packed. That's good for the trails. For me, less so.

My hands are so clammy I have to subtly wipe them on my pants every few minutes so I don't drop my tablet. My heartbeat is thrumming in my ears, and my thoughts are like an upended toolbox. There's probably something useful in there, but I'll have to hunt to find it.

"This is so exciting," Lila's saying. "Mayor Martinez is really championing the project. Did you know he's a big biker? You probably do."

Enrique Martinez visits Get in Gear regularly, and he's voiced his enthusiasm for this project over the last month. That doesn't do anything to settle my stomach, currently riddled with anxiety like mold in a hunk of blue cheese.

I need a strong drink. A long bike ride. An evening next to my fire listening to a Greek mythology audiobook. Wren's soft body tucked up next to mine on the couch. I need—

Arms come around me from behind, a warm cheek rubbing against mine. "Okay there, Callahan?"

"Wren." I clasp her arms over my chest. It's not an SSRI or a shot of whiskey, but it helps. "Better now."

"I like the jacket." She runs her fingers over the lapel of my navy corduroy suit jacket I layered over a flannel shirt. "You look like a hot, dangerous professor."

This woman. "I feel like a kid who didn't study for his final."

Even though I have the source material memorized.

"You've got this," she whispers in my ear, her lips grazing over the shell. "This is *your* vision. Your plans. You know every last detail. And you are going to rock these people's worlds."

I don't deserve her, but I'm never going to let her go.

"Thank you for being here."

She shifts forward and faces me better. "What? You think I was going to coach my boyfriend and not come cheer him on? No way, kitten."

My eyes must light up at that shared nickname because she leans back in. "Would it make you feel better if I smack your butt while you walk up to the podium?"

I laugh out loud, my mood truly lightening for the first time this evening. "It might."

"In front of your parents and everything, huh? Saucy."

"What?"

She straightens but keeps her hands firm on my shoulders. She tilts her head behind her, a secret smile peeking out. I turn and have to laugh again.

My parents are in the seats next to hers with Charlie and Leo

—holding hands, not that I have the brainpower to ask about that —next to the aisle. They're in suits and frilly dresses, clearly taking time away from the event at the lodge to join us. Hope and Griffin are here, along with Tess and Ian. Lila's boyfriend, Grant, is next to Palmer, Laurel, and the rest of my Get in Gear crew. Even Jamie from Blackbird's is here, waving at me from three rows back.

"You showed up." I'm talking to any and all of them.

"You should have told us about this, you big dope," Charlie says.

"We're always here to support you, Shepherd," Mom adds.

"But the gala—"

"We can miss the silent auction," Dad says. "But we can't miss being here for you."

Leo holds out his fist for a bump. "We're your pack, bro."

I bump his fist, trying to make sense of that. They're my what?

I tilt my head to look up at my goddess. "What did you do?"

"I threatened them all with bodily harm if they didn't come out here to show you how important you are to us. We're no Grandpa Callahan, but we can be your rock, too."

This woman who cloaks herself in cynicism like battle armor has the softest, most loyal heart at her center. Gathering everyone together to support me—the guy she used to proudly proclaim was her *nemesis*—must have cost her some vulnerability. A moment of open-hearted risk wrapped up in her "don't defy me" attitude.

"Wren." I reach up to pull her in for a quick kiss. "I love you."

"That's because I'm awesome." She kisses me again. "But so are you. This is going to be a slam dunk. In biking terms, that's like...going really fast down a hill."

"Thanks for putting it a way I can understand."

She touches her nose against mine. "And I love you, too."

"They're about to start," Lila says, quieting everyone.

Nerves ping through my chest with fresh enthusiasm. My family's presence won't cure me of my anxiety. I might still panic when I get up there, whether it's obvious to anyone in the audience or not.

But having everybody important to me in the front rows grounds me at my core. Whether I deliver my presentation flawlessly or totally blow it, they're here for me.

All because of the spitfire woman I love.

———

"We should crash more parties." Wren gazes up at me as we slow dance in the lodge's barn.

"We had an explicit invitation." My parents left as soon as my presentation ended but told us to come by once everything wrapped up at the town hall meeting. We're underdressed for the evening, but we're not the only ones. Most of the rest of our friends showed up at the gala, too, ready to dance and mingle and bid on Leo's signed Hornets gear.

My eyes popped out of my head when I saw the amount Grant spent to win a signed jersey. Leo would probably give it to him for free now, but it's for a good cause.

Wren focuses on something past my shoulder, steering us that way. I bump into someone and turn to see the man of the hour. Dancing with my sister.

It's going to take me a second to adjust, but I'm fine with it. As long as I ignore how low his hand rests on her waist, I'm totally fine.

"You did great tonight." Charlie said as much right after I finished the presentation, but I can appreciate her praise more now that the buzzing noise in my head has died down. "I'm proud of you."

Lila's already heard positive reactions from council members and residents. Her eager texts will probably double now as we plan for the next steps in the process.

"Hey, I'm proud of *you*. Look at this place." It's hard to believe this is the same space that used to be a catch-all for machinery, animals, and Grandpa's collection of old tools. Now, it shines like a new penny. "You had a dream, and you went for it."

Leo swipes a finger beneath one eye. "Stop, it's getting too emotional in here."

"Are you sure you want to deal with this guy?" I ask my sister.

She tips her head toward Wren. "Do you want me to ask her the same question?"

"Nope." I spin us away, ignoring their laughter.

"The answer's yes," Wren says after a minute. She's got one hand on the back of my neck, making it hard for me to concentrate. "I do want to deal with you. Just a little."

"A little, huh?" We slow in the middle of the dance floor. My throat tightens as if I'm standing on that stage again, even though Wren is the only one close enough to hear me. "Thank you for everything you did tonight. Getting everybody to show up. Being there for me. It meant more than I can say. I don't know how I'll ever thank you."

She lifts a mischievous eyebrow. "I have some ideas about that."

I lean closer, ready to hang on every word. "Really?"

"Do you want to go to New Zealand with me?" She bites her lower lip but plows on. "I was thinking in the spring. *Our* spring, their fall. It should still be warm enough to enjoy the beaches but not so busy we're surrounded by touristy crowds."

I draw her to me until our bodies are flush together. "Wren. Yes. Absolutely, yes."

Her smile is like the first rays of sunshine over the mountains on a summer morning. "Good. I already told Mom and Tess I'm taking the time off. So...all we have to do is make some plans."

"I would like to make a lot of plans with you."

She rolls her eyes but doesn't sell her exasperation very hard. "Big goals there, Callahan?"

I lean down to touch my nose to hers. "I want everything, Krause."

I'm not sure just what she's willing to reveal in this crowded space, surrounded by family, friends, and acquaintances who will surely gossip about us the moment our backs are turned. But she stretches up to meet me, throwing her arms around my shoulders in an enthusiastic kiss.

When we part, she shrieks. My heart pounds pretty hard, too. Ada and Isabel are standing so close to us, they might as well have their arms around us. No surprise, both are grinning like their bingo numbers just came up.

"We're just so delighted you two made it to the gala," Ada says.

"So happy to see you *both* here." Isabel smiles up at us so hard, it's a little uncomfortable. Like a clown making direct eye contact in a crowd.

"And looking so happy together, I might add."

"Very happy."

Smug has never been more perfectly personified than in these two wonderful, meddling women.

"We owe it all to you," Wren says with only a hint of sarcasm.

Ada and Isabel nod at each other, accepting full responsibility for our relationship.

"I knew you just needed a little push," Isabel tells me.

"The tiniest shove in the right direction," Ada adds.

Wren nods along. "The ittiest, bittiest nudge to kiss each other's faces off."

I pull her closer. "I never needed extra encouragement about that."

Ada giggles. "Maybe we should leave you two alone, hmm?"

It's not as alone as I'd like to be, surrounded by about three hundred other people.

Isabel looks past us into the crowd. "I wonder who else here needs a little push?"

Ada taps her fingers together like an evil mastermind. "Let's find out. Have a good night, you two."

They shimmy off through dancing couples, no doubt searching for their next potential match.

"Who do you suppose is next?" I ask.

"That's their problem." Wren slides her hands up my shoulders, gazing at me as if nobody else exists. "The only romance I'm interested in right now is ours."

EPILOGUE

WREN

THIS MIGHT BE the most disgusting thing I've ever seen.

Griffin's eyes are full of tears as Hope walks down the makeshift aisle in her parents' back yard. He's watching her like she hung the sun, moon, and stars, and a few comets for good measure. Have some dignity, man.

Next to me, Lila's a step away from blubbering.

I get it. Hope looks like an artistic angel, wearing a sleeveless gown with a puffy tulle skirt adorned with brightly colored fabric flowers stitched along the hem. It's freezing out, so she paired the dress with a thin wool boatneck sweater that looks more stylish than I've ever tried to be.

Also, she's probably the happiest she's ever been. As she slowly glides closer to us holding her dad's arm, I can see the tear tracks on her cheeks. She's grinning so hard, her face is going to ache tomorrow. Seems over the top to me. It's just the day marking her special love with Griffin.

With a tiny circle of her closest friends and family watching.

And she chose me to stand beside her sister to witness their vows.

Because we've known each other forever, and I would do anything for her.

I might be crying too. So gross.

I find Shepherd in the small audience. He knows exactly how to break me out of my melodramatic moment: he smirks. Why does the sight of him have my body breaking out in goosebumps? Sure, it could be the thirty-five-degree weather, but I wasn't trembling before, either. It's all him.

We've had one month of Shepherd-Wren bliss. People in Sunshine seem to think it's some remarkable thing—and by that, I mean people think they need to *remark* on it. Constantly.

"Didn't you used to hate him?"

"I bet you're eating your words now, honey."

"What took you so long?"

That last one's the hardest to answer. The first two are easy: yes and yes. But what took me so long to realize the guy who came into my bakery every week to antagonize me was actually the love of my life? Not that I call him that. Way too sappy. But LOML equivalent. Soulmate? Sure. That's a more sensible description.

All I really know is that I'm grateful I finally wised up.

Hmm. Also, I apparently spaced out during the vows. Whoops.

Griffin dips Hope in a showy kiss, marking that they're now Mr. and Mrs. McBride. They're the cutest. I'm so happy for them.

Lila and I pair off with Grant and Griffin's brother, Caleb, and follow the happy couple through the yard and into the house. Lila and I go straight for the wood-burning fireplace in the living room. Hope found these really stunning wide-neck cable knit sweaters for us to wear, which could have been almost warm except that our sea-green skirts are paper-thin satin. At least she let us wear white Chuck Taylors underneath them in honor of the very chill day.

And sandals would have directly led to frostbite.

"I didn't even know micro-weddings were a thing." Lila's mother has her arm around Griffin's mom as they walk through the living room. "I had my doubts, but it turned out lovely."

"I can hear you," Lila says. She was Hope's de facto micro-wedding planner. Whatever she suggested, Hope scaled down by a factor of ten.

"You're a woman of many talents," Kat McBride says to her.

Grant stands behind Lila, smoothing his hands over her arms to warm her up. "That you are, princess."

Hope's mom puffs up as she watches them. I can practically see the thoughts in her head. Tulle and lace. A hundred guests. Moonlight Lodge's barn for the reception, festooned with imported flowers. I bet she's hoping to plan a big blowout wedding next time around.

August runs over to join me at the fireplace. "Did you see me, Wren? I dropped the petals *and* carried the rings!"

"You were an excellent flower boy-slash-ring bearer." I peeked from inside while he had his moment wowing everybody in attendance. Hope and Griffin don't know any other little kids, so August got the responsibility of both jobs.

"Little babies like Colton can't do that." August's smug expression says he doesn't feel bad about taking a job from Griffin's one-year-old nephew.

"At least you're humble about it, kid," Ian says.

Tess's pirate looks dapper in a navy wool suit coat. It clashes beautifully with his red man bun and beard, but he makes it work. Tess obviously thinks so—she's got both arms wrapped around him like he's her anchor.

"Jodi deserves some praise, too." Tess nods at one of Ian's aunts, who officiated the wedding. "That was the most beautiful ceremony I've ever heard."

Oops. I probably should have listened harder. Maybe somebody got it on video.

Jodi holds an arm out, and Amy slips against her side. They're even more sophisticated than the rest of us, with Jodi in a tan turtleneck sweater and brown twill jacket, and Amy in a similar sweater dress. They're like a matched set. "I've learned a lot from a lifetime of love."

"A lifetime?" Ian repeats. "You two are barely older than I am."

Tess gently pokes him in the stomach. "Which is how old again?"

Ian takes her hand and kisses her knuckles. "Tread carefully, angel, or I might throw you over my shoulder and take you home."

"I want cake!" August pipes up.

"You're right," Ian says to him. "We need to eat some of your mama's decadent creation first."

August nods. "Then you can throw her over your shoulder."

All these happy, sappy couples. So where's my man?

Finally, Shepherd walks in from the yard trailing behind Leo and Charlie. Surprising no one, Leo and Griffin have become fast friends. Leo's such an easy-going guy, he's sort of the litmus test for people around Sunshine now. If Leo doesn't like you, you need to reevaluate your life's choices.

Leo joins our crowded circle around the fireplace. "Is this where we're placing bets on who gets married next?"

He's got his eyes trained on me, which is not cool. "Look at that one." I point at Lila, who's snuggled up to Grant. "They're clearly the next marriageable couple."

Ian huffs. "I want to take offense to that, but I'm not sure if I should."

"Let it slide," Tess says. "If you start taking offense to things Wren says, you'll never be happy again."

"Plus, that just makes you an easier target." I shrug as if there's nothing I can do about it.

"I think it goes Charlie and me," Leo says, earning a swift shake of the head from his intended. "Then Lila and Grant." He points at each couple in turn. "Then Ian and Tess. Then you."

He points straight at me, which is honestly rude. I'm dead last? Seriously?

Also, why am I *upset* about that prediction?

Shepherd takes his place next to me, sliding his arm around my waist and snugging me to him. As far as comfort from weird insults goes, it's my favorite.

"For the record, Leo predicts Super Bowl matchups at the start of every season, which is arguably the thing he knows the most about." Shepherd shoots him an innocent look. "You've gotten how many right?"

"Not really relevant at this juncture," Leo mumbles.

Charlie does him a solid and kisses his cheek. "We probably shouldn't put bets on other people's love lives."

From the way this group of guys is sizing each other up, I'm pretty sure they're going to do exactly that the next time they're alone.

Now I kind of need to know the odds Shepherd puts on us.

Hope and Griffin walk in from a back room. They lift their joined hands in triumph, their joy radiating through the house with the brightness of a thousand suns. We applaud for them, everyone from Mom and Daniel, who are with the other parental types, down to August, who's the most enthusiastic clapper.

"Thank you for joining us today," Hope says when we finally quiet down. "You know we wanted something small and low-key. But we didn't want to get married without all of you with us."

"I did," Griffin says. His brother wolf-whistles.

"You're the most important people in our lives." Hope's voice breaks, and Griffin holds her close. She looks at each of us around the room. "Our parents. Our honorary aunts. Our siblings. Our very best friends in the whole wide world."

Dammit, she had to get me crying again. Shepherd pulls me tighter to him, but that just squeezes out more tears.

Hope leans forward, pointing at August. "And, obviously, our little buddies who make everybody's lives better just by being them."

August cheers while Griffin's brother raises his small son's fist.

Hope dabs beneath her eyes with the backs of her index fingers. "We wouldn't be who we are without you guys. We love you so much."

"And there's cake in the kitchen, let's eat." If Griffin had a mic, he'd drop it.

I like him for a lot of reasons, but we're on the same page when it comes to getting mushy: not with an audience.

The crowd slowly moves from being too much for Hope's parents' living room to being way too much for their kitchen. I stay by the fireplace, still warming my ice-cold legs.

"Okay there, Krause?"

"I'm just cold. This skirt has a really high slit."

He tilts his head to examine my long stretch of exposed leg. "Not high enough."

I cross my arms and try to give him my best unimpressed look, but he's gone all blurry. Again.

He runs his hands over my back. "Are you sure that's the cause of the tears in your eyes?"

"Shh." I look past him, but nobody's paying any attention to us. They're too focused on getting to the cake Tess made.

"What's going on in that beautiful head of yours?"

I thought I'd seen the last of this dumb weepiness when the wedding ceremony ended, but Hope's speech brought it back to life.

"It's just a lot of change over the last year for us girls. We were all happy enough a year ago." I cringe. "Maybe not Lila, who'd just found out her ex was cheating on her. Anyway. We were fine, you know? Solid sevens and eights on a scale out of ten. And then you doofuses came along and showed us the scale really goes to fifteen. And you made us happier."

I groan and tuck my forehead against his chest. "Never mind. I'm talking stupid. It's wedding brain. Ignore me."

He massages my shoulders, his low chuckle rumbling through him into me.

"It's not stupid. I know exactly what you mean. I was a solid seven on the happiness scale a year ago, too."

I tilt my face to look up at him. "And now?"

He smirks down at me. "Sixteen."

He really is the best.

"I love you, Callahan."

"Oh, Krause. I love you, too."

He kisses me, pulling my body flush against his. He cups my jaw, almost speaking to me through every slide of his mouth. Whispering plans. Making promises. Giving me hints of things to come.

When he draws back, I realize Leo's walking through the living room, a grin almost too wide for his face flashing at us.

"Just for that," he says, "I'm bumping you up a rung on the marriage bracket."

BONUS EPILOGUE

WREN

"THIS IS MY FAVORITE SO FAR." I stand facing the ocean at Onemana Beach, my arms outstretched as the waves wash over my toes. It's hotter than I thought it would be for early March, but I'm not complaining. A warm breeze ruffles my coverup skirt, my thin linen top billowing around my waist. My dual braids are almost shot this late in the afternoon. I'm windswept and sunburned and have several hellaciously itchy bumps around both ankles.

But we're here, and I'm loving every second of it. Itchy bumps aside.

Shepherd wraps his arms around me from behind, resting his chin on top of my head. "You say that about all of them."

"I mean it about all of them. Look at this place. Beautiful green trees on shore. White sandy beach along the bay. Pure blue ocean stretching out in front of us. Yup." I nod, making his chin bob above me. "My favorite."

We've been in New Zealand a week already, with six days of exploring left to go. We decided not to overwhelm ourselves with too many options, so we're sticking to the upper end of the North Island for our stay. We move from tiny house to tiny house, beach bums with nothing better to do than sit in the sand and take a dip in the ocean. I've got my swimsuit on beneath my clothes, ready to get back in the water at a moment's notice.

"There's room in the beginner classes for us every day we're here." Shepherd releases me so we can stand side by side. He nods down the beach toward a small surf shack. "If you want to give it a try."

I sigh. *I've* got nothing better to do than sit around. He's trying to convince me this is a good time to learn how to surf. He's a big fan of doing things, that one.

"Mmm." I try to work up a grumble, but it's not very serious. This trip is too out of the ordinary to pass up something like that. When will I get the chance to surf in New Zealand again? "Okay. Tomorrow, though. Tonight, I just want to watch the sun set and eat all the noodles we have in our hut."

He swoops in to kiss my cheek. "That's my goddess."

Ugh. The happiness in his voice is the best sound ever.

"It's really your fault, you know."

He rumbles an agreement. "Most things are."

"You keep getting me to do things."

His smirk softens. "Are you okay with that?"

Why is my throat getting tight, like my heart jumped up in there? This is so ridiculous.

"Yes," I say softly, as if it's some big deal. "I want to do all the things with you."

Shepherd's smile ignites something comforting and warm beneath my ribs. "You had to go and give me the perfect opening, didn't you?"

"For what?"

He pulls something out of the pocket of his board shorts, takes a step back from the surf, and drops onto one knee. He opens the little velvet box in his hand, gazing up at me as the setting sun paints him with golden highlights.

"Wren Kitten Goddess Krause," he starts.

I snort, wrecking the moment. He's undeterred.

"You are my favorite person in this world. I love every part of you, the good and the bad, the sweet and the salty. I might especially love the salty."

I laugh again. He really does love it when I'm crabby. My perfect other half.

"I want to spend every day with you, from your grumpy 'Good mornings' to your sleepy 'Good nights.' It will take a lifetime to learn everything I want to know about you. I am never going to finish falling in love with you, Wren. Will you marry me?"

I drop to my knees in front of him. "All the yeses."

We kiss in celebration, with just enough push and pull to remind us what we love about each other. I'm barely thinking when he pulls the ring from its cushion in the box. It's a square-cut solitaire, which I only know is called a princess cut from hanging out with Lila so much.

And maybe the occasional peek at jewelry websites. I've been secretly hoping, what can I say?

"I thought classic elegance suited you," he says, watching me admire the ring. "But it's got a secret..."

He tilts it toward me so I can see the inscription inside the band.

Krause + Callahan

"You are such a cheeseball," I whisper. He knows it's my highest compliment.

"You love me," he says as he slides the beautiful ring onto my finger.

He kisses me again, a sweet, soft precursor of vows to come. I hold his face in my hands, look into his eyes, and admit the truth.

"I'm obsessed."

ACKNOWLEDGMENTS

To my readers, thank you for joining me on Wren & Shepherd's journey! It's been so much fun to drop hints about them since book one, and it's so satisfying to finally bring them to their happily ever after.

Thank you for reading this first series set in Sunshine, Oregon! I'm amazed and humbled by your interest in these characters. If you look closely, you'll find the breadcrumbs I dropped about who will show up again in the next series. Some of them are Texan-sized breadcrumbs!

Claire, you are the best critique partner and an awesome friend! I'm so glad we stumbled on each other amid the nonsense of IG!

Amanda K & Amanda P, thank you for your excitement and encouragement!

Kaci, thanks for the idea of Wren demanding more room on the couch during movie night!

Cindy, as always, thank you for polishing my writing so it can shine! I love working with you!

Melody, you rockstar! You always amaze me with how perfectly you capture my couples!

To the original Mo, I miss your face, girl!

To my children, I love you! You crack me up, you keep me on my toes, and you make my life immeasurably richer. So gross.

And finally, to my husband. I think you know where the butt smack inspiration came from! I adore you.

ALSO BY GENNY CARRICK

The Love in Sunshine series

Cinnamon Roll Set Up

The Loch Effect

The Magnolia Ridge series

ABOUT THE AUTHOR

Genny Carrick is a fool for happily ever afters, especially if there's a whole lot of laughter along the way. She writes rom-coms about sassy women, the cinnamon roll men who fall for them, and swoony moments outdoors whenever she possibly can.

When she's not lost in romantic reads, she's probably up to something crafty or trying to get her dog and two cats to love her.

After a quick detour in Texas, Genny returned to her true love, the Pacific Northwest, and lives with her brilliant husband and two hilarious kids.

Stay up to date with book news at gennycarrick.com